Fight
FROM THE
HEART

L.B. DUNBAR

www.lbdunbar.com

L.B. Dunbar

L.B. Dunbar
Books. Kissing included.

Originally published as Fragrance Free © 2014 Laura Dunbar
Fight from the Heart © 2020 Laura Dunbar
L.B. Dunbar Writes, Ltd.
www.lbdunbar.com

Cover Design: Shannon Passmore/Shanoff Designs
Editor: Kimberly Dallaire
Editor: Melissa Shank
Editor: Jenny Sims - Editing4Indies
Proofread: Karen Fischer

Other Books by L.B. Dunbar

Silver Fox Former Rock Stars
After Care
Midlife Crisis
Restored Dreams
Second Chance
Wine&Dine

The Silver Foxes of Blue Ridge
Silver Brewer
Silver Player
Silver Mayor
Silver Biker

Collision novellas
Collide
Caught – a short story

Smartypants Romance (an imprint of Penny Reid)
Love in Due Time
Love in Deed
Love in a Pickle (2021)

Standalone over 40 Romance
The Sex Education of M.E.

The Heart Collection
Speak from the Heart
Read with your Heart
Look with your Heart
Fight from the Heart
View with your Heart

A Heart Collection Spin-off
The Heart Remembers

The Legendary Rock Star Series
The Legend of Arturo King

L.B. Dunbar

The Story of Lansing Lotte
The Quest of Perkins Vale
The Truth of Tristan Lyons
The Trials of Guinevere DeGrance

Paradise Stories
Abel
Cain

The Island Duet
Redemption Island
Return to the Island

Modern Descendants – writing as elda lore
Hades
Solis
Heph

Dedication

To my father, whose words of advice have always stuck with me.

"He says, 'When you gonna make up your mind,
When you gonna love you as much as I do
When you gonna make up your mind,
'Cause things are gonna change so fast...'"

©Tori Amos, "Winter" from *Little Earthquakes*

L.B. Dunbar

Prologue
Something In The Way

[Pam]

My tears are nearly blinding my eyes as I peel onto the highway.
Damn the chief. Just damn him and the entire crew. I can't believe he wouldn't let me near him—my own father. I have no idea yet what happened other than an accident. As an EMT, I'm trained to respond and wired to help others. I wanted to be there, but everything you're taught in training demands that you don't take care of family. The position is too personal, and by my initial reaction, it's warranted that the fire chief tried to hold me back.

"Pam, you can't handle this." His stern voice had commanded me to back down, but I'd struggled with the man larger than me in height and girth.

"That's my dad, Joe."

When the call came through, I'd been on duty.

Possible hit and run.

There was no possible about it. My father laid sprawled on the side of the road in our small town, and no additional vehicles were present. The sheriff was in hot pursuit of a suspect, but it made no difference to me. Innocently walking home, only two blocks from the local favorite Town Tavern, my father was down.

Joe Carpenter, my boss, did everything he could to block me from the scene.

"You don't want to see this," he warned.

I swipe at my eyes as I accelerate south on the highway, hoping to catch up to the ambulance. I'm not athletic, but I ran as fast as my short legs could take me back to the fire department a block away and hopped into my Jeep. At this time of night, the highway is relatively clear minus the slowest moving vehicle ever in front of me. I swerve left in hopes of

L.B. Dunbar

passing it but can't estimate the oncoming traffic of the two-lane highway.

"What the fuck!" I scream, cursing the car ahead of me while willing it to move faster. I bang on the steering wheel for emphasis. I *need* to get to the hospital. As we continue moving slower than the speed limit, my blurry vision shifts right as the car in front of me decelerates. Another string of profanity fills my Jeep until I notice a car off the side of the road, down in the ditch near the treeline.

Don't look, I tell myself, begging the car before me to move it. But inside me, my training kicks in. *Pull over and help.*

But my dad, I argue, and in my head, I hear his voice.

You've been trained for this. It's your calling to assist. It's because of your generous heart.

"Fuck," I yell again, slapping the steering wheel one more time as I pass the accident and then pull over.

Forgive me, Daddy. The prayer might be contrition for passing an accident. It might be hope that he'll hang on until I get to the hospital. *Please, Daddy.*

Slamming off the ignition, I exit my Jeep and race down the gravel shoulder. A bright red Corvette plastered into a tree isn't hard to see despite the dark night. The windshield is shattered. The driver's door is wedged shut. The air bag deployed. With the driver's window down, I'm able to call out to the driver.

"Hey buddy, are you alright?" I don't want to be here. I need to get to my dad, but this scene doesn't look good. I reach through the open window to feel for a pulse. *He's alive.*

Everything tells me I can't get the driver's door open. The front of the car is like an accordion, pinning the door in the closed position, but somehow, strength finds me, and I pop the door. I puncture the airbag with a small pocket knife I grabbed before exiting my Jeep. This guy's head has a gash on it and lolls to the side when the airbag deflates. I catch him as he tips toward me.

"Whoa, pal."

It's then that eyes red-rimmed and glassy gaze up at me.

8

"Are you an angel?" he whispers, and I stare down into the darkest, most haunted eyes I've ever seen. My heart hammers, and I attribute it to my anger. This man is on something. Drunk, high, it doesn't matter to me. Is he possibly the suspect who hit my father? How could I save him when I want to strangle him for hurting the man most precious to me?

"I'm the devil," I hiss in warning because if this man hit my father and fled, I'll never forgive him. "Or maybe you are."

The man gags, and then he turns his head to vomit at my feet.

Gross. Definitely the devil himself.

As my blood races and adrenaline courses through my veins, my father's voice comes back to me again.

Fight through the pain. Fight from the heart. Love hurts, but it also heals.

For the first time ever, I don't know that I can take my father's advice.

9

Chapter 1

Must Be The Flu

Two and a half years later.

[Pam]

I hate that I'm in love with my boss.

I actually have two jobs, so it's not my day-job boss. It's my *other* boss—an annoyingly needy grown-ass forty-year-old man. I've worked for him for over two years and still wonder most days why I do it.

Because you think he's hot, and he pays you well for your time.

Yes, but should it be about money and looks? I'm literally arguing with myself while I massage my pounding temple. As a single woman, I'd survived the dreaded Valentine's Day only to come down with your classic flu. Stuffy nose. Sore throat. Cough. Aches. Chills. All I want to do is curl up in bed—my bed—in my apartment.

Not here. Not at selfish Jacob Vincent's house while I wait to let the house cleaner in.

You live alone. It's not even dirty in here. My chest pinches as I cough. It's almost as if by cursing Jacob in my head, my body wants to punish me.

His home on the shore of Lake Michigan is just outside our small town of Elk Lake City. Boasting floor-to-ceiling windows along the wall facing the water, this contemporary mansion strangely reminds me of how Edward Cullen's residence was depicted in *Twilight*, the books, not the movies.

Jacob likes to argue with me that the movies never get it right. It's all about the written word. Books do it best.

And he isn't wrong. As a fiction author himself, his writing was what first attracted me to him. *To his books*, not him personally.

It was not love at first sight when we finally met in person.

Jacob Vincent is nothing short of edgy and rugged in a boxer kind of way. He's lean but muscular. Feisty and jumpy with deep, dark eyes like midnight and a head of short hair to match. He doesn't have a scruffy beard so much as a jaw covered with artful stubble unless he's in writer mode. Then he might go days without shaving, giving him the lumberjack effect. Either way, he's a good-looking man in the way a man can be when he's had his nose broken a few times, scars on his forehead and cheek that mar his perfection, and several tattoos on his body. From his physical appearance, you'd never imagine words are how he fights best.

And right now, I'd like to throat punch him for requesting I be here to let the house cleaning service in.

Just give her a key, I'd argued before he left on a ten-day holiday with his girlfriend.

That's right. The man I'm in love with also has a picture-perfect girlfriend, tall and lean with big boobs and a tight ass. Not like me, who is curvy in all the right places but just not the right places for a man like Jacob Vincent. She's Malibu Barbie, and I'm just the shape of Michigan. I'm not horrible to look at, but I'm no model like his woman.

Jacob refuses to give a key to anyone other than me and his stepsister, Ella. Though she lived here for a while, she's in New York now, so I'm the one who feels like I'm on my deathbed as I wait for a service to clean a house that isn't even dirty.

Am I bitter? Of course not.

Lying on one of two leather couches in his great room, I try to focus on the large glass panes overlooking the lake in the distance. The trees are brown and barren this time of year. The world outside seems Medieval-ancient, and I'm starting to feel the same way even though I'm only thirty-six. I'm so grateful Valentine's *smalentines* is over because I hate the reminder that I'm still alone at my age—lonely and in love with a man I can't have.

The doorbell rings, and I push myself upright, the pounding in my head accelerating as I try to stand. Bending at the waist, I cough uncontrollably again and kick the leg of the square coffee table. Shit, that freaking hurt. As I hobble to the door, the throbbing in my toe matches

L.B. Dunbar

the pulsing rhythm in my head. My brain feels like it's hosting at a club dance party—*thump, thump, thump*—but I'm not enjoying myself. My hunched position makes me look old, and I feel as ancient as the bare trees behind Jacob's house.

"Miss Pam, you no look so good," Mrs. Kewadin says in broken English. The Native American woman enters along with a rush of cold Midwestern winter air, and my shivering causes my teeth to chatter.

"I'm not feeling so great," I tell her, slowly returning to my perch on the uncomfortable leather couch.

Why can't he have normal furniture like my mother's old sofa? Something where you can sink into the cushions and feel the warmth in the worn fabric.

"I'm going to just lie here for a bit," I say over my shoulder, limping because of my toe and holding my head so my brain doesn't move too much.

Stop thinking about stupid stuff, and it might not ache.

Collapsing on the couch, I bring my knees up to my chest and try to get comfortable, allowing Mrs. Kewadin to do whatever needs to be done now that she's in the house.

I don't know how much time passes as I drift into that weight-pressing sleep when you can't move a muscle, but you're cognizant of your surroundings. The vacuum drones. The glass squeaks from cleaning. The furniture is sprayed with polish. My body melts into the cool, crackling couch while I shiver, drawing my knees tighter to my chest.

My thoughts drift to when I first met Jacob. A memory of my deceased dad.

It's all a jumble, and then I sense a presence before me.

Daddy? I'm hallucinating if I think my father has come to visit me from beyond the grave. It's the kind of fictional story I like to read. Fantasy, thriller, sci-fi, and horror are my jam. However, in real life, I don't need a ghost haunting me.

Lilac? The masculine voice drifts to me as if I'm underwater. Definitely not my father as only one man calls me that name.

"Are you an angel?" he asked me when we first met. The next day, he decided I was more of a woodland nymph with a distinct fragrance—*syringa vulgaris*, the lilac.

Perhaps it was love at second sight for me then.

Lilac. The manly voice grows louder, sensual even with a raspy, low tenor. Again, not my father. It almost sounds like Jacob, but he's not due home until tomorrow morning, thus the need for my presence today. I wonder if Mrs. Kewadin is almost done. I really want to go home, but I'm not certain I can move from this spot. I'm not comfortable, but the thought of getting in my Jeep and driving to my apartment in town does not sound like a wise idea despite the temptation of my bed.

"Lilac, what's the matter?" The depth of the concerned tone surprises me.

I moan Jacob's name as if he's standing before me. I can't open my eyes. They burn behind my heavy lids like my throat, which doesn't want to work other than to groan. A fever has taken over, and I shake despite the aches in my body.

Something wraps me, shifting me, and I cry out at the movement.

No, don't move me. I'd just found a warm spot on that damn cold couch.

"Hang on, Lilac." The voice becomes more distinct.

"Jacob?" *Is it really him?* My head rests against a hard shoulder, and I'm cradled into a warm chest. *This is nice. So nice.* My nose presses into skin, and I inhale. Cloves. The sweet fragrance of tobacco tickles my nose, and I can't help myself when I mutter, "You smell delicious."

A deep chuckle rumbles the chest at my side, and I sense us ascending.

Where are we going?

Within minutes, I'm lying on something more comfortable than a leather couch, sinking into the depths of what's under me. I miss the strong arms holding me and the comfort of nestling against a warm body, but layers of fresh-scented clouds of softness cover me, pressing down on my sore body. *This is nice, too.* Heat slowly seeps into my skin, and I melt into a sweet abyss without ever opening my eyes.

13

L.B. Dunbar

"Thank you," I mumble to the imaginary Jacob. Lost in my pulsing head, I have no idea where I am, but a smile curls my lips as I drift into sleep with thoughts of my hot boss.

Chapter 2

Deliriousness

[Pam]

Slowly, I open my eyes to the light behind my lids. Taking in the dim room, I notice the vaulted ceiling. The starkness of the wall. The dark windowpane, and the comfort of an unfamiliar bed. I roll my head to the other side of me and push myself upward on a shaky arm. My head screams in pain, but I'm focused on the man beside me.

Please tell me I'm dreaming.

"That must be some hangover you're nursing, Lilac." The raspy tenor ripples over my skin, and my arm bends, collapsing me back to the bed. I look up at him with fearful eyes.

This is not happening.

"I'm not hungover." I don't recognize my own voice, rough from disuse and dehydration. My throat is killing me.

"I'm just teasing," Jacob says, blowing out a breath. With his legs stretched out before him, he sits with his laptop on his thighs and glasses perched on the end of his nose. He almost looks studious, but once those glasses are removed, his appearance will shift to tough, edgy, and almost hostile.

"What are you doing here?" I question, staring up at him as my brain slowly processes—*I'm in Jacob's bed.*

"Seeing as it's my home, it makes sense for me to be here," he jokes as he removes the glasses and sets them behind him. I've been in Jacob's room before but never when he's been present. *Hell no.* I've been up here to instruct the cleaning lady or snoop around when he's out of town. A low bookcase placed behind his bed acts as a headboard of sorts. The bed stands in the middle of his room, near the large floor-to-ceiling window facing west. There's a little reading-writing area with an overstuffed chair, ottoman, and floor lamp on the other side of the bookcase. The

L.B. Dunbar
bathroom is located behind that section. It's an unusual setup for an unusual man.

"A better question is what are you doing here, Goldilocks?" Of all the nicknames Jacob calls me, he's never called me this one before. I might resemble the errant child with my chin-length straw-blond hair, styled in loose curls on occasion, but presently, my hair is greasy and plastered to my head. If I'm Goldilocks, he's one grizzly bear, and this bed is just right, but I'm still wondering what I'm doing in it of all places.

"I let the house cleaner in. You weren't supposed to be home until tomorrow." My tone is defensive. I was to get in and get out, not under his directive, but my own. I'm upset he took a two-week vacation with his girlfriend, which reminds me . . . *I'm in Jacob's bed.*

As I attempt to push my body upward again, my quaking limbs cause me to struggle. "I need to go home." Tears fill my eyes at the possibility of moving as well as the reminder Jacob has a love life that does not include me. It normally doesn't matter. I understand our positions. He's the boss, and I'm the assistant. Only, I'm not in the proper headspace to deal with my emotions.

"Hey," he softly says, moving his laptop and turning to me. "You aren't going anywhere." His hand moves forward as though he intends to touch me. As if he'll cup my jaw and tell me he's always wanted me in his bed.

That would be a fantasy—which he's good at writing, and I'm good at reading—but it's one neither of us lives.

"How did I get up here?" I ask, looking around the room while his hand retracts. I'm hoping to hide my disappointment, and then I remember I'm a sweaty, shaky mess. I'm sick.

"I carried you. What do you need? Water? Some food? Tea?"

I turn back to him, startled by his suggestions and overall kindness. It isn't that Jacob's particularly mean to me. He just acts indifferent. He teases me, and he flirts sometimes, but it's just his personality. He likes me as his assistant, but we aren't anything more to each other.

Ignoring all his questions, I ask one more important than the others. "Why am I in your bed?"

16

"With the way you've phrased that, I'd think you don't want to be in my bed. And here, I've been wanting to get you in my bed forever." He winks at me. The smug bastard winks.

This is not happening. I'm hallucinating because I have the flu, and my temperature has made me delirious. On that note, I glance down at myself and realize I'm not wearing what I came to his house in. Instead, I'm wearing a large T-shirt that smells very much like Jacob. The clove fragrance is intoxicating, and I shouldn't be thinking of his scent or anything else about him—like how close he is to me, or how he's looking at me right now, or the fact . . . *I'm in Jacob's bed.*

"Did you undress me?"

Jacob holds a hand to his chest, feigning offense. "If I didn't know better, I'd think you're upset that I took your clothes off." He slowly smiles, finding humor in his own words. "You know I've been dying to do that for years as well."

He's a liar. He's a lying liar who lies. Jacob Vincent has never once wanted to remove my clothes or take me to his bed, and I don't even know why we're having this discussion. I glance down. I'm not wearing a bra, only my underwear and his T-shirt. My head pops up, eyes widening. Oh my God, Jacob has seen me naked—all large-breasted, curvy-hipped, not quite flat belly of me.

I'm mortified. Like dear God, come and take me because I can never look at this man again.

"Relax, Lilac," he says, his lips slowly curling. "I didn't check out the goods." However, as he speaks, his eyes lower, more like a flick downward before flashing back up to my face, which heats the rest of my body. I'm suddenly warm everywhere, only I can't kick off the covers because I'm hardly wearing anything.

My thoughts race. Have I shaved my legs recently? When was the last time I trimmed the privates? Did he notice the roll of my belly? My eyes close. My throbbing headache pulses faster than my heart.

"Lilac, could you please lie back down? You need rest, angel."

The softness of his voice could break me if I wasn't already weak and wondering what was happening. He twists again for the top of his low bookcase and hands me a glass of water, then holds out two pills.

L.B. Dunbar

"Nurse's orders. Every four hours."

I stare at him. He doesn't know any nurses. He's more of a recluse, so he hardly knows anyone here. He's a writer-in-the-woods kind of guy. I had to sign a non-disclosure agreement after we met and he asked me to work for him, so I wouldn't reveal who he was or where he lived. I don't dare ask him who he knows that's a nurse because I'm certain I'll hear about some skank he was with when he was on a break with his on-again, off-again girlfriend. They've been together as long as I've known him.

Willingly taking the two pain pills, I sip the water, hoping the fever reducer will kick in quickly so I can dress and get the heck out of Dodge.

"You aren't going anywhere," he warns me as if reading my thoughts.

"You know I have another job." I remind him of my work at Mae's Flower Shop, but Jacob only shakes his head.

"And you aren't going to your *other job* anytime soon. You're sick, and you're not leaving me." His head pops up. "I mean, here. You aren't leaving my bed." His voice drops on the last statement, and the heat of my body alleviates. How I've longed to hear those words said with such intention, but he's only making the demand because of my condition.

"Which brings me back to why am I in your bed?" His stepsister has a room on the opposite end of the house. She isn't using it, and I could be in there. He also has a guest bedroom on the first floor behind the kitchen. I could be in that room as well.

"Because I want you close to me. I can take care of you better in here." He looks away from me, reaching for his laptop as if signaling the end of this conversation. I'm dismissed. Taking a moment, I observe his profile. Those etched cheeks. The slight crook to his nose. The pout of his lips. The line of stubble along his jaw. He has a sexy, fighting Irish vibe about him. However, he's hurting while he's hunting for gold at the end of some unforeseeable rainbow. Jacob never seems truly happy. He smiles, and he jokes, but he also drinks a lot to take off the edge or maybe keep something at bay. He's almost full of as much pretend in his personal life as the fictional situations he puts on the pages of his incredible books.

18

His head turns back to me. "Lie down, Lilac." His voice commands, but his tone is tender. I do as he says although I remain confused by his orders and my position. While I'm still watching him, he returns to his laptop. My lids slowly lower at the sound of furious keyboard clicking. What world is he creating so he can lose himself and escape me beside him?

+ + +

I wake coated in a layer of sweat. The lamp dimly illuminating the room earlier this evening, or morning, or whatever time it was, is off, and the bedroom is enveloped in darkness. Something warm and heavy rests around my middle and the largest heating blanket lays along my back and against my legs. I wiggle my toes and touch the tops of bare feet which do not belong to me. A subtle shift behind me rustles the sheets and I stiffen.

"You okay, angel?" Jacob's sleepy voice twists my insides. His breath tickles the back of my neck, and I shiver.

"I'm warm," I whisper, despite the cool trickle down my spine. I'm almost afraid to speak. He must be dreaming. He doesn't know he's holding me. He doesn't know what he's doing.

"That's a good sign, right? Fever's breaking." My body has been struggling between chills and heat for nearly two days.

"I think," I say, hoping he releases me and moves away. Instead, his arm tightens over my middle, and my back rests against his chest. Through the thin T-shirt I'm wearing, his chest feels firm and bare. Warmth radiates from him to me. My legs twitch, feeling the coarse hairs of his against mine.

Holy Count Dracula. Is he only wearing boxer briefs behind me?

Jacob is not ashamed of his body. In fact, he's rather proud of it. He works out religiously in his home gym, equipped with weights and boxing equipment. His physique is that of a fighter, and he's merciless once he gets going on the punching bag. The muscle of his arm flexes around me, and he nuzzles deeper into my neck, inhaling my skin.

"You smell sweet," he whispers.

19

L.B. Dunbar

"You mean like sweat," I correct with a huff.

"Nope, sweet, like your namesake, Lilac." *That isn't my name.* I'm Pam Carter, but Jacob has taken to calling me Lilac almost twenty-four seven as if no other name exists. Then again, when he's angry, my given name comes out. It's rare that he's angry with me, though. I've heard his fights with Mandi. *Yes, Mandi with an "i".*

Mandi, sweet as candy, she's known to say during interviews. She's a model or something, and thirteen years younger than Jacob. I'm actually not certain what she does. She's more like a bored heiress with too much money and a serious lack of body fat.

My legs shuffle as they ache, rubbing against Jacob's, and he adjusts behind me. Something pokes me in the backside, and I still.

Is he? . . . He can't be . . . Not with me.

"Jacob," I whisper, wanting to wake him from his slumber and remind him I'm the one he has his arm around. Not his girlfriend but me, his assistant. The woman he claims saved his life. "It's me, Pam."

My voice speaks louder, but at the same time, my fingers stroke down his forearm over my midsection. Without thinking, I scratch back up the length, tenderly dragging my nails over the coarse hair. Back and forth, I stroke from wrist to elbow, and repeat.

"Hmm. That feels nice, angel." Something brushes my shoulder. *Did he . . . did he kiss me?*

Maybe I'm the one dreaming. Maybe I'm the one unconscious and slipping into an abyss of pure wannabe. I want to be Jacob's girlfriend. I want to be his lover. I want to be his best friend.

And all of these wants make me ridiculous.

I still and pat his arm with a short, sharp slap. His fingers curl into a fist, knuckles brushing over my breast before clutching the fabric of his tee at my chest.

"What did you do that for?" he grumbles into the back of my neck.

"Just want to make sure you're awake and realize you have your arm around me. *Pam.*" I emphasize my name again.

"Don't know a Pam," he teases. "Only know my Lilac, who is typically sweet and lets me sleep. Now, can we please go back to that?" He chuckles, rubbing his nose along my skin and then slipping his arm

20

off me. He rolls to his back behind me and the loss of his body leaves mine instantly cold. I curse myself for suggesting he pull away, but the rational side of me screams it's for the best.

Jacob Vincent would never truly be interested in a woman like me.

Chapter 3

For The Record

[Jacob]

I'm so hot for her, and I'm fucking hard as a hammer. With her back to me and my head turned in her direction, I sweep a hand down my abs and into my boxers to adjust myself. Nothing I do gets my dick to go down. She's sick, but still so sweet and her curves—*damn*. I jolt in my shorts, turn to face the ceiling, and scrub both hands over my day-old stubble.

I shouldn't be in bed with her. I shouldn't be near her, touching her, or thinking of her, but for the past two-plus years, Pam Carter has consumed me. My Lilac. An angel in the night who saved my life when she should have let me die. I've had a death wish more than once although I've never acted upon it. I'm reckless, not stupid, yet some say they go hand in hand.

Lying next to Pam is both reckless and stupid.

Especially after a ten-day trip with Mandi. It was hell. Mandi Hamilton and I have had one of the most tumultuous relationships in the history of relationships. We fuck. We fight. We break up. We get drunk. Then we see one another at a party, and the cycle starts all over again. I used to think it was almost fun because I'm a sick fuck like that. The hate fucking. The heated arguments that shifted to aggressive make-out sessions. The thrill of taking her at a moment's notice. However, the excitement of Mandi came to a screeching halt when I looked up into the eyes of a vision of innocence one night.

Lost. High. Crashed.

And there she was.

"Don't you dare die on me," she'd said. I took those words to heart. I would not leave her. I wouldn't dream of dying ever again.

I also didn't think I'd see her after that night. That night when an angel looked me in the eyes.

Of course, I hardly remember the moment, but she came to visit me the next day, and I put all the pieces together. I'll never forget the woman with eyes that not only wanted to scorch me for driving under the influence but also forgave me for some reason. She was my penance, and I didn't deserve her.

Rolling my head back in her direction, I stare at the outline of her body. Despite the dark, the highlights are accentuated, like the hills and valleys of a map. The curve of her shoulder. The dip to her waist. The swell of her hip. My arm had been around her and my hand rested between her large breasts. My dick brushed against her firm ass, and I'm so freaking stiff.

Ice Cream. Frozen lakes. Snowstorms.

I need to concentrate on anything that will cool me off.

Her legs rustle under the sheets, and she twists to face me. Thankfully, she's slipped back to sleep, and I'm praying she didn't notice how hard I am.

I'm not really the nurturing type, but for reasons I can't explain, I want to take care of her. I like having her this close to me and feeling like she needs me. She's always doing everything for me, and I don't always show her how much I appreciate her and how important she is to me. She's not like anyone I've known before, except maybe my stepsister, Ella. It was such a shock to find Pam curled up on my couch— a bit delirious, definitely chilled, but as if she was waiting for me.

What would it be like to come home to a woman waiting for me?

Pam is so different from Mandi. She doesn't want to pick a fight. She doesn't want to criticize. She doesn't complain.

I also note the physical differences, starting with the softness of her golden hair. Even plastered to her head from days of sleeping and without a wash, she's beautiful. She's this contradiction of innocence and temptation. With big denim blue eyes and bouncy blond waves to her chin, she wears bright lipstick in shades of red or hot pink. Her clothing is either too vibrant or all black. And her interests lean to the dark and morbid. She loves the shit I write.

Well, most of the time.

L.B. Dunbar

Her hand lays flat on the sheet. There isn't much distance between us, and I twist myself to face her sleeping form. My fingers hesitantly reach for hers, curling around them. She's warm, exuding heat, and I hope this means the fever is breaking. I don't like to see her weak. She's strong every other day, but then again, there's a vulnerability underneath her tough exterior with me.

She's too good for you, Jacob.

It's the main reason I've always kept my distance. I tease. I flirt. But then, I rein it in. I will not cross a line she does not want crossed. She's never given a hint of interest in me, remaining standoffish even when I joke with her.

I trust her implicitly, and trust isn't something I give easily.

Her fingers react to mine over hers and grab onto them. Touching her sends a thrill through me, like lightning striking the damned or Frankenstein's monster coming to life. Both concepts are similar. The monster was destined for a horrible life the moment he was born, and the same has happened to me.

I close my eyes, holding her fingers in mine, and think back on the torture of the past two weeks. Thank God, Mandi and I have finally come to a firm agreement. *No more.* The trip was a test of wills. Will we be together forever, or will we finally end this suffocating relationship? She wanted marriage. I wanted out.

Ten days to sort out feelings I already labeled as zero. It took a lot of alcohol to make it through the days *and nights* because I have absolutely no feelings left for Mandi. That makes me a coldhearted dick, but I don't care. All my emotions are wrapped up in this woman across from me, holding my hand like I'm suddenly her saving grace in a storm, and I so want to be deserving of saving her. For all she's done for me, I want to be something to her, but I also know I'm not worthy of someone like her. I'm a sick bastard for even thinking such a thing, but my heart doesn't want to stop rattling in the cage of my chest, begging for release. My dick has its own struggles, unwilling to settle down when she's around. I'm never going to sleep tonight.

+ + +

24

In the early morning, I slip from the bed and head downstairs to my office for a few hours of work. I'm writing my next fantasy thriller and need to concentrate, which I cannot do with Pam next to me.

"Good morning." Her soft voice eventually startles me, and I look up from my computer, over my glasses, at her curvy frame leaning against the doorjamb of my office. She's a vision, but she also looks like hell.

"You shouldn't be out of bed," I tell her, taking off my glasses and standing from the desk chair. I'm wearing jeans and a flannel shirt, but I'm barefoot. She's wearing my tee, exposing most of her legs, and my dick struggles behind my zipper once again. I cannot get myself under control.

"Would you mind if I shower?" she asks sheepishly, and I smile at the guilty look on her face. See, I'm a sick man because I'm thrilled to set her up in my bathroom. My shower is this amazing hexagon shape with only one side against the tile and the other five sides glass. A rain showerhead streams into the middle. Thinking of her naked body under the drenching spray with soap sliding down her lush curves makes me a mess of hormones I shouldn't even have at forty. But damn, I want her in ways I should not.

"How about a bath?" I state, seeing as she can hardly hold herself upright without leaning against the entrance to my writing space. She chews at her lip. She wants to say yes. Without giving her a second to hesitate, I step up to her, scoop her into my arms, and head back up the stairs.

She shrieks before she speaks. "Jacob, you don't need to carry me. I'm too heavy."

"You're as light as an angel's wings," I tell her.

"Oh, my God." She laughs, loosely wrapping her arms around my shoulders. I want her to hold onto me—really tighten those limbs around me and hold me—but she doesn't. "That's sweet but false."

She's self-deprecating, and while I sometimes let it slide by continuing to tease her, I don't want to hear it today.

L.B. Dunbar

"Don't think about yourself like that," I command as I climb the stairs. Once we enter the bathroom, I lower her to the closed toilet seat while I start the tub. It's an air tub with jets because sometimes I work out harder than I should and need the muscle relief. The thought of those jets going off and pulsing at parts of Pam causes my entire body to vibrate.

Crystal snowflakes. Frozen eyelashes. A tongue stuck on a cold pole.

I need to get myself together.

Testing the water, I stopper the tub and stand back. Pam watches me, her head leaning back, face upward like she wants to tell me a secret. She's worn that expression many times in the past, and I've always wondered what her thoughts are. *What won't she tell me?*

"When was the last time you ate?" I question instead, noticing her pale coloring. She shrugs. "What would you like to eat?"

She chuckles, shaking her head.

"You don't think I can cook?" I question.

"I know you can't, remember? Mrs. White and then Ethan."

Ah, Ethan Scott, my former in-home chef who fell in love with my stepsister. It was kind of nice having another man around the house, even if I was only present for a week, and he was here for five before Ella ran off. I shake my head at the thought of my sister and Ethan. It's not that I don't like the idea of them as a couple. I hate how they haven't found their way back to one another yet. For her sake, and I suppose his, I hope it happens soon.

As for Mrs. White, that cougar-driven hussy hit on me more times than a desperate housewife on a vacation in Vegas. Ella, my stepsister, did everything she could to chase her away, and even though Mrs. White was a good cook, I'd been grateful. A woman nearly fifteen years my senior serving me dinner in her sheer lingerie was too much for me. It might be another guy's thing, going for the older woman, but not mine. It's almost laughable that I'd been cougared at forty. Isn't it supposed to be a forty-year-old woman going for a younger man, not someone fifty-five, reminding me of my mother hitting on me? Like my mother, the woman who ran off and left her kid so she could screw half of Los

26

Angeles before I was even ten. Oh wait, she did that while she was still living in our home.

I realize the hypocrisy of my statement as Mandi is some thirteen years younger than me.

"Yeah, well, I can cook," I defend, wiping away thoughts of my wayward mother and my equally frustrating former girlfriend.

"Frozen pizza." Pam snorts.

"It encompasses the four food groups. Whole grains, vegetables, protein, and dairy." I tick off the categories on my fingers while she skeptically looks at me.

"Except the kind you eat is made from enriched white flour, has processed cheese, probably uses a tomato-paste substitute, and the meat product is questionable." Her eyes roam down my body, doing nothing to calm its already stiff status, and adds, "I don't know how you look like you do when you eat that shit . . . I mean, stuff."

Let it be noted, Pam Carter just swore, *and* she complimented me. I'm not making that up.

"You think I have a nice body?" I tease. Her face heats to this pretty pink shade I've seen a few times on those cheeks.

"You know you do," she says, her voice lowering as her gaze drops to her lap.

"Maybe, but I'd like to hear more about it from you. What exactly do you think is nice on my body?" Placing my hands on my hips, I turn my head, giving her the side of my face, and wait. A minute passes. When I glance back at her, a hand covers her mouth.

"Are you laughing at me?" She looks like she wants to burst out in giggles.

What's wrong with me? I work out hard. I have a six-pack that could quench your thirst. I've got the little hip dip that narrows over my pelvis and points at my dick. She can't see that part of me, but still.

"You look ridiculous like that," she states, taking in my pose. "Don't do that again." She's teasing, but my hands fall to fists at my sides. I get it. She isn't attracted to me. Despite the hard core of my body, it's not a body she wants.

27

L.B. Dunbar

"Whatever," I say, blowing off the hurt inside. I'm not a sensitive guy. Over the years, I've made my skin tough enough you could bounce a penny off me. Nothing penetrates me like it did when I was a kid.

Her shoulders fall, and I note the tub is almost full.

"Your forearms are your best feature," she says, surprising me. I glance at my arms, one covered in tattoos, the other clean. "You're strong, but you're also gentle, even if you don't want to admit it. You have serious arm porn."

"Arm porn?" I choke out when I peer over at her. Her gaze leaps to my eyes.

"And your eyes. They're this deep, rich dark color like the sky at midnight, and when you laugh, pinpricks dance in them like shining stars."

I . . . what?

"They also look like they hold a great secret. Like something is locked behind the dungeon door, and I've often wondered what's beyond them besides the creativity of your stories."

Holy . . . nope. Not going there. There is no way Pam can ever know my secrets. The horrors in my memories. The scenes that torture me.

"That sounds a bit too romantic," I mock, my voice rougher than necessary.

"Well, I'm not a poet." Pam sits straighter, her fingers curling at the hem of my tee which she's already tugged over her thighs. She knows I despise romance novels. Give me blood and guts, strange creatures and gore, and hate, and anger, and demons and I'm all in.

When I don't say anything else in response, Pam speaks again. "Never mind." Crestfallen, she slumps her shoulders, and I sense I've hurt her feelings. She couldn't mean any of it, though. Does she think the darkness is beautiful? Has she actually noticed my eyes that in-depth? Does she really see me as trapped inside myself?

One can only hope, but hope is also a romantic notion, and something I don't subscribe to. I learned early on it's dangerous to hope. You'll be disappointed every time.

"Bath's ready," I mutter, stepping toward the door, needing to distance myself from her and the burning sensation of hope in my chest.

+ + +

Setting a clean T-shirt and the smallest pair of sweats I can find outside the bathroom door, I leave Pam alone. I'd love to ask her if she needs anything else. Me in the tub with her. Someone to dry off her body. A person to have sex with against the sink. But I decide against all those things, trying to wrap my head around what she said about me.

Is she attracted to my arms and my eyes? She hadn't actually said that, just admitted that both body parts were *attractive*. And I'm being ridiculous. I have other things to do than analyze Pam's comments.

Returning to my office, I read back what I wrote this morning. Time passes slowly, and I consider checking on Pam for the hundredth time. Suddenly, I hear a clatter from the other side of the house.

After quickly standing, I pace to the bottom of the staircase, which is right outside my office.

"Lilac," I call out, thinking she's still upstairs. When silence follows, I conclude the noise, whatever it was, was nothing. Turning back for my office, I hear another clattering sound coming from the kitchen, and I race across the great room, through the swinging door to the state-of-the-art kitchen, and stop short. Pam isn't wrong. I don't cook in here despite the top-of-the-line appliances.

A pot sits on the stove, and an unopened can of soup rests on the counter. Rounding the large island centering the cabinets, I discover Pam curled up on the floor. Her back leans against the cabinets while her knees are drawn up to her chest, and her head rests on her knees.

"Lilac," I cry, squatting down next to her. She slowly lifts her head to look at me.

"The bath took all my energy. I should eat, but I can't even open the can of soup." Her voice trembles as if she might cry, and I swear if she does, I'm a goner. Despite the endless tears and drama of Mandi over the years, to see my strong Lilac fall apart would break me.

"Okay, angel," I say, scooting forward for her and scooping her up again. "I'll make the soup. Let's get you back in bed."

29

L.B. Dunbar

"I don't think I can sleep," she mutters, curling into me for the first time out of the three that I've carried her. Her arms wrap tightly around my neck, keeping her securely against my body. The sensation of her holding onto me does something funny to my insides, and my heart hammers at my ribs.

"You don't need to sleep. But you do need to rest, though, and eat."

"Can you handle soup?" she weakly teases, and I twist my neck. It's the wrong thing to do. With her face only an inch from mine, and her body in my arms, I want to lay her out on my couch and have my way with her. I want to kiss those lips usually covered in hot pink or bright red. I want to touch every inch of her and enter her, repeatedly.

I shudder at the thought, and Pam's arms loosen.

"You should really put me down. Let me walk. I need to stretch my legs."

I don't want to let her go, but I do as she asks, setting her back on her feet. Pam stumbles, and I catch her around the waist. Those innocent eyes look up at me, questioning why I'm touching her.

Isn't it written on my face how I feel about her?

"I need to get you upstairs and back in my bed," I give as my explanation. She stiffens under my arm, and I realize what I've said.

"I mean, back in bed." *Period.* That little round dot that ends a sentence. Not emphasizing mine, with me, holding onto her. Just back to my room. End of.

"Okay." The word catches in her throat as my arms slip tighter around her waist, still looking at me in this funny way. One day, she's going to open her eyes, though, and slip from my hands when she finally discovers what's in the dungeon of my head.

As I assist her back up the stairs, her leaning into me, I remind myself I'll do everything I can to make certain she never sees the darkness in me. We'll keep living this fantasy, where she works for me and I pine for her, and the conflict in my soul will not harm the brightness of her heart.

Chapter 4

Mom Calling

[Pam]

Once I've crawled back into Jacob's bed, I lie on my side, angling myself in such a way so I can stare out the window. It's strange that he has the bed positioned so the glass is at the foot of the bed. Then again, it's peaceful lying here, looking out at the cold lake and the dormant trees. It's a morbid view, and I wonder if visions like this help Jacob with his storytelling. He writes some dark, twisted stuff, and I've loved it and hated it over the years. I wouldn't say I was a super fan, but I am. I blog under the disguise of Blood and Blossoms, incorporating the two halves of myself.

When I started blogging, I was an EMT for the local Elk Lake City fire department. Blogging was a stress reliever from the day job. I was reading books anyway, so why not discuss them? After a dozen years, two simultaneous accidents ripped me apart. I couldn't recover from that night, and I stepped away from a job I loved to pursue another avenue of my life that I adore—flowers.

Mae's Flowers is a garden center north of my small town just off the highway, and I'd put in hours there as extra income when I was still an EMT. Over time, Mae and I became good friends, and she offered me a full-time manager position when I needed a change in life. I still blog as a stress reliever although the only stress in my life is Jacob.

Thinking of the devil, he enters the room with the soup on a bed tray, a glass of water, and more fever medication. A single flower sits in a tiny vase that looks strangely like a pepper shaker.

"Where did you find that?" I laugh, noting the purple crocus.

"It was peeking up in the yard." He offers this information as if the early spring flower litters his yard, which it doesn't. The flower can actually bloom through snow, and it's a striking contrast to find something so bold against a cold backdrop. I smile to myself at the small

L.B. Dunbar

gesture, and he sets the tray over my lap as I sit upright. My short hair is still damp from the shower, and the sweats he gave me are too large for my short legs. He also left me another T-shirt of his that smells divine.

"Did you change the sheets?" My hand spreads over the freshness of clean linens.

"I thought fresh ones might feel better against your skin after being sweaty from when your fever broke." He glances away for a second. "I also put your clothes in the washer." It's a sweet gesture—changing the sheets, washing my clothes—and it certainly explains where my things went. Then I consider it means Jacob saw my bra and underwear, the mismatched set I was wearing and the size of the comfy panties. He's seen my breasts if he undressed me, although he swears he didn't look.

Why would he look? He just had Malibu Mandi days ago.

Reaching for a spoon on the tray, I blow on the soup before scooping some of the broth and bringing it to my mouth. Jacob is watching me. He's made himself comfortable on the edge of the bed, and his eyes follow the direction of the spoon entering my mouth and closing my lips around the warm liquid. Nothing tastes better than chicken noodle soup when you're sick. I swallow, uncomfortable with his intense stare.

"This is good," I tease of the canned product that Jacob only had to open with the flick of a wrist and pour into a pan to heat. "You're a great cook."

The corner of his lip crooks. "Now, you're just being mean." His eyes sparkle like I mentioned earlier—midnight with an array of stars. *What constellations rest in those orbs?* I've known Jacob for two and a half years, and I still can't read him most days. I've never spent so much unstructured time with him.

"Once I eat this, I should really change and go home."

"Lilac, quit trying to run away. Nurse's orders are you stay put."

I tilt my head, hating the question I'm about to ask. "Jacob, do you even know any nurses?"

"Yes. One. Her name is Mary."

I let the information settle in for a second, and then I nearly drop my spoon.

"Mary?" I pause. *Oh, my God.* "Did you call my mother?!"

"Yes, I did, and you know, I'm a little offended she had no idea who I was."

"Because you're a famous author and who wouldn't?" I mock.

"Because she's your mother, and she had no idea we were friends."

Friends. *Are we friends?* "I signed a non-disclosure agreement that I wouldn't share any details about you, your whereabouts, or your writing," I remind him.

"Yes, but I would have thought you'd tell your mother." He sounds aghast. Jacob knows I'm close with my family. We all live in the same small town within only a few miles of the home we grew up in. Our closeness as adult siblings has increased over the past two and a half years due to our father's death. As for our mother, well, she's just a force, and you don't mess with Mary.

"There's no one I trust more than my mother, but even she could have let it slip and told someone I work for you." *Another reminder that I'm your employee.* We aren't friends, not in the sense I want to consider friendship. I'm in love with him, but he's not in love with me. Thus, we have a line we do not cross.

"Well, she knows who I am now, and her orders were for you to stay in *my bed* for a week."

"My mother did not say that," I drone, not missing the emphasis. Why must he torture me so much? Not to mention, I don't have a week to rest and recuperate. I have another job I need to get to.

"I need to call Mae," I state, suddenly counting off the days in my head. Jacob was due back on Monday. I was here Sunday. I think it's now Wednesday.

"Handled."

My eyes leap to his. "You called Mae as well?"

"I did. She was also rather surprised to hear from me. I thought she was your best friend."

How the hell does Jacob know that? I don't talk much about Mae. Maybe I drop the occasional phrase *I have plans* when it comes to her, but again, I never give away too much personal information to him.

33

"You know, people should really know where you are, Lilac." His voice softens as his eyes drop to the black and white duvet on his bed. He speaks out of concern because of his sister. She was attacked, and Jacob beats himself up over it, as if any of it was his fault.

"I've told my family and Mae I work for a man who has a job that I can't discuss, but I'm safe working with him."

Jacob's head pops back up, and his eyes focus on mine. "You feel safe with me?"

The question startles me. *Shouldn't I?* Jacob has never done anything to frighten me. He drinks too much. He works out intensely. I've learned from his sister, Ella, he has a temper, and it stems from his childhood, but I've never seen it. I've always assumed he works things out in boxing exercises or by writing his novels.

"Of course," I assure him, and his brows pinch while he bites his lip.

Okay, maybe he's scaring me just a little right now because he's giving me a look like he wants to pounce. Like he wants to toss me back on the pillows and have his way with me. And that's not frightening in the least bit. What I should be afraid of is my own imagination and projecting it on a man who would never do such a thing to me.

I'm so ridiculous. It must be the fever.

"I'm done with the soup," I say, swallowing a sudden lump in my throat.

"You only took two sips," Jacob admonishes, staring at my lips. "Finish the bowl and then you need a nap."

I've slept so much in the past two days I don't know if I can sleep any more, but my body does feel like mush. Jacob seems to sense the war within me, so he makes a suggestion.

"Let me finish the chapter I'm working on. You eat your soup, then we can watch a movie or something in a little bit." He speaks as if he's pacifying a child, and I want to punch myself in the face for loving it so much. Other than reading his manuscripts on occasion at his house, I don't spend time with Jacob directly. We speak often via text or email, and somehow that morphed into the other things I do for him, like finding him a live-in cook and house cleaning services. He claims he asks me to do these things because I know this town. I know who to trust, and he trusts me. However, the day he asks me to pick up his dry cleaning is the day I quit him regardless of the pay.

I nod to accept his present offer, and he stands, leaning toward me. Again, the fantasies take over, the one where he'll lean down and kiss my temple. He hesitates a second, and then straightens as if reading my thoughts. Quickly excusing himself, he disappears behind me, through his sitting area and out the entrance of his room. Neither his room which is the entire north end of the house nor his sister's room on the south end has a door, just an opening to their private spaces. A loft bridge connects the two sides, but the siblings rarely entered each other's bedrooms.

I consider myself a friend to his stepsister. Ella has had a rough couple of years, and I know the feeling. She needed to find herself—outside of Jacob, outside of this town, and even outside of Ethan Scott, her one true love. I helped her with that when she escaped to New York. I didn't think Jacob would forgive me at first for helping her leave, but he came around, apologizing for overreacting toward me. It might be the one time he's truly been angry with me and asked my forgiveness afterward. I finish the soup with additional wandering thoughts. I'm curious about Jacob's surprise that I hadn't told my mother about him.

Mary Carter is what everyone would call good people, and I admire her for raising four kids and surviving the death of my father, who was the love of her life. His passing was difficult on all of us in our own way. My father and I were close. He knew how lost I was in my early thirties, and it's something I like to think I recognize in Jacob. He has a put together look on the outside, but he's dying on the inside. His dungeon door is locked tight, and I'll never have the key to understanding him.

+ + +

To my surprise, I nap for three hours after the soup and eventually wander down to the entrance of Jacob's office again.

"Jesus, I thought you would never rise," he teases, glancing up at me over the rim of his glasses. These are relatively new to him and give him a sexy professor appearance. With rumpled hair, the flannel shirt, and bare feet, Jacob takes sexy to a new level of torture for me.

"Why didn't you wake me?" I question.

"Because you're sick, Lilac, and you need the rest. But I'm starving." He stands and pats his rock-hard belly, which thuds in response. I've never seen him without a shirt, not even the other night when he laid behind me in bed, but I have a strong imagination of the tightness in those lower stomach muscles as I've seen him in fitted tees.

"I don't think I can handle pizza," I warn him. Jacob has an obsession with frozen pizzas.

"What do you feel like?" His voice drops when he asks, as do his eyes to my legs. The sweats he gave me are too big, and a ripple of something unwarranted seeps through my body under his gaze. I hate when he speaks in that seductive manner because he doesn't mean anything by it. He's only teasing me.

"I'd love scrambled eggs and toast." A little protein and some bread sound divine.

"Coming right up, breakfast in bed." He winks at me, and I grin. He's such an ass in an adorable way. As he nears me, he stops at my side. "Back in bed, Lilac." His voice drops even lower, and over my shoulder, I look up at him. He's so close to me, closer than necessary for a man heading to his kitchen. His fingers brush the back of my hand. Another ripple of excitement quickly turns into a tornado whirling through my midsection.

"Yes, sir," I whisper. Jacob bites his lip, his eyes dropping to mine once more. There's a tic in his jaw, and the vein in his neck strains.

"Lilac." A warning resonates in the nickname. For the first time ever, I'm deliciously frightened of Jacob. Not for the first time, I imagine what it would be like to kiss him. To have the lip he's chewing press against mine. To feel his tongue slip past my lips and tangle with mine. To have his body over me.

Heat rushes my face while Jacob stares at me.

Without a word, I roll from the doorjamb and turn to the staircase, slowly taking it upward and sensing Jacob watching my retreat. There's nothing sexy about wearing his too large sweats or his oversized tee, so

I have no idea what he's looking at other than the expanse of my backside, probably noting it isn't tight like Malibu Mandi.

L.B. Dunbar

Chapter 5
And The Oscar Goes To . . .

[Jacob]

She's going to be the death of me. It's evident watching her climb my stairs she isn't wearing underwear under those sweats, and I want nothing more than to tug them down and take her right there on the steps. Not to mention, she's not wearing a bra under the T-shirt I gave her, and I want to lift the shirt and place my mouth over one of those weighty globes. Pam has a lush body, and she just does it for me without even knowing it. And dammit, I'm hammer stiff again, and I've already taken care of business in the shower once this morning.

I head to the kitchen, in hopes to cool off and prepare our eclectic meal of her eggs, my frozen pizza, and a bowl of popcorn for the movie. She's right. I'm not a cook. I want food without effort on my part. It's one reason I hired Ethan Scott last fall. If someone doesn't feed me, I can forget to eat. I also hired him because I had a six-week book tour, and I needed someone to look after my stepsister, who was living with me at the time.

Pam and I have already discussed her part in aiding my stepsister's disappearance last fall. All's forgiven although I was pissed at Pam at first. Ella's the one who did the soothing over, eventually calling me and explaining her thought process, her feelings, and how she wanted to get help, but on her own terms. It's noble actually, but as soon as she hinted I needed help—I needed to face my past—it was time to shut that conversation down. I ended up easily forgiving Pam. How could I not? She's the only friend I have.

Thinking of Ella, I give her a call while I'm working on the makeshift dinner.

"Belly," I tease when she answers. She's thirty years old, but I still call her by the nickname I gave her when she came to live with me and my father. Her mother was sixteen years younger than my dad and a former model. Both parents doted on Ella as they shaped and molded her into the shining star they wanted her to be. She equaled dollar signs for them. On the other hand, I was a huge disappointment to my father, and my stepmother was indifferent. I had nothing to offer her, so she had nothing to give me except Ella. Her daughter was ten years younger than me but looked up to me for everything. Kindness. Friendship. Protection. And I failed her on the last one. I brought an unsuspected villain into her life, and he scarred her. It was all my fault.

"Jacob," she exhales with excitement. "I haven't heard from you in days. How is the writing going?"

"The writing is good."

"Wow, what a way with words," she teases. Once my sister moved to New York, I diligently checked in on her, and it drove her crazy. I just wanted her safe, happy, and whole. Even though I'm not much of a romantic myself, I did think the one thing that could give Ella the happily ever after she deserved was Ethan.

"How was your trip?" The question is asked through clenched teeth. Ella hates Mandi and held nothing back about how bad she thinks the relationship was for me. For the past six months, she's been telling me I should find a woman like Pam. When I think about it, Ella's been saying Pam specifically. I should be looking at Pam.

"It's finally over." There's relief in saying the words. I'm not the best communicator, and I don't like conflict, especially not provoking it, but I had to be straight with Mandi. I didn't love her, so there was no future for us.

"For real this time?" Ella teases. She knows the push and pull history of our reckless relationship.

"Yes, smart-ass, it's really real this time." Decisions were made with Mandi, and Pam was waiting in my home when I returned a day early. It almost feels like a sign, but signs mean hope, and I refuse to accept that kind of voodoo. Pam was sick and passed out on my couch, not expecting me and certainly not waiting for me.

"I'm so proud of you, Jacob. How grown-up and adult of you." She laughs.

"How are things with you?" I hesitate. I haven't seen her in weeks.

39

"Actually, I have news for you."

I almost drop the phone when I learn my stepsister is back and permanently staying. She quickly gives me the details, and I promise to visit her new place.

If ever there's something to fill me with hope, it's the true happiness in my sister's voice.

"I'm so happy for you, Belly," I say, meaning every word.

"It's your turn," she says, her voice lowering a bit. "You deserve happiness, too."

I snort. "Well, hearing you happy makes me happy."

"Now, you're just being cheesy." She pauses. "But you're a good big brother." The shift in her tone tells me all we don't say to one another. She loves me, and the small sliver of my heart that allows love reciprocates.

"I'm the best," I mock, and she laughs.

"Yeah, the best. Okay, talk soon," she says.

"Take care, Belly." I worry about her. She hasn't always been good at taking care of herself. Then Ethan started caring about her, and everything changed. It restores my faith in the possibility that love can really strengthen a person. *Other people.* Not me. I don't really know what love is other than what I feel for my sister, and that's a different kind of love.

Placing everything on a tray again and tucking a bottle of scotch under my arm, I carry the small pilfering up to the bedroom. Pam is sitting upright with pillows at her back and the television on.

"I don't understand how to work this thing," she jests, holding up the four remotes necessary to get to the channels. I don't watch TV often, but for the best viewing, I had the set secured to the wall near the corner, opposite my side of the bed and closer to where Pam sits. The angle allows me to watch it in bed if I wish, and I've never been so excited to watch something because Pam will be next to me.

"What would you like to watch?" I ask after setting the tray near the foot of the bed.

"I'm not picky. Anything is fine."

My brow hitches at her, and she shrugs so I pull up one of my favorites.

"*Frankenstein?*" she questions, reaching for the plate with eggs and toast. "What version is that?"

"Kenneth Branagh. I love to pick apart all the ways he got it wrong," I admit. "The book is better."

"I know." She sighs, a smile curling her lips as if she knows me so well. Even without the hot pink or bright red lipsticks, her lips are full, and for the millionth time, I wonder what they would taste like. Right now, I imagine scrambled eggs, and I've never been so envious of a food before as I watch it enter her mouth and slide down her throat.

Sweet Jesus, get a grip, man.

I take a seat on my side of the bed. As I pour myself a scotch, Pam watches me before turning her attention back to the start of the movie as if it's the most interesting part. She's no longer eating.

"Is everything okay?" I intend to tease her, but my tone turns sour, mocking. Mandi would always tell me I drank too much, which was ironic considering the shit she put up her nose.

Pam shrugs. "Your house. Your rules."

"What does that mean?" An edge still taints my voice.

"Nothing." She shrugs again.

"Don't blow this off. Do you have a problem with me drinking?" Then I reconsider my question. I'm not justifying myself to anyone, not even Pam. Fuck this. No one will make me feel bad for a drink. Without waiting on her answer, I down the glass to prove the point to myself.

A heavy silence falls between us, and I hate the uncomfortableness more than the burn of the scotch.

"What?" I snap, uncertain why I'm barking at her.

"You know my dad died from a drunk driver," she says under her breath. Her quiet tone is like a sucker punch to my gut. I remember the timing of her father's death all too well, and I huff, giving off a dismissive sound. I also know Pam's been known to imbibe on occasion, so I don't understand what I'm missing.

"It's one drink," I mutter. "Maybe you'd like one?"

L.B. Dunbar

Pam doesn't look over at me, keeping her eyes toward the television. "Probably not a good idea, considering the meds and a lack of food."

I notice she's placed her plate back on the tray, hardly eating the eggs and only taking one bite of toast.

"You need to finish that." I nod at the plate, not interested in discussing my drinking.

"You're kind of bossy, you know that?" she mutters, reaching back for the plate and taking a few more bites.

"So I've been told," I reply as she's the one who has accused me of such a thing. *I'd like to boss you around this bedroom.* Instead, I concentrate on eating my pizza, ignoring the sudden buzz of drinking the scotch too fast, and staring at the movie I've seen too many times before.

I'm not saying I'm an alcoholic. Which is the first sign I might be one, right? But I don't dismiss the fact I do enjoy a drink or two, and sometimes too often. Tonight suddenly feels like a time I don't need it, so why did I bring the bottle up here? Force of habit, I suspect. I've used the scotch to dull my thoughts, numb the pain, or just make me forget life in general, but I don't want to forget this night. I have my Lilac in my bed, doing something outside our norm of work, and I like it. I like her here, and I'm ruining it.

"I always feel sorry for the creature," Pam blurts out, interrupting my thoughts.

"He's freaking ugly," I state, staring at the hideousness of his being.

"He's misunderstood," Pam says with compassion. "He's been rejected by his creator, who is a father figure, albeit a poor one, and all he wants is love. He senses it's a natural connection in families and between couples."

Her assessment hits a little too close to home. My father has rejected me. I've never been in love.

"You're familiar with *Frankenstein*?" I question when I shouldn't be surprised. Pam is well-read and versed in the gothic genre.

"Yes, even us country bumpkins have read classic literature."

Cringing, I defend myself. "I didn't mean you hadn't read it. I meant you are sympathetic with the plight of the monster."

42

"He's not really a monster, though. He's called the *creature*, and he's only trying to survive. And more notably, survive on his own in a complicated, unforgiving world." Another evaluation hitting the mark on the monster sitting next to her in bed.

"You know he's not Frankenstein," I remind her, annoyed without reason at her remarks about the fated creature.

She guffaws. "Frankenstein is the name of the doctor, not the creation. The story is really about the doctor as a monster, not the creature as one. It's about how love is innate but needs to be nurtured to blossom. The doctor should have compassion, but he doesn't. The creature shouldn't love, but he does, and that desire for love consumes him to the point of hate."

Alright, now I do need another drink. I reach for the scotch and pour. I don't need a psychological investigation into a story so similar to my own. I want to rip apart Kenneth Branagh's warped depiction and laugh at it.

See, a monster myself.

I sense Pam's eyes on me as I down the second glass, but I ignore those knowing eyes. She sees what I'm doing—drowning myself.

"I never asked you about your trip," she interjects next, changing the subject to one that upsets me even more than our previous topic. I'll need this entire bottle to hold a conversation about my suddenly ended love life. The thought gives me pause. *But was it actually love?* The seductive attempts by Mandi. The whines, pleas, and begging for more. The coldhearted stance I had to take with her. The fact my dick couldn't rise for her anymore, and my heart finally said enough.

"It was . . ." I can't lie. "Not great."

Pam's head spins in my direction. "Really? I thought it was a vacation." She knows about Mandi on a surface level, meaning she knows I've had someone in my life. Mandi is the one who met me in various places around the States. Mandi is the one I'd argue with on the phone, and Mandi is the one I asked Pam to send flowers to once.

I'm such an ass.

"It wasn't. Vacations are supposed to be restful, and this one wasn't." I sigh and glance up at the movie. It's the scene where the

L.B. Dunbar

creature's lover is killed. *All he wants is to be loved*, Pam said. Spot-on assessment.

"Let's just watch the movie," I snap, harshly. Pam's gaze presses into the side of my head, but I don't turn back to her. I'm not comfortable with how well I think she sees me at this moment.

"Are *you* okay?" she asks. I don't want to discuss myself any more than I want to talk about Mandi.

"I'm always fine," I tell her, reminding myself. I can get through anything with a drink.

By the time the movie ends, Pam has snuggled lower in the blankets, and I want to bury myself in a hole for barking at her.

"Mandi and I aren't together anymore," I finally tell her, feeling as if the confession will make up for turning our evening sour. "The trip was a time to discuss our feelings," I mock, "which included how I don't have any, and she has all the feels for love and marriage."

"You don't want to marry her, or you're just against marriage in general?" Pam asks, turning her head to look up at me.

"Both," I immediately answer. Pam's eyes widen at the admission. I don't even have to ask to know she's a woman who wants marriage someday. A husband. A home. A family. Those are things I could never offer a woman, and especially not a woman as good as her.

She's still looking at me when she adds, "I don't think you're without feelings, Jacob. Look at how you are with your sister."

I huff as it hardly compares to relationship statuses with women as a whole. I don't do relationships, at least not well—case in point being Mandi.

"Want to watch something else?" I ask, hoping to drop the subject.

"You can," she offers, fighting a yawn. "I'll probably fall asleep during it."

"I can go downstairs," I suggest, although I don't really want to leave the room.

"You don't have to do that," she says, her voice softening.

"You're saying I can sleep with you again?" I tease in hopes to break the tension between us.

44

"It's your house, right? Your rules," she says with a bitter tone so unlike her. I especially do not like how it's directed at me.

"Good night, Lilac," I whisper, wondering what it would be like to say it to her every night.

"Good night." She rolls to her side, placing her back to me, and I hate myself even more for ruining this night. Then again, that's what a monster does. He ruins things. He destroys them.

I reach for the bottle of scotch, but something stops my hand. My fingers shake and blur as I pause just before touching the glass container. I turn back to Pam's form in my bed. I have something good right next to me, and I'm an ass for ignoring the pull I feel toward her.

But ignore her I must because monsters don't deserve good things in their life. I retract my hand from the bottle, though, and reach for the TV remotes instead.

Chapter 6

Delicious dreams

[Pam]

I sleep fitfully, but not as restlessly as the man next to me. At some point, I slipped off his sweats, not liking the confinement and extra material under the too comfy blankets on Jacob's bed. He also removed his own clothing, remaining in his boxer briefs as he did last night, and slid under the sheets. He isn't anywhere near me tonight. His body heat helped with the fever and perhaps that's something my mother told him although I can't imagine her going so far as to tell Jacob to get nearly naked with me. My mother didn't even know who he was until he called her. I'm going to have so much explaining to do. To Mom. To Mae. Ethan Scott's the only one who knew of Jacob's existence because I got him a job with Jacob last fall.

I'm thinking these things when Jacob calls out, "No." His legs jolt, and his body flinches. Spinning to face him, I hold my breath.

"I said, no." His arm twitches, and I slowly sit upright. His head moves from side to side on the pillow and then stops as though he's been slapped. His breathing is heightened. His chest rises and lowers exaggeratedly. The sheets have lowered to his waist, revealing the fine lines of his abs. A dim illumination glows through the large window wall as the moon is in the sky somewhere.

"No," Jacob groans again, and I hesitantly reach out a hand, resting it on his shoulder.

Saying his name, I gently jiggle him. His skin is hot to the touch, and for a second, I worry he's caught what I had. I'll feel terrible if he gets the flu from me and sharing this bed. Then his entire body jolts again and I press harder at him.

"Jacob, wake up. You're having a bad dream."

His body stills. "Angel," he whispers. His forehead heavily furrows.

I repeat his name, and his hand snaps upward. My throat is cupped, and I'm flipped, pressing back into the mattress. Jacob's body is instantly over mine, the weight of him heavy enough to take my breath. He isn't squeezing my throat, just holding it as he stares down at my face, but his eyes are wild. He doesn't see me, and I whisper his name.

Lifting a shaky hand for his face, I intend to cup his cheek and help him focus, but his free hand shoots outward, capturing my wrist and pinning it to the bed near my head. He continues to breathe heavily, his chest pressing against mine with each heave. His nostrils flare as we stare at one another.

"Lilac," he whispers, and tears fill my eyes for some reason. I'm not afraid. He won't hurt me, but something's hurting him. The fear and anger in those midnight eyes darkens all the stars. His heart hammers against my breast while he's covering me. One of his legs is between mine, but he slowly shifts so the other meets the first. On instinct, mine spread to accommodate him, and the sheets tangle between our legs. He shifts his body lower, adjusting between my thighs. Gently, he releases my throat and slides his hand to my chest, flattening his palm over my racing heart.

"I didn't mean to frighten you," he whispers. "I'd never hurt you, Lilac. Never." His voice strains as he stares at his hand just above my breast, concentrating on the rapid beating. He speaks as if begging me to understand, begging me to accept that he would never cause me harm.

"I know you wouldn't." His quick reflexes and sudden reaction were a response to whatever was haunting his dreams.

"What happened?" I question.

He shakes his head. "No. I'm not going there with you." He's slipping away from me, retreating into his head. He'll move off me any second and pretend this didn't happen, which might be for the best. I'm hyperaware that he's hard and resting against my core. Everything pulses—that spot between my thighs, the blood in my veins, my heart behind my ribs.

His eyes focus on my lips, which I nervously lick.

L.B. Dunbar

"I want to kiss you." His voice is that low rasp that sends a thrill up my middle. He must still be dreaming. Perhaps, he's not fully awake and doesn't realize it's me, although he's called me both Lilac and angel.

"Jacob, it's Pam," I tell him as if he isn't seeing me. His brows pinch.

"Yes, Lilac. My angel." The hand over my heart slides back up my neck and jumps to my forehead, swiping back my hair, watching his fingers touch the side of my face. His attention returns to my lips. "Kiss me."

"I've been sick." Of all the desires I've ever had, I've never wanted his mouth so much as I do now, but the rational side of me says he doesn't know it's me under him. Logic dictates I decline his suggestion.

Then Jacob does something I'd never expect. He curls his hips so his thick erection presses harder against me, and my legs spread wider while my head slightly tips back. I chew my lip to fight a needy groan. My head warns *don't do this* while my body says, *I want, I want.*

"I need to know that you're real." He lowers his mouth for my neck. The spot his fingers curled around moments ago is pressed by tender lips. His mouth opens as he sucks at my skin, followed by a tongue that hesitantly licks me before another sip. Then he nips me and I'm on fire. His body moves down mine as the kisses grow in intensity, peppering my throat before dropping to my chest. He tugs the collar of his too-large-for-me tee aside and continues to kiss me, each one urgent, hungry even.

This is crazy, but I can't seem to deny him. Lower and lower and lower, he moves down my body, tugging the material to expose a breast. He stills as he looks at the swollen globe, and one of his legs shifts. His head pops up to look at me.

"You removed my sweats."

"I was too warm." I should be telling him to stop. I should be warning him not to do this to me. My heart cannot take the passion brewing in him. He needs to recognize it's me and not someone else. However, my body overrules my thoughts. So I do nothing when Jacob hastily moves the sheets, and his upper body settles between my thighs as he's moved his entire body lower. It's a wonder I'm still breathing as my heart hammers faster than ever. But more importantly, a part of me drips with desire for him, and I'm not wearing underwear. I assumed the length of his T-shirt would cover me. Jacob would never know the difference, but my hot core is against his firm abs, skin to skin.

"Jacob," I warn, hoping the sound of my voice will remind him once more it's me because this cannot be happening to me. Cannot be happening between us. I reach for the side of his head, curling my fingertips against his short hair.

"Must kiss you," he mutters, not asking but demanding. He shifts once more, and his mouth latches onto me in a place long ignored. I nearly spring from the bed. My back arches. My head tips back. My eyes roll as his tongue laps across folds ready for his attention. Sensitive skin that has never experienced the eagerness in which this man is taking me. The flat of his tongue swipes upward, curling over my clit. The tip dips inward, and I moan like a hussy on steroids because nothing has ever felt this good. His mouth closes over the tender nub and sucks hard before delving forward once more, splitting me open and sweeping through me like I'm a succulent peach.

My head rolls on the pillow. My hips thrust upward. His hands clamp my thighs down to the bed as he devours me like a starving man.

"Jacob," I cry out as a rippling begins at my toes and races upward. This will be like nothing I've had before. His tongue moves faster with my cry. His fingertips dig harder into my thighs. My hips unabashedly rock against his mouth, and I break. In sweet bliss, I call out his name, electrified by the pleasure. My skin prickles. The fine hairs stand on end. From my toes to my fingertips a spark burrows through me, and I'm so alive at this moment. I'm more aware of my body than I've ever been as the orgasm draws onward.

Finally, I can't take any more. I collapse back to the pillow, and my head catches up to my body's betrayal. "Enough," I state, pressing at Jacob's head. We need to stop this. I shouldn't have given in to him. He'll break me if we continue because it's not just my body that wants him but my heart.

Oh, my God. We just . . . and he did . . . and we can never be the same again.

Slowly lifting his body, Jacob gazes up at me, the evidence of what he did to me coating his lips, but I quickly look away, mortified by my behavior.

"Thank you," he whispers and crawls from the bed. Disappearing behind the bookcase, I hear the bathroom door close and the shower turn on. Rolling to my side, I wonder what he's thanking me for and how I'll recover from what he just did to my body.

Chapter 7

Physical Addiction

[Jacob]

After taking care of myself in the shower, working roughly in my own hands to lessen the pain, I'm surprised to find Pam still in my bed. I took advantage of her, and I should have let myself suffer from blue balls because of it. After the dream I'd had, I needed her. I wanted to release the energy coursing through my veins. I'd fought the desire to plunge into her, the desire to lose myself in her, but I still had to have her in some manner. I had to taste her. I had to know she was real and under me, and willing—so willing to let me please her. Her cries. Her moans. Her body. In my dark fantasies, Pam gives into me repeatedly, allowing me to do what I want with her body, and her body responds. This was better than any dream. There was no disguising what happened to her . . . or me. I'm never going to be the same. She has dripped into my soul, cascaded over my heart when she should have told me I was an asshole for taking something from her.

She'll never forgive you.

When I return to bed, her silence hammers home my thoughts. She's curled into herself on the edge of the bed. She's too far away both physically and emotionally. I curse myself.

"Lilac," I whisper, but she holds herself still, pretending to sleep. My hand reaches for her back, hesitating like it did toward the bottle of scotch. I hate that I blatantly drank before her earlier. She's the drink I need. She's the sweet nectar I suddenly desire. Alcohol wasn't enough to drown out the demons but bring them forward and haunt my head while I slept. I shiver with the lingering thoughts and images from the dream.

"I'm sorry," I whisper, but whether Pam hears me or not, I don't know. I collapse to my back and stare at the ceiling. Then I roll to my

L.B. Dunbar

side and face her back. My hand flattens against her, giving in as I had to the temptation of being close to her. "Don't hate me."

She can do anything else, but I don't want her to hate me.

+ + +

When I wake alone the next day, I'm not surprised. I deserve her distance, but I'm a masochist and immediately text her. I've awakened rock-hard and ready to explore more with my little assistant, but it's probably for the best she's gone. I hate that she's run off, but I can't face her. Then again, I don't want her to feel like I used her—*which I did*— or regret it—*which I don't*. Heading to the shower once again, I miss her responding text until I'm dressed for the day.

Working, it states, but I wonder if she's telling the truth. Her friend Mae said Pam could take all the time she needed to recover. I wanted that recovery time to be endless and occur in my home, but I've messed that up, and I don't know how to fix it. This is why I don't do relationships. The monster hurts. He doesn't heal. I'm terrible at apologizing and asking for forgiveness although I had to do it once before with Pam when we fought over my sister's leaving.

I did a pathetic job of it last night.

Hanging my head, I stalk to my office with a plan to write out the negative emotions coursing through my veins. There's no creature I hate more than myself.

By Saturday, Pam has ignored me for two solid days, and I'm coming out of my skin. I don't mind being on my own, but after having my stepsister as a roommate for almost a year, I didn't realize how much I appreciated another human being in my house. I recognize a need for deeper companionship although I'd never have someone live with me. It was enough to make me consider marrying Mandi for about five seconds. I could have married Mandi and had all the companionship I ever desired, but my heart reminds me that I just wasn't that into her. With Pam's absence after those days of her illness, my loneliness feels heightened to new levels.

52

Unable to be productive in any other manner, I go out for a drink instead of my nightly schedule of drinking alone. I'll only have one I promise myself. The local's favorite in Elk Lake City is Town Tavern with booths down one side, a long bar down the other, and tables in the middle of the rectangular space. A pool table stands in the back. I've heard Pam mention she comes here with her family once a week, and I know Ethan has joined them. Taking a seat at the bar, I mindlessly gaze at the television behind it, nursing my scotch.

"Penny for your thoughts," says a mousy feminine voice at my side, and I turn to find a sultry brunette leaning against the bar. She's wearing a tight V-neck sweater that exposes a hint of heavy cleavage and reveals a sliver of her belly.

I'll give you a dollar to go away.

"That would be more than they're worth," I tease without humor.

"Want to talk?" she questions. Leaning forward, she presses said cleavage together, making the swells nearly pop out of the V in her sweater.

"Not worth the words either," I mutter.

"We don't need to talk then," she coos, and I stare at her. It's been almost two months since I've been laid. The ten days with Mandi produced nothing, and the month-plus prior was a flop as well. As I just wasn't feeling it for her, I couldn't muster the physical reaction that normally came easily to me. The same is happening with this woman.

"Ever hear of Jacob Vincent?" I question, knowing this could go one of two ways. Sometimes, I measure a woman's intelligence by whether she's heard of me or not. Other times, I don't want her to know a thing about me and the anonymity helps me lose myself for a bit. I don't actually want either response tonight.

"Nope," she says, giving me a smile that might work on other men but not me.

"Thought you were leaving, Vicky," the bartender addresses her, and she huffs as she looks up at him.

"Changed my mind, Baz." The bald man's eyes meet mine for a second, and he reads my disinterest in her.

53

L.B. Dunbar

"Think you need to change it back," he tells the woman, coming to my defense, and I'm grateful as I don't want to make a scene. I just want to sit here, beating myself up.

"I was the one just leaving," I state to save face. "I'll just settle up." After downing the rest of my scotch, I reach for my wallet while the front door of the bar opens, and two women walk in. I don't pay them any attention as I lay a twenty on the bar and stand to leave. When I look up and notice Pam taking a seat at a booth with another woman, I park myself back on the stool.

"On second thought, how about another, and a drink for my new friend, Vicky." Falsely smiling at the brunette, I keep my focus over her shoulder, watching Pam place an order with the waitress and then lean forward like she's revealing all her secrets to the woman before her.

Chapter 8

Sunshine and Rain

[Pam]

"Spill," Mae says to me the second Sandy takes our drink order and leaves the booth. I don't typically hang out at Town Tavern other than on Thursdays with my siblings, but Mae wanted all the details of my days with Jacob, and we didn't get a chance to speak at work.

Mae and her husband, Adam, own a series of businesses. First is Eden Landscaping, inherited by Adam years back. When Mae and Adam met in college, Mae followed Adam here, and he eventually opened the retail garden center called Mae's Flowers for her. Her business has grown over time to include a year-round facility selling everything from tulips to Christmas trees as well as a thriving gift shop with gardening products and books, and garden-related novelties and decorations. That's where I came into the picture. Mae needed help running it all, and I began working part-time while still an EMT. When everything fell apart for me a while ago, I started working full-time for her. Even before all that, Mae and I clicked, and we've become good friends.

"It's all embarrassing to admit because I was so sick," I tell her, which she already knows because Jacob called her to say I'd be missing a few days of work.

"He sounded rugged and rough, as if his voice alone could strip you of your panties."

She isn't exactly wrong, and when my face heats, she narrows her eyes at me. "Busted," she teases as our drinks arrive. Mae stares at me, waiting for the details while I grapple with how much I want to share.

"Nothing happened," I lie. How do you tell your best friend the man of your dreams did something to you that you can't forget but should have never let happen? "He might have come on to me, but he didn't mean it."

L.B. Dunbar

"No man accidentally comes on to a woman. Either he did it on purpose or he didn't do it at all."

"We were sleeping together and—"

"You what?!" Her screech turns a couple of heads in our direction, and I'm rethinking our being at the Town Tavern. While the country music plays, it might not be loud enough to drown out our conversation, and I don't need some nosy Nellie overhearing us. It's bad enough people look at me and wonder why I'm alone after all these years. Those who know the truth still look at me with sympathy. I'm damned if I do and damned if I don't, and I refuse to think of Brendan tonight.

"Not *sleeping*-sleeping, just literally sleeping in the same bed together."

"You were in his bed?" she shrieks again with a grin that shows teeth. Mae's expression and good humor are contagious on a good day, but I don't need her enthusiasm blasting my business to the entire bar.

"Mae, keep your voice down," I state, scanning the place and then landing on the devil himself.

Jacob.

Mae looks over her shoulder in the direction of my frozen gaze and then back at me. "Where?" she questions, and I realize I've said his name aloud. I've never seen him in town. In the two and a half years I've known him, he hardly comes to Main Street.

I turn back to Mae uncertain how to respond. Jacob told me he was surprised I'd never told my mother who he was nor have I told my best friend. *I thought women did that shit.* Maybe they do, but I hadn't because of the NDA. I took his privacy seriously. Glancing back at him, I see a woman sidled up next to him, and they look cozy.

Assuming I have his newfound permission to tell my best friend about him, I tip my head in his direction. "That's him. By the bar."

"Holy shit, Pam. He's hot. You need to lick that, or I will." This is Mae's reference to marking someone you like. She would never cheat on Adam. He's actually cheating on her, or so she suspects, but she hasn't been able to prove his affair. I think she's crazy because Mae is great. So why would her husband cheat on her? Then again, what do I know about investigating adultery? It was happening under my nose once, and I

56

never sniffed it out. At work, Adam dotes on his wife with sweet cheek kisses and an arm around her shoulder. I don't want to surmise those tender touches disguise bigger issues, but I hadn't seen it in my own past relationship. I missed the signs because of tender touches such as those.

"Now, I need to know everything," Mae prompts.

"I was in his bed." I pause, waiting for hysteria to hit her again, and when it doesn't, I continue. "And he'd been dreaming. I woke him up, and he..." *Pinned me to the bed, spread my thighs, and went down on me.* I can't tell her this. I don't want to share the details for two reasons. Besides being embarrassed to share them, I want to keep them all for me. "He misunderstood who I was. He has a girlfriend."

Only he told me Mandi and he were no more. I'd heard that before, though, so I don't have much faith that they are really over. They are constantly hot and cold for one another.

Mae watches me after I mention the girlfriend. "How can he misunderstand who you are? Maybe you need to back up and start at the beginning of this . . . working relationship." Being as I've never told anyone about Jacob, it's hard to know where to start. The accident. The accusations. His calling me angel. He is a famous author and I'm a blogger who wrote him a not-so-favorable review. That was another part to our strange circumstances, but even that I'm not certain I can mention.

"Mae, I signed an NDA to work with him, so I can't tell you more than I work for him. But it's never interfered with the garden center." I don't want her thinking I've used my time at her shop doing blog stuff.

"His voice could melt panties, and looking at him, he could break hearts," she teases. "Does this have the potential for friends with benefits or full-on heartbreak?"

Glancing back at Jacob sitting next to that woman, I find his eyes are aimed at me. My fingers twitch to wave, but I don't know if I'm allowed to acknowledge him in public. Wrapping my hands around my margarita glass, I look back at Mae.

"Heartbreak." I sigh. Being in love with my boss has no other option, and after what he did to me, I don't know if I should keep working with him.

L.B. Dunbar

"We don't need another Brendan," Mae states softly, and my eyes hold hers.

"No, we don't," I whisper, and thankfully, the subject is dropped.

Forty minutes and two margaritas later, Mae and I have moved onto her concerns about Adam and the possibility of his affair. We're laughing while it isn't funny when Sandy brings us another round.

"From the man at the bar." Her nod is so vague, but I assume it's Jacob. Catching his eye again, I notice the woman is absent.

"Thank you," I mouth to him, only his brow pinches like he doesn't understand, and Mae interrupts.

"Don't look now but someone at the bar is checking you out." My eyes travel the length of the bar and catch on a man seated with his back to the counter, and his gaze on us. He lifts his glass, and Mae lifts hers in response. I'm confused. Is the drink for her or me? When he stands from his stool, I do a double take.

Is that . . . it can't be?

"Spencer? Spencer Campbell?" I question and slowly stand from the booth. I reach out for him, and he steps into the hug I offer. I haven't seen Spencer in years. He knows my history with Brendan as he was one of his best friends.

"I knew that was you. How are you, Pam?" he questions, and I stare into the blue eyes of a man who was once a boy I crushed on before Brendan. With blond waves of hair, everything about him screams surfer boy, only our lake is missing the surf.

"What are you doing here?" I ask, meaning Elk Lake City. Last I'd heard, he'd moved away.

"Been back for a few years. I run a water adventure shop in Traverse City." Three towns over, Traverse City caters to outdoor water sports and summertime activities, but we only really have three months to enjoy the great waters of Lake Michigan. "I was visiting some friends and thought I'd stop here for a beer before heading back to the city."

Friends. Brendan and his wife.

"Thanks for the drinks," I say, waving my hand at his generous gift and suddenly remembering we once kissed back in high school. "Want

58

to join us?" I ask, though I'm uncertain what more I'd say to him. It's been years—eleven exactly.

"Don't want to interrupt your girls' night out. Just wanted to say hello. It's so great to see you again. You look exactly the same," he states as his eyes roam down my body, and I blush. It's nice to be checked out, especially by an old crush, but it's also incredibly awkward knowing our mouths have met, and he knows my past heartache.

"Why don't you give him your number, and you can get together another night?" Mae offers for me, and I turn on her, eyes bugging out. *What do you think you are doing?*

Mae reaches toward Spencer and wiggles her fingers. "Here. Give me your phone and I'll give you her digits." Spencer looks sheepishly from me to Mae and hands over his phone.

"You don't have to do that," I say to him, keeping my voice quiet.

"Actually, I'd love to call you," Spencer says, and that's when Jacob makes his appearance at the table.

"Lilac," he addresses me, his voice terse as his hand slips to my lower back.

"Jacob," I say, narrowing my eyes. *What does he think he's doing?*

"Lilac?" Spencer questions, and I look at Mae for help as Jacob's hand nearly burns a hole through my sweater. Mae mouths, "*Lilac?*" to me, and I want to curse her as the worst best friend ever.

"That's a strange name," Spencer says, drawing my attention back to him.

Ignoring the jab at my nickname, Jacob states his name without offering a hand. "Jacob Vincent."

"Spencer Campbell."

That's it, conversation over. The two men are opposites—one is sunshine and the other rain.

"So, I guess I'll give you a call," Spencer says, holding up his phone and giving it a shake.

"You do that," Mae encourages, and I want to drown her in my margarita.

"Nice to see you again," I say, knowing there's no way surfer boy Spencer Campbell will call me, especially after my pushy friend and my glaring boss made the past three minutes the most awkward of my life. Spencer leans forward, boldly giving me a cheek kiss and then excuses himself. As soon as he steps away, both Mae and I visually follow his retreat until Jacob steps in front of me to block my view.

"Want to introduce me?" he demands.

"Want to be introduced?" I ask, crossing my arms, wondering why he chose now to come to the table and what he's playing at for someone who wants to remain a secret. Being the mystery man in the woods and all that.

"Jacob Vincent." He introduces himself, holding out a hand to Mae.

"Mae Fox-Holland," she says and then looks at me, mouthing, *"Panty-melting."*

"Can I speak with you a minute?" Jacob states, his eyes zeroing in on me.

"You know what? I'm going to head out. Why don't you take my seat, and you can talk here?" Mae suggests, scooting herself to the edge of the booth. Jacob steps back, allowing Mae to exit, but I reach for my friend.

"Don't go," I say, suddenly feeling guilty that our girls' night is over. She needed tonight as much as I did.

"We're good," Mae assures me and stands from the bench seat. "See you Monday."

After a quick hug, Mae walks away, and Jacob turns on me. "Perfect as I need to see you at my place tomorrow."

"Is that all you had to say to me?" I ask as we remain standing next to the booth. When he doesn't answer me directly, I reach for my purse, searching for my credit card.

"You're all set. It's all on my tab."

"Thank you. You didn't have to do that. Now, if that's all you had to say, I guess my night is over too." I'm bitter about this fact. I wanted to hang out with Mae, talk about men in general, and just enjoy some laughter.

I walk around Jacob and head out the front door to Main Street. The February air is bitter cold like I suddenly feel. Jacob had no right to walk over when he did, nor did he need to run off Mae. Not to mention, seeing

Spencer has brought on a wave of regret and memories of Brendan. Crossing my arms to huddle against the cold, I walk toward my apartment.

"Where are you going?" Jacob calls after me.

"Home," I say over my shoulder, not stopping due to the frigid temperature.

"Where's home?" he questions, catching up to me and keeping pace with my rapid stride. I stop and stare at him.

"After all this time, you don't know where I live?" I'm floored. How can he not know? I mean, I don't expect him to have my address memorized, but how does he not remember I live over the pharmacy? It's all a reminder that Jacob doesn't know me. He likes to keep me at arm's length, and that's what makes the other night even more confusing.

"I'll walk you home," he suggests, and I huff, mist forming outside my mouth in the cold night.

"It's right there." I point at the pharmacy across the street at the end of the block.

"I'm still walking you across the street then," Jacob demands, and we walk in silence a few steps. "Look, the other night—"

"We don't need to talk about it," I cut him off.

"But I don't want you to think—"

"I don't think anything of it," I lie.

"You don't?" he questions, his tone almost sounds hurt, and I chew my lip to prevent clarifying.

I'd love for you to do it again sometime, but that probably isn't a good idea. As badly as my body wants it, my heart can't take it.

"I understand you were under duress from a bad dream, and I was there. Perhaps you had me confused with Mandi and—"

"Don't do that," he snaps.

"Do what?"

"Don't make this about Mandi. There was no confusion. There's no comparison." The tone of his voice emphasizes our differences.

"Yes, thank you for reminding me I'm not your type," I snap, unable to hold back my sarcasm.

"Not. My. Type," he stammers.

L.B. Dunbar

I stop, holding up a hand before he can continue. Changing topics before I burst into tears in the cold temps, I speak. "We don't need to see one another tomorrow, Jacob. Just email or text me what you need."

I begin walking again, but Jacob follows.

As his personal assistant, I set up his social media posts and handle reader interaction in a Facebook group. Despite not being his type, we quickly learned we have something in common—our love of books. Only I hated one of his. This caused him to ask me to beta read for him, then I became his critique partner and eventually started to work for him. Most days, I wonder why I still do it.

Because you love him.

Then on other days, I wonder why he keeps me around.

The silence in my head answers my own question. I have no idea.

"Are you going on a date with him?" Jacob interjects.

"I don't see how that's any of your business."

"It's not, but are you?" His persistence pisses me off. *Why does he care?*

"Have you been drinking?" I ask, changing the subject.

"What? No." He shakes his head in frustration as he drones, "Not this."

"Can you drive home?" I question, concerned about him.

"Yes. Stop. It was like an hour ago, and it was only one," he argues.

"I saw you at the bar."

"I had one drink." He's emphatic as he stares at me, and I return the glare. "I ordered a second scotch and then changed it to a seltzer and lime."

Interesting.

"What about the girl?" We've reached the back steps leading up to the pharmacy apartment.

"What?" he chokes out, his dark eyes narrowing in on me. "No girl."

"I saw her at the bar next to you."

"Come on, Lilac. You sound like a jealous love—" He abruptly stops, and I look away. "Wait a minute." His voice shifts, excitement filling it. Next, I'm backed up to the pharmacy wall, and Jacob is crowding my space. His hand comes to my throat, tender but pinning me in place.

"Hey." His voice softens. "Hey." My eyes drop for my feet, which I can't see because Jacob is filling my view. "Are you jealous?" The word stammers from his lips while a smile fills his voice. I don't respond. Instead, I close my eyes to shut out his nearness.

"Lilac." My name is a call in the night, sultry and deep. "You have nothing to be jealous of. Not another woman. Not Mandi. Pam, you're fucking beautiful."

He's so close he could kiss me. His breath warms my lips. My heart hammers under my winter gear. Tears fill my eyes. I want to believe him. The compliment is said with such sincerity, but he can't possibly mean it.

"Lilac." My name on his lips again is a plea, but I can't give in to him. We made a mistake. *I* made a mistake by not stopping him the other night, by giving in to my body's desire and pretending Jacob did what he did to give me pleasure. I even hoped he got something out of it. He thanked me as he finished, as if I'd done something for him instead of the other way around. It was all confusing, and I don't want to be confused. I want to get to my apartment and warm up.

"Good night, Jacob," I say to him before I push him away and race up the stairs, fumbling with the key before stepping into my apartment and letting the tears flow.

Chapter 9

My Type

[Jacob]

She's fucking jealous.

What the hell is she jealous of? Despite the negativity brought about by that emotion, I'm gloating over the fact she might be jealous of another woman with me because that means she cares about me.

But have I misread some things between us?

Not your type. However, the words echo through my head as I watch her race up the stairs and disappear into the second-floor apartment. What does she mean she's not my type? She's exactly my type. She loves classic gothic tales. She wears Converse, and she humors me about frozen pizza. She's got those curves and the sweetest pussy, and now that I've had a taste, I want another bite. I don't want her to compare herself to Mandi because they are total opposites, for the better.

Then I think of the guy in the bar.

Fucking surfer dude.

I know his type. He's all *gnarly* and *cool, dude* and *what's up*. Is that what she wants? Perhaps *I'm* not her type. The braniac literature lover wasn't much of a stud back in the day, not until I started working out and boxing. I'd never been a fighter, and my father was quick to remind me how much of a wimp he thought I was. Whenever I didn't play in all the sports he signed me up for, it was always the fault of a coach. They didn't see my potential, but even my father didn't believe I had athletic talent. In public, the coach was to blame. In private, I was the issue. I wasn't stronger, faster, better equipped. I wasn't the star athlete he wanted me to be, and he thought beating it into me would work.

It wasn't until I was older and desired the strength and speed on my own terms that I learned to fight . . . and fight back. He never saw that first punch coming, and it was the last one he spent on me.

Shaking off the memories, I quickly walk back to my car in the freezing night air. Slamming my door after falling into the front seat, I start the engine, listening to the deep purr of the SUV.

She pushed me away.

I was close enough to kiss her, and she pushed me.

She doesn't think we need to see one another. Fine, I can respect her wishes.

Only the next day, she almost runs into my stepsister and me on the landing between the second-floor apartments over the pharmacy and an empty storefront.

"Ella?" Pam questions before stepping up to her and wrapping my sister into a tight hug. This is another thing about Pam. Since the moment my sister came to live with me, Pam opened her heart to my sibling and ignored her scars. With patience and kindness, Pam befriended Ella as much as Ella would let someone in, and this endeared Pam to me even more. My sister has been through a lot, and Pam accepted her.

Ella wanted to show me her new office and future storefront, which is located next to Pam's apartment.

"What are you doing here?" Pam questions, implying the second-floor balcony.

"I'm renting this place," Ella states with pride in her voice, and I'm equally proud of her. She's come a long way from all that's happened.

"You need to tell me everything," Pam insists, giving Ella a puzzled expression at first but then reaches out for my sister's arm, encouraging her to be open.

"Let me talk to Ethan. We need to plan a girls' night," Ella cheerfully suggests, and Pam gives me a skeptical look. I ruined her outing last night.

"I'd like that," Pam states, her attention still directed at me.

Ella looks back and forth between the two of us, and my mouth opens.

"Aren't you going on that date soon?" I'd kick myself if I wasn't still worked up over the possibility that she might say yes to that douche with his blond wavy hair and his fake tan in February. He's taller than me by a few inches, but I could totally take him. In fact, I might enjoy the fight, but he probably doesn't know how to pack a punch.

"What date?" Ella asks, turning to Pam in surprise.

"Ignore him," Pam moans, reaching out for Ella and giving her another hug. "I've got to get to my mom's, but I'll call you."

She turns for the staircase without another word to me. My sister and I stand still, watching Pam's retreat.

"Pam's going on a date?" Ella asks me, narrowing her eyes.

"I don't know," I huff, scrubbing a hand down my face.

"When are you going to admit you're in love with that woman?" Ella teases me.

"Don't know what you're talking about," I state, taking a step forward. The lie I tell myself actually hurts for some reason. I don't know how to love someone, and even if I did, I'm certain I'd ruin it.

"Keep telling yourself that," Ella jokes behind me as we descend the stairs from her new office space. "But let me tell you, there's no point in denying something wonderful, Jacob. Perhaps it's time to take the risk."

While I'd like to think my sister knows what she's talking about— she didn't ever think someone would love her nor would she love—it doesn't seem so easy for me. Ella's scars sit on the surface of her skin while mine run deep within.

Chapter 10

A Blizzard of Emotion

[Pam]

Almost a week passes without seeing Jacob until I receive a text. **Need you at the house.**

Is he kidding me? A blizzard is predicted, so I call him to tell him the weather report.

"Better bundle up, buttercup," he says and hangs up.

Driving to his house, I curse him during the entire ride. *Insufferable. Egotistical. Wretched jerk.* Just who does he think he is? A better question might be why am I so easily doing his bidding. However, the simple answer is he pays me. Our friendship grew out of the blogger-author relationship, but we also have a kindred spirit that Jacob doesn't see. He needs someone to love him for who he is, and I think I could be that person.

Perhaps, I'm a bit of a masochist.

When I pull into Jacob's driveway, the garage door opens as if he's expecting me. His house is built on a bit of a hill, with the garage underneath the north section of the home where both his office and bedroom stand. As soon as I enter the garage, the door closes behind my car. I have a key to help myself into the house but find the doors unlocked.

Jacob meets me at the top of the steps.

"What took you so long?" he questions, and I glare at him, tempted to turn back around and leave his sorry backside.

Too bad his backside is not sorry in the least but perfectly sculpted, firm, and tight.

"Have you seen the weather?" I ask. It's starting to really snow, and it's not pretty and gentle but coming down sideways. "We need to make this quick so I can get home before I'm stuck here."

L.B. Dunbar

I'm in a mood, which the weather matches, and I can't deal with Jacob's moodiness.

Jacob stares at me without an ounce of consideration for my fear. I cannot stay here with him again. If he was half as evil as the villains he writes, I'd think he planned this snowstorm. As I don't believe he's able to dictate weather patterns, I dismiss the thought.

"I want you to read these three chapters. Mark them up. Bleed on this thing." He hands me the pages, old-fashioned in his ways to print and proof with a regular pen. We've also done edits electronically, but he prefers a first draft in this manner at times, and apparently during a snowstorm is the time. Thankfully, I didn't have to work at the garden center, so I take the papers thrust at me and help myself to one of the two couches in the living room. The leather couches are at a ninety-degree angle to one another with one facing the large wall of windows with a view of the lake while the other faces a stone fireplace reaching the vaulted ceiling. The room is considered a great room with the dining room table large enough for twelve behind the couch facing the fireplace.

Without glancing back at Jacob, I begin reading while I feel his eyes on me. Finally, he steps back into his office. It's been an unsettling day for me, and I decide this is what I need—to get lost in a book and rip apart Jacob's writing.

Unfortunately, roughly twenty minutes later, the lights begin to flicker. *Oh God, no.* The snow outside the glass panes is so thick I can't see the lake, which is out there somewhere. It's like being inside a snowglobe with the snow on the outside. It's beautiful and frightening at the same time. The wind whistles, and the lights flicker again.

Jacob enters the living room and glances around the lit room. "It's getting bad out there."

"Yes, thank you, Sherlock," I mock. I told him the weather wasn't conducive to me being here. I'm still angry that he demanded I come here as if it's so urgent I can't read these chapters from home, but I have calmed a bit from my original irritation.

"Maybe we should start a fire," he states, just as the lights blink again. I swear it's as if he willed them to flicker to prove his point. Walking up to his fireplace, Jacob stops and stares at the large opening.

"It's not gas," I tell him, knowing he loves convenience.

"I know that," he snaps at me while glaring at the fireplace as if it could build a fire itself. I set the chapters I was reading to the side and stand next to him. Ignoring his sass, I continue.

"You need to set wood in there and start the fire with kindling and newspaper."

"Thank you." His sarcasm is warranted. We're both on edge, but he still doesn't move. Instead, he glances toward the window, which we can't see out. "You'll be stuck here again for the night."

His tone has me questioning if this upsets him or concerns him. Either way, he has nothing to worry about. We will not be having a repeat of what happened while I was sick. I'll sleep on the fricking couch by the fireplace.

The thought of a fire reminds me of my dad and being a kid on camping trips. "Did you ever go camping as a kid?" The question pops out as I'm curious.

"My dad didn't believe in camping. It was dirty and for people without money for hotels."

Yikes. That's rude, and one of the first real mentions of his father. Jacob never talks about his parents while Ella has spoken of them on occasion.

"Okay. Newspaper and kindling." I glance up, and Jacob stares back at me. He has neither of these items. "Cardboard?"

"Maybe some frozen pizza boxes in the recycling bin," he suggests. That will have to do.

"If you could go get more wood from your garage, I can look for cardboard and get this started." Giving him something to do other than building a fire seems to please him, and I grumble my way through his bin, finding some scraps of paper and the boxes he suggested. A set of matches rests on the mantel, and I set up the fire, recalling how my father taught me from nights of camping as a kid and bonfires on the beach as a teen. Jacob makes several trips, really piling up the wood in his living room and accepting the reality of things.

As he dumps his third stack, the lights give a final wink and go off. "Your furnace runs off electricity," I remind him.

L.B. Dunbar

"Yes, Mrs. Electric Company. I know," he grouses, and I smirk. This means the only heat source is this fireplace, so we'll both be camping on couches tonight.

"Did you back up what you were working on?" With the electricity flickering, I'd hate for him to lose whatever he was writing on.

"You were holding in your hand what I was working on. I was waiting on you." The undercurrent of attitude in his tone is not appreciated. "Let's pull one couch closer to the fire."

If it were anyone else, the setup might be romantic, but knowing all I know about his dislike of romance, this is not going to be a romantic evening. This is necessity, and it looks like we're sharing a couch for the time being.

Once we rearrange the furniture, placing one couch only feet from the blazing fire, I settle back on the cushions in a corner while Jacob falls into the opposite corner. Somehow, a bottle of scotch appears near the leg of the couch. Jacob pours himself a glass, not offering me one. I assume I'm to keep reading, which I do as best as I can under firelight and the diminishing light of the day.

"Why didn't you introduce me to your friend the other night?" The question startles me from reading.

"I did introduce you."

"But only after I asked you to do it." There's something in his voice I can't read.

"I signed an NDA, remember?"

"Are you embarrassed to work for me?" The genuine concern in his tone surprises me.

"What's there to be embarrassed about? You're a famous author. I was respecting your privacy."

He sniffs and takes a sip of his drink. His body slouches back on the cushions, his head resting on the back of the couch.

"When I was a kid, my father was embarrassed by me. He rarely introduced me to people as his son. He was very proud of Ella because she was such a beauty, but not so proud of me, his flesh and blood."

I'm stone still as he speaks, astonished by the admission, especially as it's more than he's ever told me about himself in relation to his dad.

70

"So you weren't close to your father."

Jacob rolls his head to look at me. "Only as close as his fist could reach."

Horrified, I bite back a gasp. "That's awful."

He takes another heavy gulp of his drink, looking away from me while my eyes beg him to turn back. His focus fixates on the fire, and I'm worried for half a second he'll toss the alcohol at the flames and set the house ablaze.

"I was close to my father but not like people would think. I didn't match the rest of the Carter clan."

"Don't depreciate yourself," Jacob states, his voice tight.

"I'm not. I'm just stating a fact. I'm not one of the famous Carters, and I struggled with the difference between myself and my siblings when I was younger. I wasn't the football star of Jess or the class clown of Tom, and definitely not the beautiful tomboy of my sister. They are all tall, lean, and athletic. I didn't know what I wanted to be when I grew up, unlike the rest of them who seemed destined to be an engineer, a small business owner, and a teacher, respectively. I sort of fell into the position of EMT, and while I loved it because I don't mind blood and guts, I fell out of love with it." I'm quiet as Jacob knows why I stopped being an EMT.

"But my father always gave me the best advice, as if he knew I didn't think I measured up or considered myself worthy. I needed to love myself as much as he loved me, he'd say."

I love you bunches, Pammie, he'd tell me. I smile to myself, recalling my father and noting the snowstorm oustide again. "His advice reminds me of a song by Tori Amos, called 'Winter.' And I don't know why I told you that."

Jacob's attention has turned back to me. "You know I'm always sorry about your dad."

"I know." I met Jacob the night my father died. Jacob was the man in that red Corvette, and I was tending to him when my dad passed away in the ambulance on the way to the hospital. I wanted to blame Jacob when it happened, but he wasn't at fault. Still, I went to visit him the next day in the hospital to rip him apart for his stupidity. *Drinking and*

L.B. Dunbar

driving, he could have killed someone. He could have been the one to hit and run on my dad, but he wasn't. I was still hell-bent on giving him a piece of my mind, but when I entered his hospital room, something changed my mind.

"Don't go there, Lilac," Jacob whispers, but it's too late. The loss of my father was difficult for me. Memories fill my thoughts for a few minutes. My father's advice. His bear-style hugs. His silent support.

"You never mention your father. Is it because of mine?" I'd actually never thought about it until this moment, but Jacob doesn't discuss his, and perhaps it's because his is still alive and mine is not.

"I don't mention him because he's an asshole and not worth my breath."

Ouch, but then again, Jacob just mentioned his father's fist, which suggests an unpleasant history between them.

"I'm sorry he hit you," I say, keeping my voice low.

"Don't feel sorry for me," Jacob sneers. He's so unfeeling sometimes, but his concern for his sister and the friendship he tried to start with Ethan prove he isn't totally heartless. He's just a contradiction, even in our arrangement.

He flirts. He holds back.

He teases. He rejects.

I attribute his moodiness to his creativity and the evil in some of the stuff he writes, but sometimes, he's just a bastard, and moody is his middle name.

"Is that why you had that dream the other night?"

Jacob huffs. " I don't want to talk about the dreams."

And that answers that, I decide.

"Here," he says, holding out his glass for me. Shaking my head, I decline. I'm not a scotch drinker. Give me a margarita any day or wine some evening, but not the heavy stuff.

"Want some wine then?" he asks as if reading my mind.

"I only like it sweet."

"I figured as much," he grumbles, the demeanor of his voice shifting as he rocks his body to stand. He sets his glass on the mantel and crosses behind the couch for the liquor cabinet with a wine fridge built into it. I should comment on his drinking, but his argumentative stance last weekend outside the pharmacy comes back to me. It's not that I think he's an alcoholic, but I do see him using the liquid as more than courage and as a crutch. Does that make me an enabler if I don't speak up? Jacob has some deep-rooted issues if his father abused him, and alcohol might be his way to cope. But how does it expand to the fact he drinks often—and too much—as an adult? I don't have it in me to fight with him tonight, so I don't question his life choices.

He returns, carrying a bottle of moscato and a glass already filled for me. "This must be leftover from my sister."

His brows pinch, and we both think on the months his sister lived here. He sets the bottle down and picks up his drink once more before returning to his seat on the couch.

"Do you miss her not being around?" I ask as long as this is revelation hour.

"I do, and it surprises me." With the shift in his tone, his surprise is genuine. "She's ten years younger than me, so we didn't live together long as children. By the time she was a teen and entrenched in my parents' business, I was gone." Jacob's eyes drift to his drink in his hands. Guilt still coils around him for what happened to his sister. Her scars. Her unhappiness. "I got to the point I could only think of me, and getting away from there was the way to save myself. It makes me selfish."

"It doesn't," I say, and he looks over at me. "It sounds like self-preservation."

From what I know, Ella didn't have quite the same upbringing as Jacob despite being raised in the same home. Jacob was underappreciated while his younger sister was revered. Ironically, they are both famous in their own right.

"I'm sure Ella understands." I speak on her behalf. She's a grown woman who's worked through acceptance of her past, something Jacob seems sorely in need of doing. He's never been in therapy that I know of. Ella started as soon as she left here, and I'm assuming it's a reason she's been able to return.

L.B. Dunbar

Jacob takes a sip of his drink, and I realize it's my turn to share. "My siblings and I weren't close as kids. We were just typical, looking out for each other, but not really tight, not until our father passed."

Jacob turns his head to me.

"Jess and I are eleven months apart. He's thirty-seven to my thirty-six. Tom is the eldest and still a class clown at forty, and my youngest sister, Tricia, was the perfect last child." There's mockery in my tone, but I'm not envious. It's just difficult having a beautiful sister who's younger than you are and married before you did. She's also a widow, and my heart broke for her when her marriage fell apart. We all had our suspicions her first husband was a loser, but we were never aware of the total asshole he'd been until after his death.

"My sister is pregnant and got engaged." The words fall flat despite my happiness for my youngest sibling. The announcement was a huge part of my mood when I arrived. While I'm at the beck and call of a man who isn't mine and never will be, my younger sister is getting married *for the second time.*

"You don't sound pleased. Is he a tool?"

"Leon—"

"Leon Ramirez?" Jacob cuts me off. "I've met him. He seems like a nice guy."

"Yeah, he's amazing. Really devoted and loving. He had a rough childhood, gangs and stuff, and Tricia's so opposite him, but good with him. He's good for her, too. She deserves happiness after her first marriage." My sister's new man can be rough around the edges. However, he's nothing like her first husband in how he treats her. Devoted and loving describe Leon best. He's also very affectionate toward her. Throw in the fact he's extremely good-looking in a rugged, edgy, sexy way, and my sister has the full package in him.

In some ways, Jacob is like Leon. A bit rough around the edges, maybe standoffish even, but where Jacob is defensive and moody, Leon is easygoing and sweet. The serrated edges to Jacob include sarcasm and flirting as a way to shield any real emotions underneath his tough exterior. My family knows Leon is a giant softy underneath his outer shell.

74

"Anyway, our parents didn't have favorites. They just loved us for our differences," I state, trying to get back to the original topic.

"Your brothers own their own shop, right?" Jacob asks, surprising me that he remembers something about my siblings.

"Yeah, Sound Advice is their electrical business they inherited from my dad. QuickFix is a side hustle that Tom had before the boys took over Dad's shop."

"You're lucky to have siblings," Jacob mutters.

"So are you," I remind him, as he has Ella. He stays quiet after that, lifting his glass for another sip.

The dim afternoon quickly melts to a dark evening, and the room remains lit only by the fireplace. There isn't enough light to read, and Jacob doesn't push me to finish.

"Why did you start writing?" I eventually ask him.

"Because Jacob has always loved reading, his favorite books include the classics such as *The Strange Tales of Dr. Jekyll and Mr. Hyde*, and *Frankenstein*, a personal favorite, but who can discredit the master of horror Stephen King and fantasy like J.R.R. Tolkien. Inventing a fantastical world or alternate universe of his own feeds his creative imagination. Jacob Vincent lives in an undisclosed place, perhaps one of his own making."

I laugh. "Well, that's very textbook and thank you for reciting what I've written about you. But maybe you could be real with me for a moment?"

"Aren't I always real with you?" he mocks.

"I don't know. Are you?" We stare at one another from our opposite ends of the couch. Jacob breaks first, rolling his head so he faces the fireplace once more.

"Is this an interview for Blood and Blossom?" he asks with sarcasm.

"This is just for me."

Jacob sits up, leaning forward to balance his elbows on his knees, and stares into the amber liquid in the glass he dangles between them. "I needed an escape. The mind is an amazing machine, and if I dug deep enough, I could create a safe place with words. Invent a land where I was the hero and killed the bad guys, or shifted into something otherworldly and saved the hurting people."

He takes a deep breath and scrubs a hand down his face.

"I wrote for me at first, to clear my head and also to fill it with something other than the reality of what I lived. As you know, I lost my way for a while."

When I'd met Jacob on that second day in the hospital, I told him about my father and how I'd thought he hit my dad. It was more a confession. If only in my head, I'd felt guilty that I accused an innocent man of killing my dad. Stunned at my apology, Jacob told me who he was, and I'd recognized his name. He admitted that day that he had issues he was trying to work through. He'd been writing since he was twenty-two when he got his first publishing deal as a senior in college. He'd lost his creativity and felt tapped out after fifteen novels. He was going too fast. He'd had too much to drink. He asked for my forgiveness, suddenly feeling his own guilt that it could have been him who hit my dad. It wasn't, but he could have hit someone else in his state. He promised me he'd never drink and drive again, and to this day, he's kept that promise. Drinking and sitting at home was a different story.

Jacob clears his throat, drawing me back to his living room.

"Anyway, then I met you, my muse, and my inspiration returned." He smiles without it reaching his eyes, but the compliment is genuine. He's called me his muse on many occasions.

What I'd really like to know, though, is what would make him give me a genuine smile?

Chapter 11
Fire In More Than One Place

[Jacob]

Two and a half years ago, I was on my way to Mackinaw Island. I'd rented a red Corvette to travel the two-lane highway, passing through small towns on my way north through Michigan when I'd had one too many hits on a joint mixed with too much to drink . . . while driving. It's hard to admit I could have killed someone. I wasn't thinking of others, only myself, and I didn't care about me. It's a moment I'm not proud to recall. I was stuck on a story and late on a deadline. My creativity felt tapped out. My love-hate relationship with a younger woman was draining.

I don't even remember how it happened, but when my eyes opened, I saw the brightest blue eyes I'd ever seen. The night was black behind her, and her effervescence glowed as her blond hair shone like a halo around her head.

I asked her if she was an angel.

The next day, she came to see me all hell-bent, devil at her heels, and ready to rip into me. While she no longer thought I'd killed her father, she was angry that I *could have been* the one. When she apologized for accusing me of a crime, though, it startled me. No one had ever apologized to me for anything, and she meant hers. She was genuine, and I was attracted to her instantly.

Then she explained how her father had died while in transit. While she saved me from the wreckage, she lost her dad. God, I'd never felt so guilty, and I hadn't even been the one to hit the man. I confessed everything to her, like she was the angel I called her the night before. I told her my name and my issues. She recognized who I was, but it went deeper than that. She knew me. She knew what I needed and helped me get back on track. From that day forward, I saw her as my muse, my inspiration, my lucky charm or what have you. I needed her in my life.

L.B. Dunbar

After her little interview question, I take another sip of my scotch and then curse myself as this shit is what got me into trouble that night. More memories return to me.

"Work for me, Lilac," I said to her at the end of our meeting in that hospital room the next day.

"Why'd you call me Lilac?" she'd questioned, tipping her head, and I remembered that blond hair like a halo around her face.

"Your scent." Entering my room on that second day, her scent triggered me, perhaps lingering somehow in my head that she was the woman who saved me. Her brows rose in surprise at my admission.

"But you also look like a woodland nymph, the one tempting that guy." I snapped my fingers.

She laughed. "Pan, the one desperate for sex with Syringa."

"Yeah, desperate for sex." My eyes roamed her body on that day, and I instantly knew she was too good for me. To cover my blatant perusal of her, I also noted, "You're wearing all purple."

She laughed at herself when she realized she was.

I almost laugh to myself as she's wearing a light purple sweater tonight.

"I'd never print what you just told me," Pam says, interrupting my memory. "But thank you for sharing the real reason, the real Jacob with me."

I smile half-heartedly. *The real Jacob.* I don't even know who that is most days.

"Have you ever considered therapy for the things you can't work through with writing?" Pam asks, her voice quiet.

"I don't need to be psychoanalyzed, Lilac." I fall back onto the cushions, placing my feet on the hearth of the fireplace.

"Maybe you need someone to talk to you," she mutters.

"I'm talking to you," I remind her. It's not that I'm against therapy. My sister is in it and has been for months. I just don't think I need it. I have my writing, Pam, and . . . I stare at the glass in my hand.

Shit.

What I really need is a good round with my punching bag. I'm tense and tight with the urge to fight, but it's not Pam I want to battle.

"I'm sorry. I'm a dick and in a mood." It's true, but that's as much as I'm telling her. My mood has to do with her. She's avoided me all week, and I don't want her going on a date with some slick surfer dude even though I don't have the right to tell her not to go. However, my mouth cannot stay shut on the subject.

"Are you going to go out with that guy?" I blurt out.

"Who?" she replies with surprise.

"That surfer wannabe."

"Spencer?" she questions.

"Spencer," I mock.

"Why does it freaking matter?" Pam asks, shifting her body to face me, and I turn to mirror her position.

"Because I don't want you to go out with him." *Fine, there's the truth, the whole fucking truth. Analyze that.* Only, she doesn't. She stares back at me, setting her wineglass on the hearth of the fireplace away from the fire.

"He's not good enough for you," I add. I'm aware I'm not making sense or being fair. I've had Mandi for years, but I can't help the jealousy I suddenly feel that Pam's been with someone recently or could go out with someone in the future.

"You don't even know him," she retorts.

"Do you?"

Her lips clamp shut, admitting more without words. *How well does she know the chump?*

"I kissed him back when I was eighteen," she says, a giggle in her voice and heat on her face. Is she blushing over a kiss? What must she think of what I did to her then?

"I didn't take you as a demure damsel," I tease. Pam loves medieval things.

"Oh, I'm no innocent." Her voice turns deep, sarcastic even, and now I'm truly interested.

"Pray, do tell," I inquire, mockingly holding a hand to my chest over my heart.

"I am not giving you my sexual history." She snorts.

79

L.B. Dunbar

"Oh, please give me your history . . . the sexual parts, all the sex and parts." My eyes lower, roaming over her lush body. I don't want her history. I want to make the present—the here and now—a sexual memory.

Easy, man.

Her eyes narrow, and I tip a brow waiting.

"I'm the relationship type. I tend to date people for long periods of time, but after my last breakup, there were a few dalliances."

"Dalliances." I laugh. "What is this, a historical romance instead of your sexual past?"

"Alright. I've had sex with a handful of men and done a handful of other things with more than those men."

My mouth falls open. "You hussy," I joke, although her mention of long-term relationships suggests loyalty. Sticking with me for over two years proves her commitment qualities, even if we aren't a couple dating one another.

"I wasn't, and then I was, I guess."

I don't believe it. Not one bit. "But you're so . . ."

"So what?" she snaps, crossing her arms.

So beautiful. So perfect. So standoffish. She has her boundaries, and I can't imagine men crossing them. Then again, any man who does would be lucky and apparently several have with her.

"You're so you," I offer weakly, and she turns her face away from me, hurt by the lack of explanation.

"Well, apparently that wasn't good enough."

"Lilac," I groan, hating when she puts herself down, and decide to offer her more about me. "I had the wild years throughout college and into my twenties. Then I met Mandi and decided it was better to have one kind of crazy in my life than a multitude of crazies."

"Because it's always the woman who is a little off balance?" Pam snarks, and I arch a brow. "Okay, maybe in your choice of woman, the shoe fits."

"You know, clichés are unbecoming," I remind her. "But I can't seem to do normal." There's a strange comfort in the fight with someone like Mandi. The volatile personality. The hate sex. Maybe it's because fighting is what I grew up with. Fighting was my perspective of love.

"I bet you could."

"I don't even know what normal means." I huff.

"Dates. Holding hands. Kissing. That's the normal progression." Pam and I certainly didn't follow that course with what I did the other night, but I also haven't really been on dates, even with Mandi. We'd be mad at one another, and then see each other at a party, a club, or somewhere mutual. Arguments ensued and sex followed in a bathroom, a hallway, or someone else's bed.

"Okay, so let's pretend this is a date. What happens first?" I ask, lifting a knee and leaning an arm along the back of the couch. My fingers twitch to touch her. The tips of her hair. The edge of her shoulder. The lower curve of her lip.

She looks at me skeptically but then decides to play along. "Surely, you've been on a date before. What would you do first?"

"Dinner," I say. "Although, does any of it matter? It's all a precursor to sex, the ultimate goal."

"Really? Sex is the only goal of a date?"

"You tell me."

"No, no, it's not," she scolds. "Dating is the discovery of another person, seeing how someone else might fit with your parts."

"Sex is about fitting parts together, too." I chuckle.

She huffs again, looking away from me. She can't disagree with me, but I want to know her thoughts. "What are you thinking?"

She shakes her head, ignoring the question.

"Why aren't you married?" I blurt out next, with no filter or feeling to what I'm asking. Her answer is a shrug, and I'm sensing there's more to the tip of her shoulder.

"Come on. Tell me," I tease, pushing her walls while my heart races at her potential answer. "Your parts never fit with someone else?"

"I was engaged once."

Fucking shit. I instantly see red.

L.B. Dunbar

"I thought we were in love and going to spend the rest of our lives together. It turns out, he was fucking my best friend, who happened to be my maid of honor, and they got married instead."

Motherfucker. "Lilac," I say softly, but her eyes remain focused on the crackling fire.

"I was twenty-five, and in a small town, word gets around when you get jilted. Thankfully, it was *before* we hit the altar, but it still stung, and it was still far enough along in the planning that I had a church to call, a reception to cancel, and gifts arriving daily that had to be returned. You can't return a wedding dress, though."

She's quiet for a second, thinking before she speaks next. "When all your friends are long-standing sweethearts and marry each other, they tend to pick sides, and then there you are, in the middle of your thirties, still by yourself."

Is this why she was upset with her sister's engagement announcement? Pam was extra feisty earlier, and while she was mad at me for demanding she come to my house, I'm wondering if there was more going on in her pretty head when she arrived here.

"Who was he?" I ask, deciding to avoid any questions about her sister's new status. I'm ready to look up the toolbag who hurt her and pummel him into the dirt where the scumbag belongs.

"It doesn't matter," she says, but it does. Someone hurt her. Ripped her heart out. I don't understand. She's an incredible woman—smart, well-read, and beautiful to boot.

"Do you still love him?"

"God, no. It's been eleven years. I've moved on, and clearly, he did before we even exchanged rings."

"Did you love him then?"

"I thought I did. I mean, I really thought he was my forever, but in hindsight, I see he wasn't any more than the rest of the long-term relationships I'd had. He was comfort and commitment, until he wasn't, and I'm the fool who is loyal to a fault."

She reaches for her wine and sips the rest. She's certainly been loyal to me, and maybe I've taken advantage of that trait of hers.

"I told you my father would say you have to love yourself before you can expect someone to love you back. Maybe that's been my problem. I haven't always loved myself first." The sadness in her tone rips my cold heart in two, like a physical cutting down the middle.

"Lilac." The call of her name is sympathy and surprise. She must love herself. She's too confident and pulled together. She's one of the strongest people I know.

"Don't pity me," she says under her breath, using my words against me.

"I don't feel sorry for you. I feel sorry for the dickhead who missed out on you and the world of schmucks who didn't appreciate the dedication of a fantastic woman." *Holy fuck, I could be speaking about myself.* "I feel sorry for me as the most selfish of assholes because I don't let you know enough how I feel about you."

Mainly because I can't. I physically cannot have her know she's my everything. I'll never deserve someone half as golden as the angel sitting across from me.

"You're . . . important to me," I add. The comment sounds weak, even to me, and I want to kick myself. I'm a man of words, so why can't I just tell her how I feel?

Pam remains quiet for too long, and we need a change of subject.

"Okay, so dinner first," I state, hoping to sound more cheerful than I feel. "What should we have?"

Her brows pinch as she looks up at me.

"I'm hoping you can teach me the process here, plus I'm starving. What should we have for dinner?" I tip a brow.

"Are you looking to have sex with me?"

I choke on her honesty. "No, angel. I'm not playing this as a means to get into your pants. I really want to know how this works." Wouldn't it be a wonder, though, if it worked on her? If she gave herself to me willingly and not because of some process to woo her with dinner first?

"So what you're saying is, you really want me to just fix you some dinner?" she mocks.

"I'm serious. Teach me your dating ways, wise Lilac," I tease and find I do want to learn how to do things properly, because if I ever considered dating, I'd want it to be with her. I'd want to do right by her.

+ + +

Following her into the dark kitchen, I hold the flashlight mode on my phone to help her look through my fridge. Next she opens cabinets. Pulling down a box of pasta and a jar of spaghetti sauce, Pam smiles at me.

"Viola. Dinner."

"How do you microwave that?"

Pam laughs. "We don't as there's no power for a microwave." *Duh.* "You also don't make spaghetti in the microwave." Pam fills a pot with water, turns to the stove, and lights a burner with a match. The flame comes to life.

"Were you a Girl Scout?"

She laughs again. "This is not Scout training. This is broke college student training."

I wasn't ever one of those, but I don't mention it to Pam. "Fine. You cook. I'll pour more drinks." As soon as I offer, I realize I really don't want another drink. I actually don't need it either. I'm in good company tonight.

"You drink too much," she states sheepishly.

"You're probably right," I say, lowering my voice.

"It's not my place to judge, but I worry about you."

I pause, lifting my head. I want to tell her she doesn't need to be concerned about me, but something in her voice stops the retort on my tongue. How nice would it feel to have someone worried about me?

"You know I value your opinion, Lilac. I want you to be honest with me in everything, not just my writing." She has been bold over the years, telling me how to handle Ella, suggesting I hire Ethan, and stepping up in all the spaces in-between. "And I didn't drink and drive the other night," I remind her.

She doesn't respond but cracks open the jar of sauce for a separate pot. She flits around my kitchen, knowing her way around it, and acting as if she belongs here. Suddenly, I have a vision of her here, doing what she's doing on a nightly basis.

"Hey," I say, reaching out for her hip and stopping her movements for bowls and silverware while the pasta and sauce cook. She stills, looking up at me in the dark kitchen. "I'm glad you're here."

The quiet that follows my admission leaves a lump in my throat. I'm ready to retract what I've said when she slowly smiles at me.

"Me too," she whispers.

"I'm sorry that guy didn't marry you, but I'm also relieved he didn't. You wouldn't be standing here with me if you had." I brush back a loose hair against her cheek. I want to kiss her just as badly as I had the night outside her apartment. I lean forward, and her eyes watch my lips. I'm so close, ready to take what I've been missing out on for the last two years, when we hear a hiss.

The water is boiling and overflowing the pot. Pam breaks free of my hold and quickly turns to settle the water. Our moment is lost to a boiling pot, and I understand how that pot feels. I'm ready to explode myself. I want this woman. I want her to know how beautiful she is. I want her to know how worthy she is. I want her to know how important she is to me, and I want to show her because my words are not enough.

"I don't suppose you have real flashlights or candles perhaps," she asks.

"Candles? Sure, somewhere." Candles would scream romance, but suddenly, I want to give those things to her, if only for the night. Then again, it's dark. How else will we see?

"If I leave you alone, can you finish this?"

Pam smirks at me over her shoulder. She's doing all the work anyway, and my phone battery won't last if I use it as a flashlight all night. I'm so unprepared for emergencies—another reason to be grateful for Pam's presence.

"I'll be back." I make my own quick work, setting up candles I found in the credenza near the dining table. Most of them look used, and I'm wondering when I burned them. I don't remember lighting candles,

L.B. Dunbar
especially the large number that seem to have a spent wick. Not giving
it another thought, I light several of the larger ones, bringing them closer
to the fireplace. There's a noticable temperature difference between the
living room and any other space in the house, so I rush upstairs for an
extra sweater for Pam and my comforter.

When I return downstairs, I find Pam standing before the fireplace,
holding two bowls of pasta.

"Wow, this is beautiful," she says, her voice soft and impressed
with the candle display.

Yes, she really is beautiful, especially with the firelight glowing on
her skin."Here." I hold out the sweater for her. "It's getting colder."

"Thank you," she says, setting the bowls on the hearth before
reaching for the sweater. I watch her tug it over her head. Her short hair
springs free, and she fluffs it up a bit from the static. Her eyes slowly lift
to mine, and she holds out her arms, emphasizing the bigger size.
"Fashionable, right?"

"Beautiful," I admit. If she blushes at the compliment, I can't tell
from the fire glow on her cheeks.

"Let's eat." Her voice turns quiet. She takes her seat on the couch,
and I hand her a bowl. Then I cover her legs with the comforter. Her eyes
follow me as I pick up my bowl and settle next to her, keeping the
comforter only over her.

Holding up my fork, I nod for her to pick up hers. "Bon appetite,"
I state, then tap the metal utensil against her. She slowly smiles before
digging into her pasta. For a second, something warm and strange fills
my body, and it isn't alcohol, and it isn't hot spaghetti. That genuine grin
on her lips is more satisfying than either substance.

We eat with less serious chatter than earlier, and I'm thankful to
leave the heavy stuff behind for a bit. Pam tells me more about growing
up in a small town and her family, who sound amazing. Ella's in love
with Ethan's parents—the Scotts—and I learn more about how the
Carters and the Scotts intertwine. As the night wears on, Pam does take
another glass of wine while I try to ignore the scotch bottle calling to me.
Her body seated closer to mine feels more addicting.

Eventually, her shoulder falls against my arm, and her head lowers to my shoulder.

"Is this the hand holding portion of the evening?" I tease. Pam straightens, returning upright, and I don't like the distance.

"Too much wine and only pasta to eat today is making me sleepy," she says around a yawn.

"Why have you only had pasta today?" I'm a fanatic about women and eating after Ella had food issues. I don't want to even think about Pam doing something crazy like my stepsister used to do.

"My boss demanded I work for him today."

"In the middle of a snowstorm?" I sarcastically mock.

"In the middle of a snowstorm." She yawns.

"Jesus, he sounds like an ass."

"He can be," she says, but I hear the smile in her voice.

"He doesn't always mean to be," I admit.

"He can't help it," she teases, and silence falls between us. I'm not hurt by what she said. She's being honest like I asked, and I can't seem to help being a dick on occasion. Still, I don't want to always be the asshole boss.

"Actually," she says, her tone still low. "He can be really sweet when he wants to be." My eyes latch onto a glowing candle, the small flame dancing. "He's even romantic without knowing it."

I hold back a snort, choosing to reach for her legs instead and hitching them over mine. Straightening the blanket, I cover our leg combination. Pam returns her head to my shoulder, and I seek her fingers.

"Hand holding," I state, curling my firm fingers with hers. I'm nervous when this isn't even a real damn date. We're just trying to stay warm, slipping into sleep after a lazy day during a storm. But there's something more happening here, and I wonder if Pam feels it, too.

Chapter 12

Cheap Date

[Pam]

We'd shifted in the night from sitting upright leaning against one another to lying down on the couch with Jacob's front to my back. The fire is slowly dying, but my body temperature is a hundred degrees. Jacob's like a human thermostat set to high, then add the comforter and the extra sweater, and I'm too warm to sleep.

Slowly, I remove his arm from my waist and sit upright. As I'm tugging his thick cable-knit sweater over my head, his hand lands on my thigh. He remains lying behind me in a seated position.

"What are you doing?" His sleep-roughened voice sends a thrill up said thigh, and I shiver despite the heat of my skin.

"I'm too warm." Holding the sweater on my lap, I fold it.

"I like you in my clothing," he says, and I recall wearing his tees and sweats while I was sick.

"I still need to return your things," I remind him, remembering I stole out of his house that fateful morning, taking his soiled clothing with me to wash at my place.

"I'm not worried. I know where you live now," he teases. "By the way, you're the worst date. I didn't even get a good night kiss."

When I glance at him over my shoulder, his eyes sparkle in the dull firelight. He looks so carefree compared to his normal hard edges. Unable to help myself, I lean down and press a kiss to his lips. Soft. Tender. Sweet. Drawing away, he catches me at the back of my neck with his hand, and he perches up on an elbow. His eyes switch from sparks to flames.

"Lilac." He breathes my name like a plea, pressing at my nape to return me to him. When I hesitate the slightest second, he lifts his head and captures my lips instead. His kiss is harder, more demanding, and I'd expect nothing less from my fighter. The man who punches the bag like he punches his keyboard—with intensity and ingenuity locked deep within the dungeon of his mind. His lips command mine, spreading them to allow his tongue to enter. Once our tongues meet, Jacob is falling back to the cushions, taking me with him, keeping our mouths connected as he kisses me like I've never been kissed before, dark and deep like him, and I want more.

Eventually, I press at his chest, releasing my mouth from his, and sit upright again. Jacob remains on his back.

"Lilac, I—" His voice halts when I remove my own sweater, exposing my bra covering large swells with firmly peaked nipples. Jacob rushes upward, a hand coming to my lower back. His lips suck at my shoulder before nipping at my neck. Reaching behind his own neck, he tugs his sweater over his head, revealing the hard planes of his chest and the fine lines of his abs. His fighter's body is a muscular vision.

With a shaky hand, I reach out for his skin. Jacob watches with rapture as I slowly glide along his collarbone, down the middle of his chest, and through the fine chest hairs. A tattoo inked over his left pec reads, *Change your destiny*. The wandering fingertip traces over the scrolling font. Looking up at him, I want clarification, but he guides my hand to continue exploring him. As my fingers lower, his abs flinch at my touch.

"Ticklish?" My voice doesn't sound like my own, both rough from my own slumber and deep with desire for this man.

"Too much," he croaks before leaning forward and taking my mouth with his again. The power in his lips astounds me, firmly demanding mine follow his lead. He's my personal addiction, and I can't get enough of his taste. Scotch. Sleep. A week ago, he had *me* on those lips, and the thought intensifies the kiss I return to him.

"Are we really doing this?" he asks, his fingers at the catch of my bra. He doesn't wait for an answer before he unclasps my bra. We probably shouldn't do this, yet I want nothing more.

He tugs the silky material forward, and my breasts tumble free for Jacob's inspection.

"So perfect." His eyes widen in delight, gazing at the achy globes like a kid longing for candy. *No, like the devil ready to feast.* Cupping the firmness of one in his palm, he lowers his head to meet the already hard nub. His tongue sneaks forward, and he traces around it before opening wide and filling his mouth. He sucks hard, his tongue wild until he pulls back, tugging at the sharp peak with his lips. He moves to the other breast and repeats the action.

Pulling away from me, he lies back while rubbing a hand up my spine. His eyes meet mine.

"Lie on top of me, Lilac." With no willpower to deny my attraction to him, I ignore the niggling warning once more that we shouldn't be doing this. *I'm convenient. I'm present.* Jacob isn't really attracted to me. He's seduced by our situation. Another night. A snowstorm. It's forced proximity attraction and nothing more.

Fool that I am, I dismiss all thoughts and climb over him, straddling him before lowering my chest to press against his. I hiss at the sizzle between our skin.

"Your body," he whispers without further explanation. "Must kiss you." He tips up for my lips while his hands rub over my back, heating my skin further under his touch. While we kiss, my body adjusts, my center finding the covered tip of his hard length. In black leggings, the cotton material does nothing to lessen the heat at my core. I squeeze my thighs at his hips.

He breaks from our kiss. "Need to be closer. Clothes. Off." The final words are a demand I agree with. Scrambling off him, I stand, and he watches as I slip my leggings to my feet, revealing a light purple thong.

"More purple," he whispers, eyes lasered in on the lacy material hardly covering anything. He shifts to sit upright and reaches out for my hips. He tugs me forward and presses kisses to my lower belly. I'm aware that I don't have a flat tummy, and the thin straps of the thong cut into my skin a bit, but Jacob pays no attention to those things. He sucks at my stomach and lowers to run his nose over the lace.

"Do you know how perfect you are, Lilac?"

I chew at my lip, unable to answer him, and he startles me by quickly standing. His hands come to my cheeks, and he leans forward to kiss me once more. His mouth is a wonderland, demanding and firm.

Taking away every kiss before him and ruining me for every kiss moving forward.

"I never would have imagined . . . well, I imagined, but I didn't want to presume I'd get this chance. I need to grab something from my office."

I nod, knowing what he needs before he steps away, but I'm more focused on the fact he admitted he's imagined something. Has he dreamed of having sex with me? How could that be?

His disappearance lets reality seep in. *What am I doing?* Reaching for the comforter, I take a seat and tug the thick material to my neck. Jacob returns rather quickly, drops packets to the floor near the couch, and then adds a log to the fire, stoking it back to a blaze. I watch him as he shucks off his jeans and boxers. At some point, his socks were removed. He loves to be barefoot, and it's a strange thing to note about him.

I look up at him with the glow of the flames behind him. Standing before me is a magnificent man, cut in a way every muscle stands on display. His thighs. His chest. His dick. He's firm everywhere, and my confidence wanes.

Are we really doing this?

Jacob tugs at the blanket I'm clutching like a shield and tosses it to the floor. I lean back, needing space to escape his hungry gaze. Lowering to his knees, Jacob wedges his body between the tight space of the fireplace hearth and my knees. He reaches forward and tugs at my underwear, forcing my hips upward a second to remove the material. He tosses my underwear over my shoulder, where it lands somewhere behind the couch.

"I need another taste," he growls. Spreading my thighs, he positions himself closer and lowers for folds already ripe with desire. He delves into me with his tongue as eager as his kisses. My legs quiver but firm palms hold me in place as he devours me like a starving man. My fingers wrap around his head while he laps and licks, and I quickly shatter. My heavy groan of pleasure mixes with the crackle of the fire.

"So good," he murmurs, kissing my inner thighs as I come down from the high. He reaches for a packet on the floor.

L.B. Dunbar

Making quick work to cover himself, he tugs me forward by my hips, then positions himself at my entrance.

"You have no idea how long I've wanted this." Startled by his words, he surges forward, filling me to the hilt in one swift movement. I arch into him. My head tips back. My eyes roll. I've never been so full, so fast. He's solid everywhere, and this part of him is no exception. I pull back to lift my legs and wrap them around his hips, heels pressing into the firmness of his perfected ass to keep him attached to me.

"Not going anywhere, angel," he warns before thrusting forward again. My arms circle his shoulders while he remains on his knees, filling me. He surges forward several times before pressing me back. Confused at first, I realize the position is so he can watch. He wants to watch himself disappear in me. As I angle back, his eyes fixate on our performance. My hips lift to crash with his rhythmic pace.

"Lilac," he strains. The thrill builds again, something that's never happened to me.

"I'm going to . . . again," I warn him, surprised at how quickly my body responds to him a second time. His hand presses on my lower belly while his thumb slips between us, working at my pleasure point.

"Please," I beg, not wanting to give up this sensation. The build swirls up my thighs and hovers over my belly. I'm so close.

Jacob shifts, and the movement triggers me to let go again. Muttering his name like a curse and a prayer, I break, clutching at him with my heels at his ass and fingertips digging into his hips to hold him to me.

"My turn," he growls. He quickly pulls out of me. "Kneel up on the couch." His hands guide me at the hips to flip and climb up on the cushion. On my knees, he follows me. I'm lost to his control.

Do with me what you will.

I lean over the back of the couch, and Jacob enters me. As he thrusts harder, hitting deeper and moving faster, I grunt and groan.

"So beautiful like this, angel." With the devil at my back, I'm taken in a way I've never experienced. Jacob's fingers clutch at my hips, nearly bruising the skin. He dives into me over and over again. Our position is raw and racy, with the fire at our back like some ancient ritual. Each thrust becomes more wild, more desperate with need until he stills, holding himself within my depths, and the evidence of his release is undeniable. His upper body leans back while his hips tip forward, holding him in place. Glancing at him over my shoulder, he's a gorgeous creature in the throes of lust.

Eventually, he collapses over me. His warm chest covers the expanse of my back, and we remain in this position, still connected to one another. With the power of his orgasm, I silently praise the glory of condoms.

"My Lilac," he says into my neck. "That scent. It just lingers."

His words make me shiver. The endearment screams intimacy, but reality crashes into me despite our position. This is only one night.

However, twenty minutes later, after we've slipped down to the couch to catch our breaths, Jacob begins kissing my neck. Then my shoulder. With a hand on my arm, he turns me.

"Can't get enough," he says before crashing his mouth to mine again. He sits up and drags me over him, straddling his lap this time. With my back to the fire, his hands coast up my sides before his mouth takes mine again. He's already hard and ready for a repeat, but he works my mouth until I can't take the anticipation. My core covers him.

"Wait," he softly says as I grind over his stiff length. He reaches around me for another packet on the floor. Quickly, he sheaths himself, and this time I guide him to me. Balancing on the precipice of him seems iconic of our situation. We shouldn't have tipped over this edge, but we did.

And we do it again, as I slide down him, slipping him inside me. Jacob's head tips back once before his eyes meet mine.

"You're so fucking perfect. Truly an angel." His eyes outline my body as I rock over him, undulating with a rhythm that matches the racing of my heart. He watches me, eyes wandering over the movement of my hips, the heave of my chest, and the gasp from my lips when he taps me in a way I'm unfamiliar.

"With the fire like this, highlighting your skin. You're a vision, Lilac. I don't know what I've done to deserve this night." There's a question in his voice, along with the confusion, but it's all a reminder

L.B. Dunbar

this is only for tonight. *This night.* I don't want to turn back time. I just want to keep taking from him.

"I feel so alive being inside you." I slowly smile at his words as his hands skim my body. My hips respond, moving on him in a way another orgasm builds. *This is crazy.* And delicious. I rock on his lap, setting a pace that drives my clit over his pelvis.

"Jacob," I whisper, a warning too quiet.

"That's it, angel. Take from me. Break for me." My lids close, and my head tips back as I feel the spiral swirl through my body. My thighs clench against his while my hands clutch at his shoulders. I break apart, mouth falling open to scream, and his lips capture mine, swallowing back my cries. His hips thrust upward, taking over. He grows wild once more, bucking upward while tugging me down at the hips. His mouth quickly breaks from mine.

"So good. So fucking good." The words pour from his mouth as his head falls back and he holds me over him, jolting inside me once more. When he comes down from the high, his lids open, and he stares at me over him. One hand reaches up for my hair, swiping along my face at the hairline before brushing back the short strands.

"Beautiful," he whispers to me, and of all the things to make me blush, it's his words.

+ + +

We eventually sleep with me curled into his chest. I'm spent after such aggressive lovemaking, but quickly remind myself it isn't love. It was lust in the heat of the moment, in the heat of a snowstorm.

I wake to something long and thick between my thighs. My lids flip open, and I notice Jacob watching me. The fire is out. Daylight fills the windows. The storm has passed, but the earth is a white wonderland.

With my back to the cushions and Jacob at my front, he's been my heat source through the night, but the firmness between my legs is warmth as well.

Jacob's fingers caress my hairline as they did last night.

94

"One more time," he whispers as if asking for old times' sake. I don't want to think about how the bubble will burst once we leave this couch. Instead, I tip up my head and brush my lips over his. He kisses me back, long and lazy as if we have all the time in the world. Eventually breaking the kiss, he reaches blindly behind him and picks up a final packet. He covers himself, skilled at the motion, and returns between my thighs. He hitches my leg over his hip, keeping us on our sides.

Without words, he slides into me, and we quietly sigh. He rocks once before flipping me to my back, sliding over me. It's the most vanilla position we've been in, and Jacob stills, balancing on his elbows. Shaky fingers brush at my hair once again.

"What are you doing to me?" he groans before rocking forward, tapping into me, and all thoughts escape me. I have no answer for him. Whatever I'm doing, he's doing to me. I'm confused while complete. I'm concerned while comfortable.

Jacob moves slowly, no longer in the rush of last night. His eyes focus on mine, but it's too much. I turn away first, but his hand on my face turns me back.

"Look at me," he begs. "I'm a monster at heart, but you're turning me into something else. I'm a creature confused at the beauty before him. How can I deserve someone like you?"

His words are too much. A tear seeps from my eye as I sense this is goodbye between us, a final act before reality strikes, and we realize what we've done. I have no idea how this will affect us other than to destroy the working relationship we have. We can't go back.

Jacob continues to move, growing more intense with each thrust. "Can't hold back. Feels too good." His stammering comments break through the haze of his previous words. My hips tip to meet his short thrusts. I'm too in my head to get where I need to go for him.

"Lilac," he warns, and my hands cup his face, drawing his lips down to me as I kiss him in sadness and fear. I'll lose him once we leave this couch. I sense the loss before we've even moved.

"Shit," he mutters, breaking our connected lips and stilling. He goes off inside me once more, and he holds his position, remaining on top of me. "You didn't."

L.B. Dunbar

He shifts to remove himself from me, but I catch him at his shoulder blades. My heart sinks as I accept that this is not personal. Despite our intense connection, this was just sex. It can't be more. Jacob doesn't want marriage. He doesn't even date. He's told me dating is only a means to sex. And these are ways I'm not the person for him as I want more than just sex.

"It doesn't matter," I finally respond to him, and his brows pinch as he looks down at me. At thirty-six, I'm reduced to my sixteen-year-old self. The girl who gave up her virginity to the wrong boy. The woman whose hopes fell on Brendan as the wrong man. I've picked the wrong man again, but haven't I known it all along? Suddenly, I'm emotionally scarred by our situation when it's been all my fault. I thought I could handle this night for what it was.

And I can't.

Jacob lowers, pressing his lips to my forehead and holding the position. Tears fill my eyes as we lay molded together, still connected when a sharp knock sounds on the front door. Jacob pulls back to look down at me.

"Are you expecting someone?"

"I don't know anyone," he replies, tipping his head as if he can see the front door from our position behind the arm of the couch. He probably can because we moved the furniture.

"Stay here," he commands, quickly separating from me. He moves off the couch and reaches for his jeans, stepping into them without his boxers. He grabs the cable-knit sweater he gave to me last night and slips it over his head. Leaving me, he rounds the couch and heads to the front door. He looks through the muted glass of the side window before opening the door a crack.

"Can I help you?"

"I'm looking for Pam Carter." Instantly, I recognize the rough male voice. "Is she here?"

Shit.

"Who wants to know?" Jacob inquires, irritation present in his voice. His body shifts, blocking the visitor from viewing inside, but I know who stands out there. I swing my legs from the couch and scramble for my sweater. My leggings are next as my underwear is somewhere behind the couch. Still seated, I tug up the material and hear the man at the door speak.

"Her brother, Jess." He speaks with the same warning hesitation Jacob did.

Jacob slides the door open farther, revealing me with my bedhead of hair and smudged makeup. Trying to straighten day-old clothing, I stand and walk with humiliation to the front door to face my brother. Eyes that match mine shift from me to Jacob and then back.

"Who's this?" Jess snaps, tipping his head in Jacob's direction.

"This is Jacob Vincent." I address my brother, no longer holding back Jacob's secrets. Jacob doesn't take his eyes off Jess.

"He the mystery man?" Jess smirks, his jaw clenching as he's working through his thoughts. Born eleven months apart, Jess looks every bit my twin, with chin-length straw-blond hair and denim blue eyes, only his brooding features don't match the more roundness of me.

"I'm her boss," Jacob interjects with steel in his tone. His body stiffens as he continues assessing my brother.

My family has known I work for someone outside of Mae's Flowers, and they've teased me for years that I'm in love with this mystery man. I've adamantly denied my feelings. Standing before my brother, I look guilty of something other than loving the man at my side.

"You okay?" Jess asks, pausing to assess my state of dress. "Thought you might be snowed in." I tip my head to see my eldest brother, Tom, sitting in his truck geared up with snowplowing equipment.

"How did you find me?" I question as I've never revealed Jacob's address.

"Emily has some find her friends app. She looked up your location when you weren't answering your phone."

I chew at my lip, uncertain of what's next when Jacob speaks.

"Since you're here, could you plow the drive? Then Pam can get out of here." Jacob's terse tone, addressing my brother, turns my head in his direction. I narrow my eyes on him, wondering why he's standing so still. His fingers are white-knuckling the edge of the front door. My

97

stomach roils. Is he trying to get rid of me? Is my brothers' sudden appearance the perfect excuse to kick me out?

"Yeah, man. We got it." Jess addresses Jacob and then turns to me. "Phone dead?"

"Lost power last night," Jacob clarifies for me, but I'm holding eyes with my brother again.

"Call Mom," he mutters.

Shit.

I never called anyone to tell them where I was. Not that I need to check in, but it was a storm, and I'm guessing Mom checked in with all her chicks to make sure everyone was safe. I hadn't answered my phone all night. Then again, I am a grown-ass adult and can take care of myself. Glancing up at Jacob, I realize I'm wrong. I'm in over my head. I've thrown myself at the fire and got burned.

"Let me get my things. I'll meet you downstairs." I pause, waiting for Jacob to say something, anything to stop me from going, but he doesn't. When I glance back at my brother, Jess's jaw clenches before he nods once.

"Nice to meet you," he mutters to Jacob, holding out a hand. Jacob stares down at it for a second before responding.

"You, too, man."

Shaking my head, I trudge back to our little nest, gathering my bra and socks before searching for my bag. My underwear is a lost cause. My jacket was near my bag, and I roughly tug it on, angry with myself. *I'm so stupid.*

Jacob enters his office without a word to me, and I return to the hall for my boots. While I slip them on, Jacob returns, standing before me. He holds out his hand with several bills in them—hundred-dollar bills.

"There should be enough for your brother's service and your extra time last night." I blink at the dullness of his tone.

"Extra time?" I hiss, then swallow back the sudden lump in my throat.

"You probably want to be paid for your overtime."

Continuing to stare at him, I can't process what he's saying. He didn't force me to stay. It was an act of nature. I wasn't working. I was spending time with him.

What the hell does he think happened here?

"I don't want your money."

"Take it. You deserve it." He shoves his hand toward me. Shell-shocked, I reach forward as if I'm going to accept his offering—for services fucking rendered—and then I smack at his wrist. The surprising strike causes Jacob to drop the bills, and I watch as they scatter to his floor.

"What the fuck?" Jacob stammers, staring back at me.

"No, that's my question," I snap back at him. "Do not treat me like this," I demand, finding strength I don't feel.

"I'm not treating you—"

"You've never been a dick to me before, so don't start now," I yell.

"I'm not being a dick. I'm paying you for—"

"For sleeping with you," I finish for him.

"That's not what happened here."

I stare at him, waiting for more of an explanation. "What did happen then?" I finally ask, knowing I won't like his answer. His silence says it all.

"That's what I thought," I whisper.

My name is a quiet echo I ignore as I turn for the staircase, stomp downward, and slam the door on my exit. I've reached my breaking point with Jacob, and it's all my fault.

Chapter 13

A Cold Blast

[Jacob]

I have no idea why she's pissed, and I stand here shell-shocked as the bills lay scattered on the floor. Bending to pick them up, I return to the living room, finding our disheveled love nest. The condom wrappers and the spent ones. The comforter has fallen to the floor. *Fuck.* I race barefoot down the cold stairs to the lower level garage, yanking open the door to find Pam already backing out of the space. With the soles of my feet freezing against the concrete flooring, I wave my arms at her retreat, but she ignores me, slipping out in the sliver of space her brothers have plowed in my drive while I stand there watching as she disappears between the thick shrubbery onto the dirt road.

I run back into the house, immediately calling her, but she doesn't answer. Her old Jeep isn't high tech, and I know she's a responsible driver, not distracted by phones unless she has her Bluetooth earpiece in place.

Call me. I shoot off the text, and then my own phone dies after using it as a flashlight for too long last night. When my electricity restores, and I can finally plug in my phone to charge, there is no response to my text.

As I thrive on work, I end up sending her the chapters she didn't complete reading via email. I need to write, but my head is a mess with her disappearance and lack of response to me. At three in the morning, the chapters return, and I stare at the empty email minus the work.

Suddenly, I feel guilty as she does have a job outside of working for me. Plus, she does all her blogging stuff, most of which she does for free, claiming she just likes books that much.

"It's a stress reliever to read and then chat about what I've read."

On that day in the hospital, when I told Pam who I was, she told me how she knew me.

Fight From The Heart

"Jacob Vincent, the author?" Born Jacob Vincentia, I dropped the last letters to make my name easier for readers to recognize. I'm not hard-pressed to meet a random fan, but it did seem strange that this angel in a hospital would recognize me.

"I write for Blood and Blossom, a blog and—"

"What?" I'd cut her off immediately because I'd heard of her. She'd hated my prior release—*Where the Wolves Hunt*—ripping about the fantasy thriller as unrealistic and almost childish compared to my other stories. As I'd loved that book, her review was harsh. Not that I normally react to reviews, but for some reason, hers really hit home, especially because her prior reviews were eloquently written, dissecting the subtleties within my stories, and even finding nuggets I hadn't consciously made. She was excellent at deciphering my work, so I didn't like her disappointment in that one book. I asked her to read for me, and so our history began. She's been my muse ever since, and I've won three major awards with her assistance.

While I'm typically cavalier about people in my life, letting them walk away if they wish, I'm not so carefree about Pam. I want to argue with myself that it's her inspiration I can't dismiss, but it isn't just her award-winning assistance. I'd miss her. She doesn't take my shit, and the underlying current that she could walk away from me easier than I can with her tells me I don't want to lose her on a deeper level. I just don't know what that level is.

+ + +

The next day, Ella calls to ask me to join her and Ethan for dinner at their new place. I jump at the chance as I need to get out of my own house. Everywhere here is a reminder of Pam. She's been an integral part of my home for over two years, and now, it's as if she's imprinted on everything. My bed. The couches. Even my pots and pans.

"What can I bring?" I ask Ella, knowing I'll need to stop at the Bear's Den for anything she suggests.

"Just you. Ethan has the rest covered." My lucky sister has a live-in chef and future restaurant owner as her lover-roommate.

101

L.B. Dunbar

When I arrive at their house, I find I'm not the only guest.

"Lilac." Her name is a breath of fresh air like the scent of her skin. In return, she glares at me like I'm the boogeyman, haunting her.

"Jacob." Her voice is as sharp, but I step up to her terse address. Kissing her cheek, I want to give her so much more but restrain myself. Ella's attention swivels from me to Pam, staring at us, but I ignore my sister's questioning gaze.

"Hey, guys," Ethan greets me as he enters their entryway. The tension is so thick. He looks at Pam, then me, and back at Pam. He steps up and kisses her cheek as I did, and I'd want to punch him if I didn't know he loved my sister. "Come on in."

Ethan leads us farther into their cozy cottage house, which appears tight compared to the sprawl of my own home. Ella beams as she looks up at Ethan, her arms wrapped around him as he gives us the quick tour. Our final stop is in their kitchen where he's preparing a meal, and Ella pours us all wine.

"To challenges," Ethan cheers, and my eyes leap to Pam, who ignores me. What Pam and I did the other night was a risk, and I haven't been so certain it was worth it. I mean, it was amazing, but I can't handle her silence. We should talk, but I hate explaining myself. *What would I even say to her?* I don't have any fucking idea. I can't tell her how I feel even though plenty bled from my lips the other night. I told her she was beautiful. I told her how amazing she felt around me. I told her how I'd been waiting for such a long time to enter her. I couldn't help myself. The reality was so much more than the fantasy. I'm rock-hard, just recalling the night, but it's evident we need to talk, and I hate these kinds of discussions.

I don't want to complicate things. It was just sex.

But as I look over at Pam, ignoring me and listening to Ethan talk about something, I realize it isn't so simple as just sex.

This is Pam. My Lilac. My angel.

After a few sips of wine and casual talk about dinner, Ethan says it's ready for our tasting, and he leads us to their small dining room. Ella sits at a right angle to Ethan, which places Pam across from her. As I sit next to Pam, the energy coming off her suggests she'll stab me with a butter knife.

We dig into Ethan's dinner, a specialty item he's hoping to have on the menu of his soon-to-open restaurant. Traditional pot roast with new seasonings, plus petite potatoes boiled to perfection and cooked carrots, which I normally don't like, but he's found the ideal consistency for them—still firm while hot. Dinner continues with a conversation about Ethan's restaurant and Ella's company, Fabulously Flawed. Her business is a clothing line she designed. Pam and I listen intently and ask appropriate questions but don't speak directly to one another.

I hate the tension.

This isn't like Mandi, who can hold a grudge and then turn on me to wind me up. This is Pam, who I fear could keep silent forever, and I have only myself to blame.

As dinner ends, Pam volunteers to do the dishes with Ella while Ethan and I take a seat in their living room with nothing more than a saggy couch and a leather recliner.

"What's the deal with you two?" Ethan says, leaning forward and directing his gaze toward the kitchen. Admittedly, I don't have many friends, and I shortchanged Ethan after he slept with my sister. Over time, he's grown on me, and I consider him a friend.

"Who knows?" I state, blowing off the question while feeling guilty. I know exactly what's wrong. Pam thinks I tried to pay her for *services* the other evening. I've never done such a thing, nor will I ever, and I definitely was not paying Pam to have sex with me.

"You know there was a time I thought you might be using Pam for sexual favors."

"What?" I choke.

"Thought once I'd met you, I'd have to hurt you if you were using her like that."

"I'd never do any such thing," I stammer, still fighting the suffocating lump in my throat.

"So if you weren't paying her for sexual affairs, when did you start giving them to her?"

L.B. Dunbar

I cough even harder now, no longer able to control whatever is choking me. "What?"

"I know a woman scorned when I see one, and you did something to her. She can hardly look at you. Was it Mandi? Did she catch you two in the act? Are you two back together?" Ethan shivers.

"Why would Pam care about Mandi and me?" It's half dismissive, half inquiry. Pam never discusses Mandi with me. Then I consider the other night, outside the pharmacy, and Pam's hint of jealousy. Has it bothered her that I've had Mandi in my life?

"Because Pam's had the hots for you for years, but this Mandi thing pushes her over the limits."

"Pam does not have the hots for me."

"She's so hot for you it's like eating a jalapeno pepper with tabasco sauce on it."

"That is not true."

"It's like a poker primed for branding, all red-orange and fiery, ready to sear and sizzle and burn." Ethan gives me a cheeky grin.

"You're making that up."

"She's so hot, it's—"

"Who's hot?" Pam interrupts, entering the room and suddenly filling all the air with her scent.

"You're hot," Ethan says.

"What the fuck, man?" I snap.

"He's only teasing," Pam says, waving a dismissive hand at Ethan. "Wishful thinking."

"What does he wish?" I question, looking back and forth between the two of them as Ella enters the room.

"Ethan likes to pretend he has a crush on me because I always turn him down."

"An arrow through the heart every time." Ethan presses one hand to his chest over his heart while simultaneously reaching for Ella. He tugs her onto his lap and looks up at her. "Until now." It's strange to watch a man kiss my sister, right on her cheek, over her scars. He doesn't see them like I do, as a reminder of a time I let her down. If I were emotional, I'd say I love this guy for the way he loves my sister, but I have no emotions.

"Anyway, thanks for dinner, E, but I've got to get going. Work in the morning, and I had a late night last night," Pam states.

"Oh, up all night misbehaving," Ethan teases her.

"Yeah, now that would be wishful thinking," she mutters.

What the hell?

"What do you need to do at the garden center this time of year anyway? It's like a second winter out there." Ethan teases her, and I'm wondering the same thing. She should be in my home, day and night, helping me—with writing, sexual favors, and spending time with me.

My chest tightens with the knowledge of how empty my house feels since she's left.

"Orders. And arrangements for a certain someone's grand opening," she teases Ethan. His place doesn't open until April, which is a little less than a month away.

"Are you guys still going to New York next week?" Ella has worked with a photographer friend to pair her new clothing line with images. She has another show in the city, and I promised I'd attend this one since I missed the last one at the end of January.

"Yeah, we're going." Ethan tugs at Ella's hip, peering up at her again, and my sister cups his face, leaning down for another kiss. It's all sticky sweet and too much sugar for me, especially with the tension between Pam and myself.

"Okay, then." Pam claps her hands. "E. Ella. Thanks for dinner. Delicious as always, Ethan. Your place will be a hit."

"You should come to New York, too," Ella blurts out, and the room goes silent. Pam's eyes shift to me but leap back to my sister.

"Uhm, that's sweet of you, but I don't think I can get the time off. When do you leave?"

"Next Wednesday evening," Ella replies. The plan is a long weekend in New York. I have a meeting with my agent on Thursday with Ella's showing on Friday night. I was even able to hook up an impromptu fight at the gym on Saturday evening.

L.B. Dunbar

Ella glances at me, her brows pinching before she gazes back at Pam. "Well, maybe next time then? We can turn it into a girls' thing."

"A girls-plus-Ethan thing," Ethan teases, squeezing at Ella again. After Ella slipped away from him the first time, I imagine he doesn't want to let her out of his sight.

I know the feeling, man.

I glance at Pam with her head down, suddenly feeling uncertain about this New York visit for some reason.

"I better be going as well. I'm on deadline." I stand and step toward the front door, taking my coat off a hook near it and reaching for Pam's. I hold it open for her as if we planned to leave together. Her brows pinch, but she gives me her back and slips her arms into the coat. I catch another whiff of her as she stands so close to me. I ache for her.

We say our goodbyes with hugs and handshakes, and then Pam and I leave. More painful silence follows us out the door once Ethan and Ella close it behind us. Pam walks ahead of me, as her car is in the street and mine is parked in front of hers. As she walks, I lean forward and scoop up a handful of snow remaining from the storm. With perfect aim, I nail her luscious ass, smashing the snowball and forcing her to finally turn and look at me.

Chapter 14

Snow Deals

[Pam]

"Hey!" I turn and yell at Jacob as a snowball hits me square in the backside. After another one hits my midsection, I lower for my own ammunition. Whipping off a ball of snow, it goes nowhere near Jacob. I lower to scoop up another ball when I'm tackled to the ground before I can fire it off.

"What's your deal?" I holler at him as he's pressing me into the wet snow.

"What's yours?" he counters, looking into my eyes until I have to look away.

"What are you doing, Jacob?" My gaze falls on the house where the front porch light remains on, but the rest of Ethan and Ella's place has gone dark.

"I hurt your feelings." The truth in his words returns my attention to his face. "I'm sorry."

Do I thank him for the apology? What about the rest of the night?

"You're mad at me," he adds. "I don't like it."

"I'm not mad," I state, huffing out a breath that hits him in the face. His eyes remain fixed to mine, and my steely resolve is melting under his gaze. I'm not strong enough to resist him, and that's been my problem lately. I've given in to temptation too easily.

"For more than two years, I've resisted you," I whisper, staring up at him with the dark sky behind his head and the cold snow against my jeans. "Why now? Why is this happening now?"

I don't even know if I'm asking him directly or just wondering out loud.

"Resisted?" Jacob questions. "What do you mean, *resisted?*"

I roll my head to the side, but Jacob grips my chin with his glove-covered hands, forcing me to look at him. Do I tell him how attracted I've been to him? Do I tell him how I feel? It all seems like too much.

"You're always teasing me, and I've just fought the . . ." *Attraction.*

"Fought what?" His voice grows rougher, his grip tighter, but his eyes say he's desperate for the truth.

"The pull, okay? I've fought the pull I feel to you. I've done everything in my power to keep us professional, but the other night . . . I don't know what happened." Frustration comes out with my words. Was it the atmosphere? The candles, wine, and dinner? Was it the hand holding and falling asleep? Or was it just that my resolve had finally broken? I couldn't fight how strongly I wanted to be with him, even if for one night.

"You're drawn to me?" His midnight eyes soften, moving back and forth across my face. He can't seriously not see it, not feel it. I've always felt as if it's written on my face, and he knows it, thus torturing me with tempting taunts and innocent flirtation.

"Yes, okay. Yes, I'm . . . drawn to you." My arms attempt to flare out but don't go far with the bulk of my winter jacket and the press of his body over me.

"Are you going out with that other guy?"

"Not this again." I sigh, tugging free of his grip. Spencer actually did call me, but he has a wedding to attend this coming weekend, and we both agreed a first date at a wedding seemed like a predilection to disaster. He was sweet as he teased that he'd be all emotional and want to marry me on the first date, and that might be a big turn-off. He has no idea how it might be a turn-on if someone so easily wanted to marry me, but a wedding does ramp up the emotions. I've attended more weddings than I care to count. Not to mention, there's the whole awkward history with Spencer being one of Brendan's friends, which leaves me wondering why Spencer would even want to go out with me in the first place.

Perhaps he's lonely like I am.

"Well?" Jacob growls.

"It's none of your business." If I told him the truth, would he be jealous? Or would a competitive spirit cause him to react?

"Come to New York with me."

"What?" My forehead furrows as I gaze up at his dark eyes. He can't be serious.

"Come to New York. My agent's been wanting to meet the woman who keeps me in line. You can see Ella's show and explore the city."

"Jacob, be serious." This isn't funny, and I'm getting irritated. The invitation is under duress or something ridiculously similar, and I don't need some pity invite.

"I am serious. I'll pay for everything."

My body slumps under his. "Throwing money at me?"

"Come on, Lilac. It wasn't like that." He stares down at me, sincerity in those eyes. I wait for further explanation as he didn't give me one the other morning. His gaze traces the edges of my face, like his finger did, drawing a line along my hair and tucking it behind my ear. It was such a sweet gesture as he peered down at me, similar to how he's looking at me now. He was over me just as he is presently, buried inside me, making me feel one with him, and separate from him at the same time. I didn't know how to handle the mixed signals.

"I wasn't trying to insult you the other morning, and I'm sorry you took it that way. I just . . ." He huffs. "You work hard. For me. In general. I didn't want you to think I took advantage of you. And I did take advantage."

My mouth falls open.

"I mean, I demanded you come to me in a snowstorm, and it wasn't sensitive." He pauses, eyes still searching my face. "But I'm not sorry you stayed. And I'm not sorry for what we did. I don't know how to define it. Maybe it's the pull you're talking about."

I try to look away, embarrassed that I want a definition. Does he feel drawn to me? He isn't saying that. It was only sex to him.

"Lilac, come to New York with me." For some reason, the moment feels too intense. His apology. His struggle. I accept it *was* only sex to him, and I'm the one with the foolish heart attached to him.

L.B. Dunbar

"You're still an ass." I cup snow into my mitten-covered hand and press it into his face. Too quickly, Jacob has my wrist next to my head. His cheeks drip with snow as he menacingly glares down at me.

"I see the master has made a monster of you. You'll pay for that." He lowers his face, pressing his cheeks against mine and rubbing his cold jaw along mine. I squirm and squeal while kicking my legs in an attempt to get him off me. We're making quite a scene in Ethan and Ella's front yard, but Jacob does not relent. Once he's smothered my face in retaliation, he pauses just over my lips.

"Come to New York." His mouth crushes mine before I can respond, literally stealing both my breath and my answer as his warm tongue delves past my lips. His kiss is frustration. As his body shifts, a knee wedges between my thighs. My legs are cold, snow seeping through the denim, but the heat of him blankets me, warming my insides. I fight the attraction again.

"Jacob," I mutter against his lips, attempting to pull back.

"New York," he mumbles, returning to my lips, dipping past the seam again. His tongue dances with mine.

I try to say his name again, but he refuses to let me speak. His lips cover mine, refusing to let me deny him.

"I'll call Mae for you. I'll tell her how badly I need you with me."

"How badly?" The heat of his mouth wants to answer for him, but I'm not allowing it. I fight the warmth and break another kiss. I need his words.

"Lilac," he begs with my name.

"I'll think about it."

He huffs out in frustration. "I don't like to play these games."

"I'm not Mandi."

His eyes skim my face. "Don't I know it."

I push at his sides, willing him off me, but he flattens himself against me, pinning me in place. "That's not what I mean. Shit, angel. You're so much more than her, just . . . I don't know what you want from me."

I want it to mean more than sex. I want his body *and heart* like he's taken mine. I don't want to fight him, my attraction, or even my anger at

110

the moment. I don't want him to compare me to her. I just want him to see me.

"Look, do you want me to tell you I felt something between us? I did. I don't know what it was, but it was amazing. I want it again. I want you." He pauses, staring down at me. "Come to New York."

The cold night air no longer effects either of us as the heat of his eyes melts me. I hate how I'm giving in to him. *Why can't I be more resistant? Why do I feel this pull toward him?*

"Will you do something for me first?"

"Anything." He exhales.

"Meet my siblings." Jacob has no friends, no family outside of Ella, and I don't want to keep him a secret anymore. Let my family meet the man I've been lusting over for years, and then tell me how foolish I've been to fall in love with him.

"What?" His eyes turn wild. "Why?"

"Because they're important to me." This is a test, but I'm not playing games. I need someone outside myself to tell me I'm crazy to want this man. I'm crazy to give in to a request to go to New York with him. I need someone to talk sense into me.

Jacob rolls off me, and I know he'll decline. "I don't think that's a good idea."

"Why?" Here's the moment of truth when he says he doesn't do family and meeting them is like stepping into commitment.

"Because I'm not good with other people." His head turns to face me. Lying in the snow in Ethan's front yard, we should be talking someplace else, but I don't want to move. Not yet.

"You do okay with me," I tease. He's an introvert, that's for certain, but he easily opened up to me that day we met in the hospital. We've been working together ever since.

"That's because you're you." He rolls to his side to face me better. "There's something about you that makes me feel free to speak."

My brows pinch. He's a man of words. He speaks all the time through his writing, but then I recall what he told me the other night about his father and the abuse. The worlds he created to lose himself or

L.B. Dunbar

save others. He couldn't speak up for himself in his real life, so he did it through his fantasy storytelling.

"Come to the Tavern, and I'll go to New York."

"Jesus," he hisses, rolling back in the snow and staring up at the dark late winter sky. "You're in the wrong business. You should be in negotiations or something."

"Is that a no?" I tease. He turns his attention back to me.

"That's a *you drive a hard bargain*, but I'll seek my retribution on you, my pretty." He rolls his entire body back over me and swipes down the side of my head with a glove-covered finger. Then he brings the finger to his mouth and bites the glove, removing it. His warm fingertip traces along my cheek, and he watches it move.

"I'll do anything you ask," he whispers, and my heart flutters faster before he kisses me to seal our deal.

Chapter 15
Family Matters

[Pam]

By seven thirty on Thursday evening, Jacob hasn't shown, and I'm second-guessing everything.

"How did you get Jacob to agree to come here tonight?" Ella asks when she first arrived with Ethan.

It's actually strange to see Ella as an addition to our weekly family gathering, but we've added Emily, Jess's fiancée, and Leon, Tricia's fiancé, over the past six months. It feels like everyone is pairing up except me, the token single woman in the group.

"What happened with you two the other night? The tension was as cold as an icicle."

I really long to discuss all the things with someone, but Jacob's stepsister is probably not the best candidate to hear my concerns. That's what Mae is for as my best friend, but I haven't opened up to her either. Ella reaches for my wrist.

"You can tell me anything," she whispers as she's told me her fair share of secrets. When I helped her leave last November, I thought it best if she start at the beginning and tell me everything. Her tale is sad and twisted, but not without a happily ever after. At the time, we needed to make a plan of action for her. The course included three months of self-discovery, setting her future in motion, and seeking therapy for her past.

"Nothing happened," I lie, playing the pretending game I've played for years. *It was only sex.* But if that's true, why did he kiss me, ask me for a chance, and agree to come here tonight?

"Jacob told me he asked you to go to New York." Ella's voice rises with her enthusiasm.

"You're going to New York?" my sister asks me. Her hand rubs over the small swell that isn't visible yet, and I want to be happy for her. She has everything she ever dreamed of.

"I'm undecided," I mutter.

L.B. Dunbar

"I hate to hear that." The deep male voice behind my seat causes both Ella and me to spin and face Jacob, dressed head to toe in black. His normally edgy expression was heightened while his eyes said he was nervous. I stand to greet him. I hold out a hand, and he stares down at it a moment before slipping his fingers into mine.

"More hand holding," he mutters, and I shake my head, biting the smile on my lips.

"You're late," I tell him.

"I'm on deadline," he states. "But my assistant wanted me to meet her family."

"She sounds like a real hard-ass," I tease.

"She can be." He smirks and leans closer to me. "But she also has a great ass, so I'll do whatever she asks."

My face heats, and I turn away from him, pointing at people around the table. "You know Ethan. This is my sister, Tricia, and you mentioned you already know her fiancé, Leon Ramirez."

Leon holds out a hand. He has cappuccino-colored skin with almost midnight eyes and a devilish smile. With tattoos on him, his dark look isn't much different from Jacob, but Leon has a more relaxed expression about him.

"They aren't so bad," Leon teasingly tells Jacob, nodding his head at our family. "Have a drink."

Jacob instantly relaxes under Leon's easy welcome, and I mouth my gratitude to my future brother-in-law.

"So, we have something we'd like to tell everyone," Tricia says, drawing the attention of all eyes at the table. They've already announced their engagement and pregnancy, so I can't take much more sappy news. I'm not jealous, not in the traditional sense. It's just that all my family members are finding their true loves, and I'm sitting next to someone I've been in love with for too long. For days, I've been wavering on his New York invitation, trying to convince myself not to accept. I'd only be setting myself up for more heartache.

"We got married," Tricia states, excitement and hesitation in her voice.

The air wooshes out of me, and the rest of my family sits in various positions of shock and awe, stunned that we hadn't all been included on this important day for them.

"Mom knows, and we asked Jess and Emily to be our witnesses," Tricia explains. "We would have had Lys and Levi do it, but they aren't old enough." Lys is Leon's youngest sister, and Levi Walker is the youngest brother of Tricia's first husband. He's like a child slash little brother she never had, and they have a unique relationship.

"I didn't want to wait," Leon says, lifting Tricia's hand with his and kissing her knuckles.

"And I didn't need the fanfare of a big wedding," Tricia adds. She's already had one with a man who turned out to be everything opposite what we could want for our sibling. In addition, her life has been a whirlwind for the past six months or so. "We just wanted to keep it simple."

"I wasn't invited," Tom states, a scowl on his face as the eldest of us.

"I'm sorry." Tricia's eyes shoot to Jess for support, but he shakes his head. It made sense to have Emily and Jess as witnesses as Leon and Jess have formed a new friendship, and Emily has grown close to Tricia.

"Well, I think it's wonderful," Karyn interjects, soothing Tom's momentary pout.

"Please be happy for me," Tricia whispers, and I look over to find her watching me. My sister and I aren't terribly close, but we are still sisters, and I want what's best for her. Leon is that best.

"Of course," I say, reaching for her hand. I am happy for her. *I'm only unhappy with me.*

"You need a party," Ethan suggests. "Let me throw you a reception."

"Oh, man," Leon mutters, looking over at Ethan. "You don't need to do that."

"That's not necessary," Tricia adds, smiling at Ethan for offering.

"I want to do it. You both deserve it, and I owe Leon for all his help with my place. We need to celebrate." Party could be Ethan's middle name, but I admit this is a show of acceptance. Ethan and Leon are good friends now. "I'll plan everything."

The suggestions break out, and the conversation shifts to when to hold the party and what to serve. Emily joins the exuberance as Jess and she are getting married this summer with an actual wedding on Ethan's property at the old red barn.

With a focus on Tricia and Leon, I figure Jacob and I are saved from scrutiny. However, too soon, my family shuffles to my guest and me. The firing squad begins.

"So, how'd you meet Pammie?" Tom teases, calling me a name I haven't heard since my dad.

"She works for me."

"Sexual favors," Ethan coughs into his hand like the teenager he once was.

"Ethan," Ella shrieks, but a wide smile curls her lips.

"Things a brother does not want to hear," Jess grumbles, but Emily smiles back at me as well. She winks. We've already discussed how her location app found me. I just happened to leave out the details of what I'd done at Jacob's house.

"Because you're the boss," Jess states, recalling when he met Jacob at the house. After I drove myself home that day, I didn't get the inquisition I expected from my brothers.

"I'm the boss," Jacob states, his head turning to face me. A mischievous energy comes off him.

"The boss?" Karyn questions. "Not the *boss*-boss?"

I don't even know what that means.

"The mystery man she's in love with?" Tricia blurts out, surprised and then equally embarrassed that she's just ratted out my emotions. Anxious tears well in my eyes, and I want to crawl under the table. I hate my family at this moment.

To my surprise, Jacob holds my hand tighter, crushing my fingers before lifting them for his lips. He kisses the tips. "That's me. The boss-boss who Lilac is in love with."

"You have a nickname for her?" Emily squeals. Jacob and I still face each other, and I blink back the tears. I'm the one who asked him to be here, yet I'm mortified at how this is playing out.

"She's my angel," he whispers to me. Then he surprises me a second time and leans forward to kiss the corner of my lips. As he pulls back, Ella's smile is so large it hardly fits her face, and Ethan chuckles before he says, "You all owe me twenty bucks."

The table erupts in hisses and discord as I listen to my family quibble over bets they placed on my mystery man and me.

"Twenty bucks said he'd fallen for you," Ethan explains, and my mouth falls open.

"That might not be fair. You have insider information," Jacob tells him, and Ethan laughs.

"Gambling isn't fair."

"When did this happen?" Ella wonders.

"When did what happen?" I question, unable to admit anything because I don't know what's happening right now. I brought Jacob here thinking my family would see he doesn't feel a certain way about me, yet he's playing opposite what I expected. I wanted the voice of reason from them, and they're turning against me.

"It's been a long time coming," Jacob admits to his sister, and I'm still not sure I believe all that I'm hearing.

As the table turns to other conversation, Jacob looks over at me, still holding my hand.

"You know what this means, right, Lilac?"

I stare at him a second.

"I came to meet your family, so you're off to New York with me." He smirks, having won his own bet and getting his way. "Our flight leaves next Wednesday at nine o'clock."

"You're proud of yourself, aren't you?" I tease.

"I'm happy you're giving me a chance." His tone turns sober, but his smile expresses his pleasure. He really wants to spend this time with me.

L.B. Dunbar

When the night wears down, and my family disperses, Jacob walks me home, holding my hand. He lifts our cold fingers to press another kiss to my knuckles.

"You know, this hand-holding thing isn't so bad," he teases, his eyes shifting to me a second. I laugh.

"You survived my family." I exhale, warm breath misting in the cold night. "Thank you for coming tonight."

"They weren't that bad, once Jess got over wanting to kill me for having my way with his sister."

"My family doesn't know you did that," I mock. However, there can't be much doubt that the boss-boss and I have hooked up. Jacob was attentive all night, holding my hand or keeping his palm on my thigh. He even swiped my hair along the side of my face a time or two, and it felt so intimate despite being so public.

As we near the pharmacy, Jacob turns to me. "Did I have my way with you? Did I ruin everything?" The hesitation in his tone tells me he's truly concerned.

"You already apologized," I remind him. "It was a misunderstanding."

"But I want to be clear that the night wasn't a mistake, Lilac." His head lowers, his fingers rubbing over my knuckles.

I step closer to him, cupping his face despite my cold hand. "Jacob, you just came out of a bad relationship. We got caught up in the night. I don't want to push you into something you aren't ready for." Maybe I'm not ready for Jacob because I don't want to be his rebound girl. His second choice.

He lifts my fingers again, curling his other hand over our linked ones and kisses them.

"Were we caught up? Or was it the pull?" His eyes look at me over his mouth on my knuckles.

"Jacob," I groan.

"So hand holding?" He shifts subjects, shutting down his question. "You've created a monster in me. I think I like it." His eyes sparkle under the dim streetlamps. "And to prove that hand holding does not need to lead to sex, I'm going to kiss you and say good night."

I start to laugh at his playfulness until a hand slips into my hair, and his mouth crashes mine. My body falls back against the exterior wall of the pharmacy as his lips master mine. Instant heat rushes my body as his tongue thrusts into my mouth, and he moves it in such a way that mimics what he did with it between my legs. It mimics what he's done to me, entering me, surging into me, filling me. It's erotic and wild, and I can't get enough. I tug him closer to me, but it isn't enough with our winter clothing between us. He tilts my head one way and then the other, not missing one spare spot of my lips before drawing back, leaving me breathless and collapsed against the wall.

Wow.

"Going to walk away now before I beg you to take me upstairs."

Beg. Please beg. But I also like how he wants to show me not everything leads to sex.

He doesn't walk away, though. He kisses me hard and fast once more and then breaks free, leaving me still panting against the building.

"Upstairs," he whispers, brooking no argument. "Now."

I think he means to follow me, but he doesn't. He waits as I race up the stairs to my apartment and enter it. My heart hammers in my chest as I fall against the door, wondering how I'll survive a weekend in New York with him.

Chapter 16

New York: A City That Needs Sleep

[Pam]

The following Wednesday, Jacob picks me up for the drive to Cherry City Airport in Traverse City, where we will fly to Detroit and then connect to New York. He offers to buy me a coffee after we check in, but I can't stomach anything so early.

My excitement builds with each step of the process until the plane taxis to the runway. My hands clutch the armrest as the speed increases for takeoff.

"What's this?" Jacob teases, taking note of my fingers white-knuckling the divider between us.

"I haven't flown in a long time, and I'm just a little nervous."

Chuckling, Jacob takes my hand, kisses the tips of my fingers, and then rests them in his lap.

"Hand holding," I mutter.

"Look at me," he whispers, and I turn my head to face him. His mouth lands on mine, thoroughly distracting me as we enter the sky and level off. Our tongues tangle as he pulls me deeper and deeper into the kiss. I've latched onto him like he's the air I need to breathe. When he finally leans back, tugging my lower lip with his, his dark eyes spark.

"Kiss me like that again, and we'll be testing admission into the mile-high club," he teases.

"You're probably a founding member," I snark.

His playful eyes narrow. "Actually, no." This surprises me.

"Most unusual place," I question, unable to let it go and hoping this conversation will continue to distract me a bit.

"My couch before the fireplace in my home."

"Jacob," I groan. It's such a line.

"I'm serious. I've never had sex in that place."

What? I stare at him. He's lived there for over two years. Then again, I've been in his home often enough to know he hasn't brought Mandi there. I assumed he might have had random hookups from town, but I'd hear of them, too. Jacob wouldn't be someone a local woman could keep a secret.

"What about you?" he asks, and I think back to all the mundane places I've had sex. A bed. The back seat of a pickup truck. There really hasn't been anyplace out of the ordinary or any place as romantic as a leather couch before a fireplace during a snowstorm.

"A leather couch in front of a fireplace in my boss's home."

"Yikes. Does he know you did that? I hope it was after working hours."

I laugh. "It was after working hours. And he knows."

Jacob's eyes brighten. "I'm sure he'll never forget the experience."

I shake my head. He's too sweet.

We're up and down from Traverse City to Detroit before I know it. Another flight and Jacob repeats the distraction, kissing me until I'm breathless and considering mile-high club admission.

I'm working on fumes by the time we get to Jacob's condo in the city that never sleeps. I'm exhausted, but I'm also wound up. I want to get inside Jacob's place and play out the things my imagination dreamed up about airplane sex. His kisses have left me wanting to be close to him again, and I'm excited to see where this trip leads for us.

When we enter his place, I marvel at the industrial look and feel. The old warehouse was converted to lofts, and the exposed brick of one wall is beautiful. That same wall has a modern wrought-iron and wood-slat staircase leading upward to a balcony with three doors. Jacob explains two bedrooms are located up there with an adjoining bathroom. He has floor-to-ceiling windows, arched under brick headers, letting in loads of natural light and reminding me a little bit of his place in Michigan. The main space is an open concept with an L-shaped kitchen in a corner, a dining table next to it, and the living area. Compared to his home on the lake, the furniture is in white tones with metal accents. It lacks comfort.

L.B. Dunbar

"And my room is over here." Jacob gives me a mischievous grin, and I'm so ready to be with him again. It's been almost a week since he met my family. He's been stuck on deadline, plus I had to work to make up for the time I asked to take off, so we haven't been able to connect. Kissing me on the plane was only a warm-up, and he steps up to me as if reading my thoughts. His mouth lowers, and he takes mine, slow and tender, and not at all like he's kissed me before. A different kind of thrill rushes through my body at the anticipation of spending some endless time with him. Tongues join our kiss, and we press against one another, hands locking together until we hear a key turn in the door.

Startling both of us, Jacob steps back.

"Jakey." A female voice screeches through the opening door as a body leaps for Jacob. He drops my hand to catch her, and her legs wrap around his hips. Long fingernails with white tips curl around his head as she peppers his face with kisses. "I knew you'd be back, baby."

Too stunned to move, to allow them privacy, I remain in the middle of the room as Jacob works to remove the monkey-woman from his body. It's like watching a failed wrestling match. Hands push at legs, which drop but immediately return to his hips once he moves to wrangle her arms. She murmurs at him until she sees me staring.

"Hello, Apple," she purrs, a Chesire cat smile crosses her too-thin face with her too-large lips. Her legs finally drop, but her arms circle his waist.

"Pam," I correct.

"I thought he called you a fruit."

"A flower," Jacob corrects, and he tugs at her upper arms wrapped around him. He presses her back without looking at me, and I'm slow to catch up on a few things.

He's mentioned me to her.

She recognizes who I am.

She knew he was coming home.

What the hell am I doing here?

"Mandi Hamilton, this is Pam Carter. Pam, Mandi." He waves a hand between us. His voice strains, but he doesn't look at me. Instead, he glares at the woman before him, who is a modern-day Wonder Woman with her dark glossy hair, deep eyes, and plush maroon lips.

"Mandi, what are you doing here?" Jacob addresses her.

"I heard you were coming home, and I wanted to greet you when you got here."

"How did you get in the building?"

She pouts at him, and I almost take that as her answer. She's stunning and a woman who looks like she's never denied her way. "My keys, baby." She speaks as if he's a simpleton, and her hand lifts for his cheek, but he catches her wrist before she touches his face.

"Watch it," he warns her, and I've seen enough.

"I'll give you two a few minutes. Maybe I could freshen up." I point at the loft, suggesting the bathroom upstairs. I need to get as far away from these two as I can.

"Lilac," Jacob pleads, finally looking at me, but I have nothing to say. My thoughts race.

We had sex.

He was just kissing me.

She knew he was coming.

How? When? Why? He must still be talking to her. He said it was over, and I know better. *I. Know. Better.* Their on-again, off-again relationship has been going on for years. It's unhealthy, Ella once explained, and she didn't have to tell me twice as just the thought of a back and forth relationship means it's not solid.

Not to mention, I'm suddenly wracked with guilt. If they're still together, and I didn't know, I slept with him as another woman's man. After that happened to me with Brendan, I swore I'd never do that to another woman, no matter who she is.

Excusing myself, I take the staircase to the balcony and help myself to a bedroom. Once inside, I lock the door and fall against the barrier. Tipping my head back several times, I will myself not to cry.

Stupid. Stupid. Stupid.

Uncertain how long Jacob will be with her, I curl up on the bed in the room and close my eyes. All I see are visions of them. Her wrapped around him. Him over her like he had been with me. Fighting the pain of them together, I eventually doze off, my systems shutting down with the heartache.

I wake a while later to sense Jacob behind me as I lay on my side. I look over my shoulder to find him on his back, staring at the ceiling.

"What happened?"

"Somehow, she knew I was coming here." He scrubs a hand down his face and lays it on his chest. His other arm is bent with his hand behind his head.

"You didn't call her?"

He huffs in response.

"She's very pretty," I say, not certain why I'm complimenting her.

"She's also all of twenty-seven." Age gap *and* Malibu Mandi—lucky man. My irritation at her presence grows as I consider how beautiful she is and how young.

"Is she back for marriage?"

"I already told you I wasn't marrying her," Jacob says, his tone dry, and I shift to sit up, twisting to face him.

"Oh, let me guess, she decided she doesn't need you to marry her. She just wants to have you in whatever manner you'll take her." This was classic, and I'd almost been that girl once in a relationship before Brendan. It's another reason I thought Brendan and I were solid. He'd actually proposed to me.

"Lilac," he groans.

"I promised myself I'd *never* come between a man and a woman." I glare at him.

"Stop it," Jacob snaps.

"What am I supposed to do here? Pretend she isn't here."

"She isn't here. She left," he says, eyes narrowing.

"But she'll be back. She'd be a fool not to return for you."

"Why? I'm no fucking catch," he snaps.

"Bullshit." We glare at one another.

"Then catch me," he says, but I shake my head.

"You don't like games. Well, neither do I. And this . . .?" I point toward the door. "I don't play. I'm not fighting some other woman for your attention, but don't worry, I won't be giving you an ultimatum. You're a grown man, Jacob. You can make your own decisions."

He sits up and tackles me back to the bed. "I chose you. I brought you to New York with me."

"Where she already lives?" She has a key to his place, which means she's easily circling within his life.

He leans toward me, but I'm still too raw to kiss him. I turn my head, and he gets my cheek.

"Way to kick a man when he's down, Lilac," he mutters to my ear.

Well, how does he think I feel? I've just witnessed a beauty queen hanging off him, and I'm wondering why the hell he'd want to sleep with me when he could sleep with that.

Jacob presses off me and scrambles off the bed. Without another word between us, he exits the room, slamming the door, and I flinch. I'm not going to fight with him like her.

I don't play that way.

+ + +

As it grows dark outside, I hear muffled voices come from below. Ethan and Ella have arrived, and I feel safe enough to leave the room. My suitcase made it to the bedroom, and I change my clothes, wanting a shower but accepting a fresh outfit as second best.

Exiting the room, I notice eyes follow my movements as I cross the landing and descend the stairs to the living room. Jacob's slanted eyes tell me he's spent the day drinking, and I'd feel sorry for him if I didn't already feel sorry for myself. I slept with a man still attached to another woman. Maybe she's young. Maybe she's entitled, but she's still *his* woman. My skin crawls.

"Hey, you guys finally made it," I say to them as eyes shift around the room, sensing the tension between Jacob and myself.

"We did, and I'm starving. I want all the New York experiences," Ethan teases.

"Let's order Chinese." Ella suggests her favorite place.

L.B. Dunbar

"Have you eaten?" she addresses me next, and I shake my head. I haven't eaten all day when I think about it, and Ella's head turns to her brother.

Jacob struggles to stand as I admit to not eating, and Ethan follows him to the kitchen area where the open space isn't separate enough to dilute their discussion.

"What the fuck is your deal, man?" Ethan whispers, but his voice carries.

"Don't worry about it," Jacob states, slurring his words.

"Well, I am worried." His eyes shift to me and back to the man holding himself up by the kitchen cabinets. "Because I'm worried about her. What happened?"

I don't need to hear Jacob to know the name he says under his breath, and Ethan tugs at his hair, holding his wild curls at the top of his head.

"What did she do?" Ella whispers to me, and I meet her eyes.

"She conveniently showed up just as we arrived."

Ella's eyes widen in horror, and Jacob turns to face us.

"I didn't ask her to be here." His voice projects, but I don't know how to respond. His eyes land on mine. "I only want time with you." He scrubs a hand down his face. He's telling me something, but I can't read him. I don't want to guess his thoughts. He's a master of words, so he needs to use them.

Looking back at Ella, I lower my voice. "She was all over him. Wrapped around him, kissing him, calling him baby." I swallow around the lump in my throat. I've made such a huge mistake being here, thinking I was someone to Jacob.

"I don't think I should be here," I whisper.

"Bullshit!" Jacob yells from the kitchen, and I flinch at the aggressive tone.

"Hey," Ethan interjects, as things are spiraling out of control. Jacob shoves at Ethan, but Ethan pushes back, pinning Jacob to the cabinets behind him. Ella screams next.

"Jacob." Something in the firmness of her voice turns his head to her, and his face crumples. *What the hell?* I don't know what I'm

126

witnessing other than a scene from their history somehow. Jacob's eyes travel to me.

"I'm sorry, angel." Ethan releases Jacob, and Jacob stumbles to his bedroom. His door closes with an audible click, and the tension in the room deflates like a released balloon.

"What the hell?" Ethan turns to us and then rushes Ella, who's visibly shaking. "I'm sorry, princess." He strokes her face, and she leans into him.

"It's not your fault," she murmurs to his chest, and for the second time today, I feel like an intruder in this room. Ella turns to me, still leaning against Ethan. "And I'm so sorry you saw him like that."

I shake my head, dismissing her distress. This isn't Ella's issue. Jacob has a problem. Several actually. His past. His alcohol. His recent relationship.

"She's so volatile for him. So destructive. Did she hit him when she was here?" I think about Mandi's raised hand and how Jacob caught it, warning her.

"Has that happened before?"

Ella's sad eyes answer the question. "He doesn't understand that's not how love works."

Jesus.

"He cares so much about you. He's excited you said yes," she weakly defends, but I don't know what to think.

"Okay, maybe we should just order the food and calm down a bit. I almost hate to suggest it, but I think we could all use a glass of wine," Ethan says. Ironically, the elephant in the room is Jacob needs help, yet each of us feels the need for something to soothe our nerves. But Jacob's alcohol issue is more than just nerves.

When the food arrives, Ella, Ethan, and I eat and discuss the city that never sleeps. Between shrimp fried rice, wontons, and eggrolls plus wine, I'm emotionally exhausted and food satisfied. Once we finish the second bottle of wine, I easily fall into bed. However, sometime during the night, I have a bed buddy. He slips up behind me, wraps an arm around me, and tugs me to his chest.

"Are you sleeping?" he asks, with a voice that sounds clearer than earlier.

"What do you want?" I mutter sleepily. Jacob nuzzles his nose into my nape, inhaling my skin just under my hairline.

"You're too good for me, and I know that. I don't deserve decent things in my life," he says. "It's why I don't deserve you, angel. I don't know what I did to have you in my life." Then he huffs. "Actually, I know what I did. I crashed into a tree, made you miss your father's death, and begged you to be my friend. I don't want to lose you."

I roll, shifting to my back, and Jacob scoots to my side. "You didn't beg me to be your friend, and as your friend, you need help, Jacob."

He sighs, falling to his back and staring up at the ceiling.

"What if you were more than a friend? What if you loved me like your family teased?"

How does he not see it wasn't just innocent teasing? I am in love with him, but I'm not admitting my emotions tonight. Not with Mandi still an issue, and his drinking a major concern for me.

"If I loved you, I'd want you to love yourself enough to get help. Because I can't just ask you to get the support you need. Like I told you earlier, you're an adult, Jacob. You need to make your own choices for yourself."

I'm not dismissing his choices, but I also can't enable them either. I said I wouldn't give him an ultimatum, and I'm not, but I can't stand by and watch him keep drowning.

"Pretend you love me. Would you leave me if I didn't stop drinking?" he questions, and I fight the urge to roll my eyes. I don't have to pretend anything.

"Would you want me to go?"

Jacob remains looking at the ceiling. "I don't ever want to lose you," he quietly admits, and while my heart should soar at the confession, it's longing for the emotion I want him to have. I want him to desire me.

"Then I guess you have things to think about," I whisper in the dark.

"I always fuck things up. I'm the monster in my own story, destroying what I have that's good."

"What's been good in your life that you destroyed? Mandi isn't good for you, Jacob, and I'm not saying that because of how I feel. I'm saying it as a friend, as someone who cares about you. It's not healthy to be with her. As for good things in your life, you have an amazing stepsister who loves you like blood."

"I damaged her too," Jacob says, still holding onto the guilt of the man who attacked her.

"That wasn't your fault, and it's another issue I think you should talk to someone about. Your hurts are like books stacked too high and inevitably going to tumble. You need the chapters of your life read and analyzed, not critiqued."

"Aren't they the same?" he questions, turning to look at me.

"I don't think so, honey," I say, softening my tone. "You need a hard look at your past and maybe the present, and learn to distinguish what's noteworthy and what's not, so you can have an amazing future."

Jacob's finger comes out to caress along my hairline. "How did I get you in my life?"

"By accident," I say with a weak tease. Sometimes I've wondered if that accident was more than an accident but some kind of happenstance. Admittedly, it'd be strange to think my father sent this man to me in some fluke of the universe—a passing of the guard of sorts. I'd like to think my dad would never make love so complicated or give me a man so complex.

Jacob huffs without humor. "Would it be too much to ask you to wait for me, Lilac? Stick with me while I figure out my shit?"

As I've already spent years on him, what would be a little more time, but I'm tired of putting my life on hold for someone else. It's not that Jacob is hopeless, but I'm the romantic who has held on to him. I guess I have things to think about as well. As I'm quiet too long, Jacob speaks again.

"Don't give up on me, angel. Not yet."

Chapter 17

Field Trips and Mind Games

[Jacob]

When Pam wakes the next morning, I've already been down to the gym to secure my place in an amateur fight on Saturday. I've had an intense workout before running miles back to the condo to get rid of the alcohol in my system, the negative results of Mandi, and the wood I have for Pam. I couldn't sleep most of the night after our chat on her bed. I hate that she's even in the guest room, and her separation is a reminder that things need to change.

I'm going to lose her if I don't change.

And I accept that it's not a personality trait or a character flaw or even giving up scrambled eggs for fried. This is letting go of the past somehow, and that *somehow* is the difficult part. I don't know what to do.

I arrive back at the condo to find Pam dressed in comfortable clothing like she's going for a walk. In an attempt to turn this trip back around to the exciting time I wanted her to have, I ask, "What's on the agenda today?"

On the plane ride to New York, we discussed things she wanted to see. We only have three days, so it has to be the highlights on this trip. I want to bring her back here again, but this might be the only chance I get with her after last night. I want to make it right. I want to make it good for her. I want her to be happy.

"I'm going for a walk in Central Park." The distinct way she says *I'm* leads me to think she wants to go alone, but that's not happening.

"You can't walk Central Park alone when you don't know where you're going."

"I'll take a map." She bends to put on running shoes.

"Which screams tourist, and I happen to know a personal tour guide who can take you anywhere you want to go."

She looks up from tying her shoe. "Really? A personal guide? Sounds expensive."

I lower to my haunches before her, dropping my voice. "He takes payment in alternative ways."

She laughs, breaking some of the tension between us.

"Kisses are applicable."

Pam gently shoves at my shoulder, and I fall back to the floor. "Too expensive."

"There's a payment plan. You can do it in installments if you wish. Even schedule when it works best for you." Pam laughs again, and it does something to my insides to hear the sound. She needs to laugh more often, and I want to be the cause. "Tips are optional."

Her eyes narrow. "Is that a pun somehow?"

My eyes widen. "You dirty little wood nymph, it wasn't, but it is now."

She shakes her head, softly laughing again.

"Give me two minutes, and I'll be ready for the Jacob Vincent tour special of New York."

"You know, I'm here with my boss. I should probably check with him. See if you're reputable as a service."

A sly smile grows on my lips. "Your boss, you say? I have an in with him, and I'm certain he'll give me the highest of recommendations." I pause, suddenly nervous. "Spend the day with me, Lilac. Let's do New York."

She nods once with a hesitant smile, and my goal is to make the curl on those lips more genuine.

+ + +

We ride in a cab to the Park entrance, and I watch as Pam takes in all the sights. Even though I have been here a million times, it's fascinating to observe her, seeing this fabulous city through a new perspective, watching someone view this special place for the first time. Arriving at Central Park, Pam pulls up a map on her phone.

131

L.B. Dunbar

"Put that thing away," I tease. "You're embarrassing me. I'm the guide. Let me lead."

Pam laughs, cautious of my expertise, but we begin to walk in silence, just taking in the organized woods around us compared to the wild wilderness around my lake home. It's peaceful here in a different way. Peace on the edge of chaos, which is how my life has felt since I settled in northern Michigan two and a half years ago. It's been life-altering.

Change your destiny.

The tattoo over my chest speaks in more ways than one. My childhood. My writing. My relationships.

After several twists and turns through the walking paths, we come upon a coffee vendor, and I suggest a cup for Pam. Lifting the liquid heaven for her nose, she wrinkles it.

"What's wrong?" I lift my cup for the smell.

"I don't know, but I suddenly don't think I have the stomach for this today."

"No worries." I carry hers while drinking mine and then drink hers as well.

"Would you like to see the City Zoo?"

"Can we?" Her face lights up, and I want to see her brightness every day. Not just in my dreams. Not only in my memories. But every damn day, I want the light of her. Maybe I can climb out of the darkness a bit, or she can just lighten the dungeon as she calls it. I shake my head, already giving too much thought to my past today. I want the rest of this day to be about her.

We walk through the zoo entrance, and I can't remember the last time I visited here. Passing exhibit after exhibit, we eventually pause at the birdhouse.

Bali Mynah. I read the name of a white bird with black-tipped wings and eyes outlined in blue feathers. It's a striking thing, although I'm not much of an ornithologist. I watch it fly around the exhibit before landing on a high perch.

"'*I know why the caged bird sings,*'" Pam recites. My sight remains on the bird, following its motion through the cage. Circling, circling,

circling before landing once more. I can strangely relate to this caged creature.

"Maya Angelou's poem is so sad," Pam explains. "But I've always understood it. The caged bird sings to mask the brutality. It needs something beautiful in life to help it through the pain. Trapped and alone, the bird needs something for herself, something that belongs only to her. Her song is that gift. The cage does not seem so lonely with a song."

My heart hammers. Breathing becomes difficult. She's just described me. Writing is my release. It became my pleasure from the anger, the bitterness, the injustice. In my worlds, in my words, I was no longer so lonely. I couldn't go a day without expressing myself with the written word because I didn't have an outlet to verbally express my emotions. The fighting eventually became the physical release I needed for negative energy. Words were for my mind what fights were for my fists.

"I'm sorry. I don't know where all that came from," Pam says, but I still can't pull my gaze from the cage.

"I'm more of a Raven man, myself, written by the master Edgar Allen Poe. Nevermore, the bird repeats. *Nevermore*." The creative word echoes around me like a motto I should keep. The word is powerful and fierce, in my opinion.

Nevermore will he love. Nevermore will he give up his emotions.

"Nevermore," Pam whispers. "It's one of your tattoos, near your wrist." Her eyes look down to my arm and lift my sleeve's edge, revealing the word scrolled as a reminder. *Nevermore* will someone touch me with his fists, but it's happened again. My thoughts leap to Mandi. It was never the same thing, but still, she'd hit me, and I misguidedly took that touch as affection. It built on our back and forth relationship. I finally look up at Pam. She'd never touch me like that. She'd never use her touch as a weapon but worship of me. She did it the night we were together.

I'm such a fool. I need to know how to keep her, not break her. I don't want to destroy what we could be.

L.B. Dunbar

I tug my sleeve back over my wrist, feeling vulnerable at her observing gaze. Next, I reach for her hand, pulling it upward to kiss her knuckles. When I lower our fingers, I don't release hers.

Hand holding.

I like this stage of the process. Whether the day ends in sex or not, I'll be happy to just hold her hand, fitting my parts to hers, as she explained of dating. I want our parts to fit.

+ + +

When we return to the condo, Ella and Ethan are out but left a note that they'd meet us later for drinks. They want to go dancing, but when I ask Pam her thoughts, she scrunches her nose

"I'm not much for publicly shaking my groove thing," she teases. Pam has a way of slipping in these little self-deprecating comments, and I don't like it. She's perfect just as she is.

"I'd like to see your groove thing shake." I want to run my hands over her curves—over and over again—but I'm keeping my distance, trying to let the shitstorm of yesterday dissolve. This morning was a start, but I still needed to apologize for my behavior last night. For now, I have my agent meeting.

"We need to head out in about an hour."

"I need to shower, dress, do my hair—" Pam is a frenzy of anxiety.

"Whoa, whoa, whoa. Simmer girl. It's not a black-tie affair. It's just a meeting."

"I still want to look nice. I want to make a good impression for you."

"Lilac, you're so fucking beautiful, you could wear a potato sack. You don't need to make an impression on my behalf because Theresa will love you."

How could she not? I love Pam. She's this burning desire just below the surface of my skin. It's a strange energy I've never felt before. I'm making a big assumption, but this seems like love, and I don't know what to do with the emotion.

"Potato sack?" She laughs. "Who says that?"

134

"I guess I do." I chuckle. What's happening to me? Every time she laughs, it's like a live wire to my heart, another jolt of electricity livening me up from the inside out. "By the way, tour duty payments. Are we running a tab, or are you ready to make a deposit?"

She tips her head. "Payment in kisses?"

I step up to her in my living room and draw a finger along the side of her face. "Payment in kisses." My eyes focus on her lips, licking my own, desperate for a taste of hers. She watches my tongue sneak out and retreat, and a slow blush fills her face. She is so beautiful—in sweats, in a dress, in a winter coat or without.

"I'm not certain I'm ready to make a payment yet," she whispers, and I understand. We've had a good morning, but it's not enough. I still need to apologize, but I don't want to just toss it out there. I want to do it right with something special. A new plan for our night forms.

+ + +

My agent is a cross between Edna 'E' Mode and Diane Keaton, and her outstretched hand and genuine smile is the warm reception I expected her to give Pam. "I can't tell you how happy I am to meet my Jacob's muse."

"The pleasure is all mine," Pam returns. We take a seat in a comfortable conference room where I'm offered a drink and decline. I ignore Pam's head turn and surprise at my rejection of the midday scotch. The meeting quickly turns to some proposed storylines and upcoming tours before Theresa addresses Pam.

"I look forward to what you'll do for him next." She means my writing, but there's an undercurrent to her words. Theresa knows Pam is very important to me.

"The creativity is all his," Pam states, continuing to sing my praises.

"Yes, but the perfection of it is all yours," Theresa adds.

Pam practically beams with Theresa's words. The meeting ends quick enough, and as we haven't had lunch, I suggest a favorite pub of mine for a burger. Emerald Isle is an Irish icon with its folksy music and female string quartet that can rock the small space on a Saturday night.

135

L.B. Dunbar

It's only Thursday, though, but the place will give off a vibe the Carter clan might appreciate outside of their weekly Town Tavern visits.

Once outside Theresa's office, down on the busy sidewalk, I'm punching in the order for an Uber when Pam flattens herself against the building.

"I just need a minute." Her voice cracks, and I notice her visibly shaking.

"What's wrong?" I ask, stepping up to her, crowding her against the concrete architecture as the busyness of the sidewalk shuffles onward.

Pam holds out her trembling hands.

"Jesus, Lilac. It wasn't anything special."

"It was important to you," she says. "And me. I wanted her to be proud."

I don't fully understand her reaction. "Theresa is proud. She knows you're my secret weapon." I wink at her but grasp her hands in mine, lifting them for my lips and kissing each palm. "You were wonderful in there. You made me sound like a god."

"The one who chases after a wood nymph?" Her joke takes me a second to remember Pan and his desire for the mysterious nymph he turned into a flowering bush.

"I'll chase you wherever you need to go," I say, leaning closer to her, and because I can't help myself, I kiss her. As much as I want to rush her and crush my mouth to hers, I keep it slow and tender, dragging it out as I feel her melting under my lips, relaxing into the kiss. We're still holding hands between us but her trembling shifts from quakes of anxiety to something else. I want to explore the change, but I'm not taking advantage of her against a public building.

I pull back, and her lids lazily open. "What was that for?" she whispers.

"Found a coupon for tour services. I'm applying the discount, deducted from your overall fee."

She giggles, shaking her head of short, loose curls. "You're so ridiculous."

It's better than being an asshole, so I'll take it.

"Change of plans for tonight. Up to spending more time alone with me?"

"What about Ethan and Ella?"

"I think they can fend for themselves." My sister and her boyfriend need their own time to make amends with this city. If they want a dance club, and Pam doesn't, I'm okay with that. I don't really want to share her anyway.

"Burger?" I ask, nodding as my phone beeps that the Uber is arriving.

Pam smiles, and it's another zap to my heart.

Chapter 18

Dancing In The Street

[Jacob]

The air is crisp when we return to my building, but I'm not ready to let the night end. We had a great time at the pub, discussing *A Game of Thrones*, a series we loved, and sharing stories about the characters we loved to hate.

"Mind if we take a walk?" She's wearing heels so we can keep it slow. I just don't want to go up to the condo yet and face my bed alone.

"Sure." We're holding hands again as we walk the dark boulevard. The night holds all the noises of a large city off in the distance. Along this street, various walk-up homes are lit up, and my mind wanders to who lives in them.

"Do you ever pick a place and write a story?" Pam asks me as if reading my thoughts.

"All the time." I exhale. "Sometimes I see something, and my imagination grabs it, then I twist it and warp it to fit what I want."

"I can't write it, but I can see it whenever I read," she says on a sigh.

Continuing on our walk, I point. "A cyborg lives there. He has four wives but wants someone different because none of them satisfy him."

"Four wives," she gasps.

"And a werewolf over there. He's been pining for a woman for a long time. She thinks he smells funny." Pam laughs as I wave a hand before my face emphasizing his stink.

My next work is titled *The Beast Within*. I wonder how she'll really feel as she reads the torture inflicted by the main character to get what he wants. He's also greatly misunderstood, and I'm counting on Pam to discover his truth. He's in love with a woman he shouldn't want but can't give up. It's all rather autobiographical in a sick fantasy-thriller type of way.

"Let's see. Alien invasion there. The woman of his dreams doesn't know he's from another planet."

Pam shakes her head at my silliness.

"Your turn." I squeeze her hand, knowing she has an active imagination as do I.

"A monster with a good heart. He lives in a condo on the main street."

I chuckle until I realize how prophetic her statement is. "Ah, my girl, still loves the gothic." My heart patters hard at calling her my girl, and I feel like a fucking teenager instead of a forty-year-old man.

As we near a small park, I draw Pam into the empty space. A singular lamp lights the area, reminding me of foggy nights in London where evil lurks in the shadows and a maiden is always alone in the dark. In our case, Pam isn't alone. She's standing with the devil, hidden within his own shadow. I step out from her, guide us to walk a large circle, and then tug her to me. As she stumbles into me, I reposition our hands to clasp between us and wrap my arm around her back. Her hand slips up to my shoulder, and I sway.

"What are you doing?" she questions, chewing her lip.

"Shaking your groove thing in a private setting."

One side of her lip curls upward

"So I don't want to get all heavy, but I need to apologize for last night."

"Jacob," she groans.

"Look, I was drinking, and it's no excuse. None. I shouldn't have shoved Ethan. He shouldn't have *needed* to push back. I'm embarrassed that it happened. I don't want you to think I'd ever act that way with you."

She's quiet for a second. "The thing is, alcohol has a reaction in people. For some, it's good fun and relaxing, but for others, it can be just like a drug, addictive and harmful to them."

I bite my tongue. I don't want to argue and justify how it won't happen again—it won't—but Pam needs more than words from me.

"For now, I'm hoping you can accept my sincere apology for the way I acted last night."

L.B. Dunbar

"Forgiven," she says, her voice hesitant.

"Even monsters have to prove themselves," I say. No anti-hero gets the girl immediately. He messes up. He tries again. He might fall a second time, but in the end, he earns true love. Pulling her closer to me, her body molds with mine, and we dance in large circles around the empty park. I hum in her ear a song of teasing and longing.

"Is that 'Wicked Game' by Chris Isaak?"

"How could you recognize that?" I question my throaty beat.

"That's one of my favorite songs."

Softly chuckling to myself, I comment. "Lilac, that man was a fucking fool for not marrying you."

"Don't," she presses, her voice tense.

"You're incredible. You're beautiful. You're kind and thoughtful. Your heart is wide open and accepting."

She shakes her head. "I'm over it. Bitterness is a drug, too, and it can eat at your soul. I don't have time for that negative energy. I want to believe in love and second chances."

"Do you? Do you really believe love exists? Do you believe people deserve a second chance?"

"I do," she states adamantly. "Love doesn't look the same for everyone. It might not even feel the same. For some, it's roses, and for others, it's violets, but it's still love."

Or lilacs in the form of a petite blond with sultry curves and a heart of gold.

And whoever he is, this man who she'll love, he'll be the luckiest man in the world.

And that pesky emotion of hope weaves its way into my soul because I want it to be me.

+ + +

When we finally return to the condo, Pam slips from me once inside my place.

"Thank you for today. For tonight." Her smile fills her face. Her cheeks are rosy from the chill of the night, and her eyes sparkle like sapphires. "New York feels a little magical."

I want it to be special to her as this is a second home to me. She tips up to press her lips to mine, and I can't let her go, desperate for another minute. My hand cups the back of her neck, holding her to me for a little longer. Taking her mouth deeper, adding my tongue, soaking her in. She breaks first, slowly pulling back from me.

"And now I'm going to prove kissing doesn't lead to sex, either," she says, stepping out from my touch.

"Lilac," I groan.

"Dating 101, Jacob. Dinner. Hand holding. Kissing." She bites her lips, teasing me with their plump swell.

"Are we dating?" I ask as she takes another step backward.

Slowly, she shakes her head. "I don't think we're there yet." However, she's still smiling at me, and I hang onto the word *yet*.

"I could just come upstairs and hold you," I whisper, feeling like a chump for suggesting such a thing, but I don't want to stop touching her. We don't need to have sex. Not *yet*.

Pam shakes her head as she reaches the staircase and twists to glance at me over her shoulder. She's seductive in this position. Her eyes say *come hither*. *Chase me*. But I don't. This is a test. Can I resist her? Can I fight that pull she said she felt to me? Haven't I been fighting it for over two years?

I can give her this. Slipping my hands in my pants to disguise what she's done to me, I watch her slowly ascend the staircase like some star-crossed lover in his mythical mansion. The beauty doesn't fall for the beast in a day.

Chapter 19

Work It Out

[Pam]

Last night, I slept restlessly, tossing and turning, torn with my thoughts. I wanted him next to me, in this bed, holding me as he suggested, but I don't trust myself. After two years of fighting off the attraction, it is suddenly in my face, and I can't accept it. Mandi's presence still lingers in my head. Jacob hasn't told me what they said to each other or how he got her to leave, and my biggest concern is that she'll return. She always comes back.

Eventually, I give up on sleep and head downstairs. I heard Ethan and Ella come in late, so I assume they'll be sleeping for hours still. To my surprise, Jacob is in the kitchen.

"I'm headed to the gym, but afterward, I thought we could hit up some of the touristy shit." His voice unsettles me, something off in his tone.

"Maybe I could come with you," I mention, and his forehead furrows.

"Uhm, this isn't a health club. This is a gym." He pauses for a second. "A boxing club."

My mouth falls open and quickly shuts. While I've seen Jacob's workout room at his house, and know he works hard against a bag and a pummel ball, I wasn't aware he actually fought.

"Like a *fight*-fight?"

"Yes," he drones, irritation filling his voice.

"Why?" I question, crossing my arms.

"It's to blow off steam," he admits. He seems frustrated for some reason. Is this about sex? Is this because he couldn't sleep in bed with me?

"Are you hungover?" I question, hating that I've asked but wondering why he's so grumpy.

"I didn't drink last night," he snaps, and I wonder if that's what has him on edge.

"Fine. I'd like to go with you."

His lips twist as he considers me a second. "All right, but you're working out as well. There's a private trainer there who can show you a thing or two." His voice is still edgy, and suddenly, I'm ready to fight. Energy churns through my body that I need to burn off myself.

"Private trainer isn't a euphemism like personal tour guide, is it?" I question, teasing him, but he steps up to me, crowding my space.

"I'd never let my trainer near you," he hisses. "You'll be working with a female trainer."

Yikes. Simmer down.

"Okay," I drone.

"Get dressed," he snaps.

Someone's woken up on the wrong side of the bed.

A half hour later, we enter a gym, and it's just as he mentioned. Boxing ring. Smell of sweat. This isn't some polished, posh club but an honest-to-goodness fight club.

"Ashling, this is Pam Carter," Jacob introduces me in that voice that's been aloof all morning.

A burnt-red brunette with a feminine athletic build sizes me up and smiles. "You did good here, Professor."

"Professor?" I tease, turning to Jacob.

"They know I write books, but they don't understand I'm not a teacher." He glares at the woman. "Pam needs some basic training while I hit the ring."

He's actually going to fight in the four-sided, roped-off arena where he'll punch someone on purpose and get hit in return. I'm not certain how I feel about this situation, but it has to be better than randomly picking fights or giving in to the temptation to start them outside a controlled environment. If Jacob needs this, it's better than some alternatives.

"Sure, darlin'." Her voice is filled with an Irish brogue. She circles the desk and leads me to a room where I'm out of sight of the main gym.

L.B. Dunbar

For the next forty minutes, I learn hooks, uppercuts, and kicks. Strangely, it feels good to punch the bag.

"Pretend it's his face," she teased, encouraging me to muster anger. I'm not certain if she means envision Jacob or call to mind Brendan, but punching something just feels right. I didn't realize how tense I'd been in New York. Despite the wonderful day yesterday, I still have energy to expel.

"Or better yet, pretend it's her," she joked. The bag almost hit me as I stopped short and turned to Ashling. "She's a tool."

I don't need to ask to know who she is talking about, which meant Mandi has been here. Suddenly, I have the strength of an elephant and the anger of a hungry lion. Tension vibrates up my arms as I slam into the bag over and over again.

When our session ends, Ashling leads me back to Jacob, who is still in the ring. She leaves me near the side, excusing herself for her next client, and dismissing my offer of a tip, stating Jacob covered everything. Feeling good but still wired, I watch Jacob work with a man slightly larger than him.

"You're losing your touch." His partner's face is covered, but his Irish brogue is just as distinct as the personal trainer. Jacob doesn't respond to the taunt but continues to punch left and right into large mitts on each hand of his opponent.

"Must be really mad at her this time, eh?" The man continues to poke at Jacob.

"Fuck you," Jacob mutters around his mouth guard, but the words are almost crystal clear.

"What'd she do this time? Max out your credit card?"

Mandi has access to Jacob's credit cards.

Jacob's pummeling increases.

"Sex with another man again?"

Mandi cheated on Jacob.

I gasp, and Jacob turns in my direction, startled by my nearness to the ring.

"Who's this pretty?" the Irish trainer flirts, lowering his mitts while Jacob stands still, minus his heaving chest. He spits out his mouth guard and introduces me.

"This is Pam. She works for me." It's said as if I'm underneath him when just a day ago he made me feel indispensable to his process. He praised my support and suggestions to his agent, and she complimented me in her own way.

"Isn't she a lovely?" the other man continues with a devious smile in his voice.

"Don't," Jacob growls.

"Got your knickers twisted over this one, eh? Or is it your balls are blue?" Without another word, Jacob punches the man outside of the mitts.

"Illegal!" the Irish man hollers with a chuckle, after taking the blow. He spits to the side of the ring. *Gross.* Ignoring Jacob's hunched stance, poised like a prized fighter, the man speaks to me again.

"As he's a wanker, want to give it a go with me, lovely? I promise to be gentle."

"I'm warning you." Jacob lunges again, but the other man catches him, successfully blocking his punch with the large mitt and laughing even louder at Jacob's reaction.

The Irish man pushes Jacob off him. "In your corner, or I'll pull you from tomorrow's fight."

"What?" The word doesn't have a chance of being contained.

"The professor here has a turn in the ring tomorrow." The trainer pulls his face guard off, revealing rusty hair and a smarmy smile. Bright but dark green eyes stare at me, knowing he's just told me something I didn't know.

"You look like you could use a go at him?" Irish man tilts his head, nodding to Jacob. If Jacob wants to fight someone, he can fight me. "Come on up here, lovely."

"She doesn't want to get in here," Jacob barks.

"Don't speak for me," I warn him and climb up into the ring. I'm pissed that Jacob has let himself be abused by Mandi all this time while I've been right here willing to love him. I'm angry he's using this ring to

145

L.B. Dunbar

release his aggression instead of talking about things, and I'm upset he hasn't told me he fights, like *fight*-fights.

The trainer holds out a hand to me once I've entered. "I'm Paddy McGregor."

"Pam Carter," I state, although Jacob's already said my name. Paddy leans in for a kiss to my cheek, still holding my hand with his. "Give him one good punch. You'll feel better."

Lifting his head to nod, I follow his gaze to find Jacob with his back in the corner, holding the ropes. He's a bull ready to charge with flaring nostrils and a heaving chest. He's worked up, but so am I.

"What's your deal?" I snap.

"Give it to him," Paddy encourages.

"She's not interested," Jacob growls. There's an entendre in his response, and this fuels my ire. Snarky word games will not work today. I stalk to Jacob's corner, getting right up close to his sweat-laden body.

"Don't pretend to know anything about me, Professor."

"You'd be surprised how much I know about you, angel. And don't call me that," he snaps, anger vibrating around him.

"And what should I call you?" I can think of a few choice words. "Why would you say I'm not interested in you? I'm standing here, aren't I? I've been by your side for years." I emphasize by stomping my foot like a petulant child.

"Or am I your rebound girl now? Am I a filler until you get back together with her? Was I just some pity fuck?" I don't even know where the questions come from, but I'm suddenly out of control, my concerns escaping me.

"Don't you dare go there," he growls.

"Oh, and where should I go, Jacob?" I hiss, leaning toward his body as he leans away from mine. He's frightened of me. In fact, he's holding himself back, gripping the rope as best he can because he looks ready to pounce. "Is it only about sex for you? Is that all you want from me?"

While Jacob's shaking his head, Paddy speaks from behind me. "I'd like to have sex with you." He's only teasing, aggravating Jacob more to get a rise out of him. And it works, as Jacob moves, attempting to go around me to get at his trainer.

My hands go up, palms flat on his sweaty skin. "No!" I yell at Jacob. "No. This is our fight." His head swings back to me, and I point back and forth between us.

"Is this about last night? Because I didn't give in to you, didn't give in to the pull." I nearly spit at him, upset that he's being such a dick because we haven't slept together again. He's a spoiled child not getting his way.

"Why did you fuck me that night? Was it just the convenience?" I need an answer. It's clear Mandi doesn't believe they are over. It's clear Jacob can't see she's an issue. Am I wearing rose-colored glasses as well? Is this Brendan all over again, and I'm not seeing things clearly?

"Don't." The fire in his eyes could set me aflame. The black pupils have turned to molten lava, anger boiling over and rolling between us.

"Then tell me," I demand, desperate to know why he did it. After two and a half years, why now? I need to know. Once and for all, I need to know if all he wants is in my pants, just some itch he needed to scratch.

"I regret nothing," he says, and it sounds like something tattooed somewhere on his skin. He makes his choices, and he lives with them. Maybe that's why he's never truly gotten rid of Mandi.

"Come on, man, you can do better than that," Paddy jests behind me, and Jacob raises a gloved hand in his direction.

"You . . ." He points at the man. "Stay out of this."

"Just trying to help out a lady."

I don't need his help, and I'm ready to interject my own defense when Jacob turns back to me.

"And you. Don't ever fucking say that to me again. I did not fuck you for money, pity, revenge, or any other stupid shit in your head."

"Stupid?!" I shriek, aghast at the insult of my emotions. "You think *I'm* stupid?"

"Lilac, I didn't—"

"You're the stupid one," I say, poking at his firm chest with my fingertip. "You've let her use you and abuse you when you have *change your destiny* written in ink right on your chest. You're the one who permanently wrote *nevermore* on your wrist where you can see it when you type but over and over again you go back to her. You're the one

147

drowning yourself in alcohol to chase away the demons." My voice cracks.

"I might have been stupid to miss a man cheating on me under my nose. No one else wanted to tell me, but people have been telling you." My hand flings out to emphasize Paddy behind me. "And you've taken her back time and time again. I loved myself enough to walk away when I learned the truth. You need to do the same. Maybe then you'll be able to see what's right under your nose."

I'm breathing so hard it's as if I've gone twenty rounds myself. Jacob's glaring back at me, eyes flaming, nostrils flaring. His chest heaves as he quietly takes my rant.

"If you're so smart, you tell me, what's under my nose, Lilac? What am I missing?" he demands.

"Me!" I cry. Then my breath catches, and I choke on the admission. His eyes widen. My chest heaves as sweat drips down my temple. We stare at one another until I step back. He reaches for me, only he can't grab me with his gloved hands.

"No," I whisper-hiss.

"Lilac," he commands.

"You need to get your shit together, Jacob. Face those demons. Fight them," I warn. "Or you'll lose me."

Taking another step back, I turn to face Paddy. "Sorry about that."

The six-foot-three muscular man wears a shit-eating grin on his face.

"That's what I need to see tomorrow night," Paddy says over my head to Jacob. Then he glances down at me. "Hope you're ringside. He'll need ye." He tips his head at Jacob. Suddenly, I know how Mandi knew Jacob was coming to New York.

"You told her, didn't you?" I question, not angry, just curious.

"He's my best fighter." Dollar signs ring in his green eyes, and it makes sense. He wanted to rub her in all Jacob's wounds, bringing up the pain and fueling it in him.

Turning back to Jacob, standing a foot from me, I dig my hole deeper. "I would never be like her, Jacob." I raise my hand, and he flinches with anticipation, expecting a blow. Maybe he thinks he deserves it if I hit him. Maybe he's equally attracted and repelled by that action, but I'd never do such a thing. I'd never physically harm him.

Instead, I cup his face, curl my fingers under his chin, and lower my other palm to his sweat-covered chest. His heart races underneath the tattoo, which speaks volumes.

Change your destiny.

"You need to listen to your heart, Jacob. Fight for what it says in there. Fight for *you*."

My hand slips off his chest, and the other releases his chin. This man changed my destiny. The night my father died, the night he was on the side of the road, everything spiraled for me. I left my job and went to work for him. I took the simpler pace of working for Mae. One night. One man. My heart told me what to do, and I've been fighting with that heart ever since. He needs to do the same for himself, in order to keep me.

For once, I want someone to fight for me.

"I'll be up front when you're ready." After walking to the rope, I slip through the openings and feel Jacob watching my retreat. Once I've hit the floor, I refuse to look behind me but hear Paddy speak.

"You should consider marrying *her*, ye bastard, or I will."

Chapter 20
Missing Out

[Jacob]

Me. It's the only sound ringing in my head. She's telling me I'm missing out on her, and she isn't wrong. But is she willing to give herself to me? What price will it cost her to do such a thing? What will it cost me?

Standing still while I watch her walk to the front of the gym, I realize the cost will be my heart and her sanity. I'll drive her crazy.

"You're a bastard," I call out to Paddy as I turn back to him, struggling with my gloves.

"You needed that," he says to me, being one of my oldest friends. I've been coming to this gym since I was in college and he was working it under his father. Now he owns the place, training kids how to fight responsibly and teaching women self-defense. It's one reason he wound up Pam, pushing her to her limit to fight me and fling out those words that stilled my heart.

Me. She knows she's too good for me. With a heavy heart and a brick in my belly, I get my gloves off and gather my things. Meeting Pam at the front, she's chatting with Ashling about the fight tomorrow night. When she sees me coming, she thanks Ashling again for her time and marches out the front door. Once I've followed, she spins on me.

"Why didn't you tell me?" she huffs, frustration clouding her tone. "Sometimes, I feel like I know you, and other times, I don't."

"Would you come to the fight?" Sheepishly, I ask as it'd be a lot for me to handle—her on the sidelines—but then again, it'd mean a lot to me, too.

"I don't know, Jacob." She sighs, crossing her arms, looking down at her feet. I don't like how she's closing off from me. "Is this even good for you?" Worry fills her voice as she tips her head toward the gym. Her ire has settled and now, her body language expresses her genuine concern.

"The gym? This is one of the best things to happen to me." I sigh, looking off at the busy traffic. "I wasn't always strong, physically or mentally. This place taught me how to build strength, inside and out. It taught me how to fight back."

Her eyes search my face, anxious in what she reads. She also has questions.

"Just ask."

"Why would you let her hit you?" Her voice quiets, and I struggle to answer. I scrub a hand down my face.

"It's hard to explain. It's not like she was beating me up. It's just . . . I don't know. Some sort of sick pleasure, I guess. We'd fight, and she'd get physical. I'd dominate the struggle." A thought occurs. "I never hit her, Lilac. If that's what you're thinking. I never touched her like that."

I step forward, but she steps back, almost slipping off the curb. I catch her by her arm.

"Lilac, it wasn't like that. It was just some kind of power play, I guess. I'm not used to tender touches and romantic caresses, okay? There's a fine line between love and hate, and slaps and hits were somewhere in-between." My father started it. He loved to hate me, or he hated that he felt he had to love me. I'd never know the difference, but he was the only parent I had, and I wanted his approval. I wanted his acceptance, and then I had to accept I'd never have it.

Her eyes drift back to the gym, and her lips twists. I have no idea what she's thinking or what she suddenly thinks of me.

"I'd never be like that," she whispers as she told me in the ring. God, the fire in her eyes. The heave of her chest. I wanted to lay her out right there and have my way with her. "I can't be like that." She glances back at me, concern evident in her softening eyes.

"I don't need it like that. I don't want it like that." There are all kinds of twisted relationships, thriving on various levels of physical interaction, but that's not what's happened with Mandi. It's been the push and pull of a love-hate relationship. I've confused the push for love, thinking it's the way I deserve things.

L.B. Dunbar

Taking a deep breath, I slip my hand down her arm, seeking her hand. "Look, I want to spend the day with you again. Let's get lost in the city. Don't think about the fight. Don't think. This trip is supposed to be about you."

She swipes back her hair, staring over my shoulder. "I don't even know what I'm doing here with you." The anguish in her voice is killing me.

"You're letting me show you this city. You're letting me show you a part of me." I wave out at the gym, but suddenly worry she doesn't like the part she's seeing.

What if my parts don't fit hers? Dating is an experiment of how pieces fit together. What if ours don't fit?

+ + +

When we return to the apartment, Ella's made plans for Pam to spend the day with her. Spa treatments of massage, nail, and hair are on the agenda. While Pam isn't the type that needs the fuss—another thing I like so much about her—I can see she's grateful for the escape. She wants away from me. I also don't like to deny my sister anything, so I swallow back the fit I want to pitch and allow Ella the time with her friend.

After pouting about a lost day, I decide to work, but my mind constantly wanders. When a text comes through, I'm eager to check it, hoping it's Pam. Only it's not.

Mandi.

"What's up with you two?" Ethan nods toward my phone as we're both sitting at my dining table. He's been working on things for his upcoming restaurant opening.

"Lilac?" I question, as she's the only one on my mind.

"Mandi first." Ethan's voice sharpens, and I turn for my phone to find another text light up the screen.

"We're over," I state, confident in my answer. When Mandi appeared on my first day here, I told her in no uncertain terms we were finished. I demanded my key, which she tossed on the floor like a spoiled child. She wanted to argue. *We had a past. We had a future.* But we had nothing. Our parts did not fit.

"Does she know that?" Ethan asks, tipping his head toward my phone.

"She does. I know it was harsh, but I had to tell her I didn't love her. I never loved her, and I wouldn't be marrying her."

"It's a tough call, but sometimes you have to be brutal, or the message isn't clear." Ethan understands. He's turned into a good friend over the past few months. "So what about Pam?"

I sigh, turning my head for the large window to my left. "Man, I am all mixed up over her. I don't want to hurt her, but it feels inevitable. We aren't a good fit."

"Why would you say that?" Ethan states, irritation building in him.

"Because Pam is perfect, and I'm me."

"But you want her?"

I nod.

Ethan softens his tone. "You've got to pull it together then, man. Show her how you aren't a bad guy at heart. You need to be the best *you* so you do deserve her."

He's quiet for a second, and I let the words seep into me.

"Look, she's been telling everyone she's not in love with you for years while blushing whenever we brought you up, and we didn't even know who you were. Now, I've known you for months, and I see why she likes you. I can see you feel the same way about her, but you're denying yourself. What's the use in that? Be happy, man. If you're truly done with Mandi, the real thing is within your grasp." Ethan reaches forward as if grabbing something. "Pam is real."

"But I'm not," I say, exasperated. "I don't know how to be real."

"You're a man of words. You'll figure it out, but while you're at it, remember that actions speak louder than words."

+ + +

By the time we go to Ella's show, I should be in good spirits. The four of us had a great dinner, several drinks, and a good time together. It's

L.B. Dunbar

been forever since I've been out with people other than Mandi and the false group of people we called friends. But I'm on edge. Mandi's been texting me all day, and it's been harder and harder to ignore them. Eventually, I turned off my phone only to have it light up again once I turned it on to order an Uber for the gallery.

At the gallery, Ella's future clothing line is paired with black and white images of famous people all with some kind of affliction. The famous rock star missing a hand. An athlete who lost his leg. A cancer patient without her hair. They're all beautiful in their own way, and Ella's clothing line intends to match and enhance them, thus the name Fabulously Flawed. It's how she sees herself with the scars on her body. The ones I'm reminded are my fault.

As I missed the show in January, allowing Ethan to make a fuss, as he called it, I hadn't seen her designs.

"She's so beautiful," Pam says, standing before me, staring at an image of my sister who modeled for one of the images.

"You're beautiful," I whisper to her ear. Her head tips back for my shoulder as she cradles a glass of wine in her hand.

"You're sweet." Her voice is quiet, soft, and a little dreamy. The wine has taken effect on her. Reaching for her upper arms, I rub up and down.

"I love the philosophy," Pam adds. *We might wear our circumstances on our skin, but it doesn't define who we are within.* It's a large statement around the border of the gallery.

"I never see her scars when I look at her," Pam says, her voice still low. Sadly, I always see the scars, still feeling guilty that I'd brought a madman near my sister. "Sometimes scars are all we see on people, though, and they're not even on the surface. They're deeper than skin."

I press a kiss to her temple, knowing she's hinting at me. "Some people like to hide behind those scars, skin deep or not."

Pam turns to face me. "You don't need to hide from me. I think you're beautiful."

Her words almost hurt. They're so raw and real. As Ethan said, she's real, and I want to be the beautiful she needs, but I'm not. I'm damaged inside and out.

"You should model something of Ella's. Or better yet, just get undressed." The tease is meant to change the subject.

"Jacob," she whispers, a light laugh in her tone.

"I'm serious."

"About the modeling or the undressing?" she flirts back.

"Both."

She laughs and places a hand on my chest. I want her touch. I want it on my skin. She told me earlier she'd never be rough like Mandi, and I believe her. I want to know what that's like. Then again, I had it the night we were snowed in, and I didn't pay enough attention. It's been weeks since that night, and I want her again.

Leaning forward, I press a soft kiss to her, but when she leans in for more, I struggle to keep it safe for the public.

A scuffle near the door interrupts us before we get too heated.

"I don't need an invitation. I'm with Jacob Vincent." The loud cry echoes through the place, which consisted of quiet chatter and subdued jazz music.

Shit.

My eyes lower to Pam's, and her forehead furrows. Ethan rushes to the front door, but this is my battle.

"I need to handle this," I say, pressing a kiss to Pam's forehead as a sense of dread fills me.

This isn't the type of fuss Ethan meant. And this isn't the woman I should be making one with.

"Mandi," I snap as I near the entrance, and Ethan turns on me.

"This is her?" Disgust fills his face as he eyes the woman who's been in my life for years. I don't have to see inside his thoughts to know he's comparing Pam to her. There's no comparison. Pam is my lilac. This woman is dead roses.

"Get her out of here." Ethan's hissing statement matches my sentiments, and I step out the door, dragging Mandi several feet down the street. The night is dark and misty as was last night when I danced with Pam in a quiet, vacant park off the busy street. This sidewalk is sensory overload with honking horns and shouts from walkers. Lights

L.B. Dunbar

blare from businesses and vehicles. It's chaos, and it's symbolic of Mandi and me.

"Let's get out of here," I say, tugging her down the street.

.

Chapter 21
Coming Clean

[Pam]

Jacob disappears with her. After I try to give him a few minutes to handle her, as he said, he doesn't return, and I move toward the front door where Ella's been standing. Tender concerned eyes meet mine.

"He left with her, didn't he?"

"He'll be back," she tries to assure me but doesn't sound convinced herself.

"You need to get back to your guests. There could be buyers here," I remind her. She has a duty tonight. I reach out and pull her into me.

"Don't give up on him," she whispers to me, but it isn't me giving up. I've been here, solid and waiting for years. Maybe it's time for me to stop waiting.

"I'll see you back at the apartment."

"Don't go," Ella says, holding my wrists.

"I'll go with you," Ethan offers, and I hadn't realized he was behind me.

"No, stay. This is important." I cup Ella's face and glance at Ethan, who has stepped next to her. "I'll be fine."

Ella orders me an Uber and gives me her keys for the apartment. Once I've let myself in, I help myself to a long bath in the guest bathroom. I hear the front door slam, and Jacob's heavy feet hammer up the staircase.

"Lilac?" His voice on the other side of the door forces me to close my eyes. The doorknob jiggles. "Lilac, please."

My head shakes as my eyes feel the burn of tears. A soft thud hits the door.

"I can't talk to you like this. I need to see your face."

Then why did you leave with her?

L.B. Dunbar

I don't ask. I choke back the question. My eyes remain closed, and I tip back my head, struggling to find my voice. "Just give me a minute, okay?"

The silence behind the door unnerves me, and I linger a little longer than a few minutes. To my surprise, I find Jacob on the edge of the bed, suit jacket off, shoes removed, and tie disheveled. He looks like a wreck, and I'm curious if he's been drinking. He sits up as I approach, wearing nothing but a towel as I'd left my pajamas in the room.

I stop right before him. His fingers curl into fists as he looks up at me.

"I'm sorry. It's all I seem to say to you."

"Where did you go?" I hate that I'm asking. I hate that I feel like it's Brendan all over again. He chose another woman over me.

"Just down the street around the corner. I didn't want anyone to see or hear us fighting." His head lowers, and I cup his chin, wondering if she struck him. Tipping up his face, all I see is the pain of a broken man. The damage is deeper than his skin, and I want to pull him to me. I want to cradle him against me and tell him he'll be okay. But I'm not certain that's true. He has to make decisions to improve himself. He needs help, and it's more than me giving him a hug.

"You were gone a long time," I say. It might have been ten minutes, but it was ten minutes too long.

"Nothing happened with her. Please, believe me. I didn't touch her." His eyes beg me, and my heart breaks. I want to trust him. I want to believe he didn't give into her. One more goodbye kiss. One more *it's over* embrace. When I found out about Brendan, we didn't have that kind of closure. It was just over. Nothing lingered.

His hands hesitantly come to my hips, curling into the terrycloth material.

"I want to be with you." His voice shakes while it drips with seduction. I'd like that more than anything, but I won't be his rebound from her.

"I can't do it," I admit, swiping a hand over his head. He tips forward, lowering his forehead for my belly, tugging me closer to him.

"I don't blame you. I don't even want to be with me."

158

I stroke over his head several times before bending to kiss the back of his head.

"Can I sleep with you?" The vulnerability in his voice breaks me in two.

"Jacob," I groan.

"I swear. I'll be good. I'll keep my hands to myself. I just want to be near you."

I sigh heavily. "Just let me get dressed."

He nods. "I'll be right back." He picks up his jacket and leaves the room, not bothering to close the door behind him. I quickly dress in short pajamas and a long-sleeved shirt and climb into the bed. Jacob returns within minutes, wearing sleep pants and no shirt. Is he kidding me? His head lowers.

"You know I run hot when I sleep."

The comment actually breaks the tension a little.

"I'm warning you," I say, narrowing my eyes at him.

"I know." His voice remains serious. I lower under the covers, and he lies next to me, mirroring my position. We just stare at one another for a long minute. I wish I could read his thoughts.

"Remember in Branagh's version of *Frankenstein*, all the creature wanted was a mate? He wanted someone to love him for who he was, ugly and scarred, and then the doctor built him one only to destroy her."

I stay quiet.

"I don't know if I'm the creator or the creature. I desire and destroy as they both did."

"What if you aren't either? What if you're just Jacob? A man who deserves good, does good."

He shakes his head. "I don't know how to do good, and what I should do is stay away from you, but I can't resist you. I feel that pull more strongly than ever, and I'm spiraling out of control."

Suddenly, I feel like I'm the one destroying him. "Have you been drinking?" I question afraid of the fight this might bring on.

"No, but I want another drink badly tonight. I was hoping to lose myself in you, instead." He's honest, but it hurts a little. He wants sex to forget his pain.

L.B. Dunbar

"You can't replace one thing for another," I whisper, and he closes his eyes.

"I know."

I reach out for him, stroking over his face.

"Remember when you were sick, and you were rubbing my arm over your waist?"

I hardly remember that, but I shrug. "Sure."

"Can I ask you to do that again? Let me hold you."

My brows pinch, but he isn't opening his eyes. It's as if the closed lids are protecting him, keeping his dungeon locked tight. Without answering, I roll to give him my back, and he moves closer to me, wrapping his arm over my waist. I slide his forearm up against my breasts, hating how instantly my nipples respond. The swells ache for his attention, but I won't be giving in to temptation tonight. I scratch my fingernails lightly over the coarse hairs on his arm, and he hums at my neck.

"That scent. You're lilacs and heaven."

Having him this close, knowing how much he hurts, feels like hell, though.

+ + +

The next day, we plan to visit iconic sites such as the Statue of Liberty, The Empire State Building, and Ground Zero. Thankfully, Ethan and Ella plan to go with us as we take this shortened tour through the city. Jacob and I are quiet around one another, cautious actually.

"No private tour guide today," I lightly tease.

"He's decided to give you the weekend special. Payment accepted whenever you're ready." Jacob's voice rings melancholy this morning, and it's not a sound I've heard from him. He's confident, funny, sarcastic, and tough, but this is a different man before me.

I'm grateful for the distraction of Ethan and Ella, but especially Ethan, who turns each stop into the full tourist package, complete with a hundred selfies, posts to social media, and running commentary as he looks up facts on the internet. New York is a world of difference from our small town, and Ethan soaks it all up. The photos remind me I should have been posting for Jacob on his social media accounts, and I make a mental note to work up some kind of trip in review for once we return. It's a whirlwind of visits until we reach the final destination.

As we stand in the silence surrounding the fallen towers, it's surreal to imagine their height and accept the eerie quiet at the memorial despite the rushing city around this now-sacred space. Tears fill my eyes for the victims—both innocents and first responders—and when the salty liquid trickles down my cheek, Jacob pulls me into him.

"This was too much," he states, but I shake my head.

"It's so hard to be on the front line sometimes," I explain, recalling emergencies and accidents over the years. There were only two that broke me, and they happened simultaneously. "The night of my father's accident and yours, something inside me snapped. I couldn't get back into the mindset I needed to be on-task. Without even realizing it, I suffered post-traumatic stress disorder."

Jacob leans me away from him only so much that he can look at my face. "How did I never know this?"

"It wasn't something I wanted tell my new employer, especially when he was part of the cause."

"Lilac," Jacob groans, staring at me with a mix of concern and compassion.

"I'm better now, but the anxiety of you possibly being involved and the adjustment to my father's loss, it was too much. I felt helpless and not of sound mind." I needed a break, which I never thought would happen. "I'd witnessed hundreds of blood and guts moments over the years, but that night, I cracked, and I couldn't be put back together. At least, not enough to return to work in the same mental capacity I'd had before."

"That's why you took the job with Mae?"

"She offered me a change of . . . destiny," I say, shifting my eyes to his jacket which covers his chest where the tattoo scrolls over his heart. "I'm better for it. My time as an EMT was up, and I never regret the experiences I had, but it was time for something different." Now I grow flowers, watch life bloom in a sense compared to working on saving a life, only to lose one or two on occasion.

"I'm sorry I was a cause of that change."

"I think it was a sign. Change is inevitable. It's only a matter of when," I assure him.

"Do you think it's too late for me to change?" he questions, his voice lowering.

"It's never too late for anything if you're willing." I reach up and cup his cheek. "Sometimes, we need to let go to move forward. That's where you're stuck, Jacob. You're letting the past still define you when you've been writing your own path for a long time."

He stares at me like I've spoken gibberish.

"I don't know how." I almost hear the bitterness in his voice, and I know it's difficult. His unsettled past has been a part of him for so long, feeding an unseen anger that it's literally a part of him. Bitterness is like a disease. It festers and grows and consumes until nothing is left but an empty soul, and I refuse to believe it's hopeless for Jacob.

"Maybe you should talk to somebody," I suggest, and he huffs.

"You sound like Ella again."

"As Ella's brilliant, I'll take that as a compliment. Maybe you should take her advice." I wink at him and turn in his arms, laying my head against his chest as I take a final glance at the invisible tragedy before me. I can't see it, but I feel it in my bones and wish those lost souls peaceful eternal rest.

Chapter 22

Fight Night

[Pam]

Tonight is Jacob's fight, and I'm a wreck. With the history I know of him, I don't want to watch someone beat him. Ethan's thrilled beside me, like a child ready to hop in the ring, while Ella clutches at his thigh and smiles at all his silly comments.

"He's gonna rip him up and tear him to shreds and sprinkle his remains like a bad first draft headed for the trash."

His attempts at humor are doing nothing to calm my nerves and then Paddy McGregor circles the ring to sit next to me.

"Not fighting tonight?" I ask the good-looking Irish man, with his sexy accent and a mischievous grin.

"I'm the organizer, and I don't fight in amateur hour." He tips his head to the ring. "But tonight's a special occasion. We have the Professor back to school some punks."

The Professor hardly sounds like a fighter name, and I think back on all the romance novels I've read, finding this room nothing like those stories. It's a gym, not an arena or illegal underground or even a country field. The short bleachers make me feel like I'm at a middle school event.

I'm wearing a dress Ella had me buy while we took a quick side trip to shop before our spa treatments yesterday. The store wasn't trendy or chic but eclectic, and I found something reasonable and different for me. Tight fitting, it hugs my curves, outlining my hourglass shape with a square-cut neckline exposing a hint of cleavage. The dress is 1950s pinup worthy. It's daring and a bit risqué for me. However, I feel sexy in it despite our surroundings. We've gone to a fight, not a nightclub, but the energy is almost the same—chaotic, frenzied, and a bit sexual.

Then Jacob walks into the main gym, and the energy shifts. Bright lights highlight the ring. His name is announced through the sound system, but I can only focus on his presence. His chest is slick. His tattoos seem to glow like freshly scrolled artwork.

Paddy leans into me, whispering close to my ear. "He fights for you tonight."

I don't know what that means, so I glance at him over my shoulder. His face is too close to mine. His minty breath scents my airways, and if I didn't know better, I'd think he was going to kiss me. Gazing back at Jacob inside the ropes, his eyes narrow to intense slits of darkness as he watches Paddy sitting near me. Paddy pats my thigh and leaves his hand there a moment longer than necessary.

Jacob's focus draws to the movement and back up to my eyes, lasering on me. His nostrils flare— the bull ready to charge—and a bell rings. Jacob moves gracefully to the center of the square, and Paddy removes his hand but slips his arm around the back of my chair. His eyes remain on Jacob.

I watch in stunned fascination as Jacob hammers at the man slightly taller, slightly broader than him. He's on a mission to take this man down, and my heart races while my stomach should feel nauseous. The other fighter hardly gets in a punch before Jacob hits him in a way that crumbles him to the ground. When the opposing fighter doesn't stand, Jacob is declared the winner.

It's over rather quickly, but my heart hammers with the rush.

Paddy leans over and places a kiss on my cheek. "Nice to see you again, lovely. You just earned me a couple of thousand." He stands, excusing himself.

Jacob's arm is stretched above his head as the victor, but he tugs it from the referee and stalks to the corner of the ring. Slipping through the ropes, he returns the way he entered, and my eyes follow his retreating back.

"Excuse me, are you Pam Carter?" A young man with dusty skin and eyes to match questions me.

"I am," I reply, looking back at the man who smiles at me.

"Jacob asked for you."

I stare at him, who couldn't be more than twentysomething, not understanding what he means.

"I'm Jamal, and Jacob would like to see you in the locker room."

Glancing down at Ella, she smiles with a knowing grin and nods for me to follow this kid. I take my coat and my purse and blindly follow the younger man.

My heart hammers in my chest as I near a door blocked by a man dressed in black and I assume is security. He opens the door for me, and I slip inside a room with a few lockers, a table in the middle, and one fuming Jacob Vincent. Free of his boxing gloves, he's still in the silky shorts, skin gleaming.

"Why were you letting him touch you?" Jacob immediately questions. Jacob stalks to me so quickly I hardly have time to catch my breath.

"I didn't let him touch me. He just did it."

"I didn't like it." Instantly, I recall Mandi jumping into Jacob's arms when we first arrived. I hadn't liked that moment either, but I'm angry about his implication toward me.

"I'm not certain you have a say."

Jacob grips the back of my neck and tugs me to him, mouth crashing against his. He's taking my lips like he fought in his fight. Intense. Motivated. Unforgiving. Pulling back almost as quickly as he leaped, he growls at me.

"*I say*, no one else can have this mouth."

His covers mine again before I have time to respond, and while I should be fighting him off and demanding he cut the caveman act, I'm melting under the voracity of his kiss. My hands slip up his sweaty chest and curl over his shoulders. He groans against my mouth before forcing his tongue between my lips, and I whimper at the bruising kiss. He pulls back only enough to lift me, and I wrap my legs around him as he carries me to the table in the center of the room. The hem of my dress moves upward.

"God, I want you," he growls, lost to his wandering hand, skimming up my thigh, squeezing at my leg.

"Tell me you want this," he begs, but I stop him.

Jacob's head lifts when my hand presses at his wrist. He stares down at me, nostrils flaring, chest heaving.

"What's this?" he demands.

"I can't do this here. I can't be with you where I know she was." My body screams to ignore my rational thought, but I can't be here, replacing her.

"How do you know she's been here?" he snaps, but I only glare up at him. With my legs still over his hips and one hand at my back while the other crumples the skirt of my dress, we stare at one another. I don't really need to answer him.

"Dammit," he hisses, pulling back and holding out a hand to help me sit. As I do, he lowers my dress to my knees. "Let's get out of here."

+ + +

Before we leave the room, Jacob pulls on loose sweats and a sweatshirt over his heated body. He tucks me under his arm.

"Stay here," he warns, squeezing me tighter to emphasize the protective position. As we leave the room, Jacob immediately sees Paddy.

"You're a fucking prick," Jacob yells at him, stepping up to the man with me still locked under his arm.

"But it worked. That's the fastest knockout we've had in a while." The gym owner chuckles at the success of a fight quickly ended, and I read between the lines. His taunts were meant to invigorate Jacob.

"When you're ready to give up writing, Professor, there's always a spot here for you, even if you are an old man."

Jacob steps forward, ready to lunge, but I place a hand at his belly, and Paddy laughs harder.

"Get her home before I steal her from you."

Jacob growls, and we exit the gym, finding a car waiting for us. Slipping inside, I turn to him. "That would never happen."

"What?" Jacob snaps, still on edge despite the fight and because of what we didn't do.

"He wouldn't be able to steal me." As sick as it may sound, I belong to only one man.

Jacob tucks me into his chest, wrapping both his arms around me, and we ride in silence until we reach his condo. Ella and Ethan are still out, but it doesn't matter. Jacob leads me directly to the guest bedroom. He's not taking me to his room where he's been with her. Not stopping in the bedroom, he leads me into the bathroom and turns on the shower. Spinning back to me, he runs his gaze over my outfit.

"This dress," he hums before spinning me and slowly unzipping the back. He gently brushes the sides, allowing the material to fall from my shoulders, and I catch it with my bent elbows. He kisses the back of my neck, sucking at my skin before pulling back. Looking at him over my shoulder, I moan his name.

"Just a shower," he whispers. With hands on my forearms, he lowers my arms, so the dress falls to the floor. I step out of my shoes and spin to face him. He tugs off his sweatshirt, lowers the sweats, and everything underneath. I stare at him in all his magnificent glory, with tattoos marking his body in various places. He continues to eye me as I stand in my bra and underwear.

"You can get in with or without them, but you're getting in there with me. I need to feel your skin close to mine." He's settled a little from the urgency of the gym and the aggressive eagerness to take me. But he's still vibrating with energy, his chest heaving in anticipation of something.

"No sex," I blurt out as my body cries out to me, *why?*

Jacob nods. "Get in." I strip myself of my bra and underwear, feeling the heat of his gaze all over my skin. Once I enter, Jacob follows me, and we stand awkwardly under the small spray.

"I was rough back there." His quiet voice hints at apology as he lowers his eyes, but I shake my head.

"What happened?" I swipe at his temple and then quickly retract my hand. He catches my wrist and brings my hand back to his face. We're standing here, naked as the day, water streaming over us, and I've never been so turned on in my life. While my head keeps telling me to tone it down, the pulse between my thighs ratchets up.

"Fight high," he explains, and I nod. "Did you like watching me?"

L.B. Dunbar

How do I respond? "I don't like you hitting someone or someone hitting you, but I can see that it invigorates you. You like it, don't you?" My hand swipes down his cheek, along his jaw and over his throat, lowering for his chest.

"I like the control. The win. It's a different kind of high than drinking."

We all have our vices in life. If Jacob has to pick only one, I don't know how he'd choose.

Cautiously, a finger of his reaches out for my collarbone and skims along it. My body shivers.

"I want to be the only one who touches you," he says, his voice calmer than the demands of earlier. The finger at my collar lowers, slipping between the valley of my breasts as rivulets of water cascade over them, trickling off my firm nipples.

Shaky hands of mine lift for his shoulders and rub over the heat of his skin, the mixture of his fight and the water keeping him warm. As I stroke down his shoulders, his finger dips lower, but I catch his wrist before he can touch me there.

"Lilac." The pained sound forces all my attention to his smoldering eyes.

"Consider this a fight," I whisper to him. "The fight to only touch but not tease."

"Oh, you're teasing me, angel." With our gaze pinned on one another, he shifts his body in a way that forces my warm back to the cool of the tile. I cry out at the juxtaposition, and he lowers to nip at my neck.

"Jacob," I hiss in warning.

"That's right, angel. Me. I'm the only one who can do this to you, but please don't stop me from kissing you."

My hands skim his body, curling over his shoulders to his shoulder blades. He's wider than me, and this forces him closer, his firm length positioned between our bodies.

"Angel," he whispers. His mouth takes mine slowly, dragging out the kiss while his hand skates over my hip, curling around to my backside and tugging me forward. Our wet skin meets, and I whimper at the firmness of him against me. My core pulses, and I want him, but I don't. My thoughts are wild but keeping him at bay is just as exciting.

The flat of his hand comes forward, and he breaks the kiss to watch as his palm slides up my thigh coming close to the mound at the apex of my legs. My hands do the same on him, nearing his hard length but not touching him.

"Never going to get enough of you," he mutters, his fingers spread but stop short of where I want him. Mine do the same on him, itching to touch him, wrap my hand around him, and tug.

This fight is similar yet not to the one he performed in the ring. It's a battle of wills. Still skin to skin but not satisfying one another. I want him to know he doesn't have to jab with someone to feel the thrill, to anticipate the high.

"Never want to lose you." The words are delightful and damning. I want him to mean them. His forehead comes to mine, and he tugs me against him again, but we still don't meet in the way he wants. My hands grip his biceps, holding myself against him. Peaked nipples press to his chest. We both exhale at the sensation of skin against skin.

"Let me in," he whispers.

"Resist," I tell him, speaking quietly at his ear.

"I don't want to fight it." He sighs. The pull is great, but there are things in our way. His head pops up, and his mouth crashes mine again, holding the back of my neck to keep me attached to him. He groans, and he hums, and his tongue joins the struggle. He kisses me like he wants to enter me, slipping his tongue back and forth, and the flutters at my belly build, but I won't give in to him.

Quickly, he releases me, looking down at himself, stiff and ready, begging for attention. "I need to come." He's so direct, so insistent. His fist circles himself, and he squeezes. His eyes close as he leans over me, his other hand braced near my head. He strokes himself while I watch. It's incredibly exciting, and I resist the urge to assist him. Instead, I slip around to his back, rubbing my hands up and down his back, leaning forward along his spine as he takes himself in hand.

"Jesus," he hisses, building a rapid pace, arm struggling as he tugs and he taunts. My fingers tickle over his skin, lowering down his back

169

and flattening over the fine globes of his backside. He nearly whimpers before groaning, and I sense what's happened to him. With head lowered to the arm bracing him, his back shudders, and then he spins.

His mouth crashes mine again, fighting me, telling me he wants to give me more. He pulls back, moving to my neck, sucking at my skin to mark me. I groan.

"Let me at least touch you." I shake my head despite the desire, despite the need in me to release as he did.

"I miss how we fit," he says with a strained voice. He looks down at my thighs, staring hungrily at them. "I love how you respond to me."

"I . . ." I can hardly find the words. I'm a fool for this man, and I tell myself this over and over again while melting under his gaze and the touch of his hand lowering down my body again. He's not the least repentant that he drags a fingertip over my breast and across my nipple, crossing the line.

"You're my inspiration. You're the woodland nymph and the fresh floral scent. You're my angel and my salvation." Hesitantly, he reaches for me, even though I've told him no.

"It's not fair," I whisper, but he shakes his head.

"A fight never is." His fingers slip between my legs, and I moan at the relief of his hands on me there. His thumb meets the sensitive nub as his fingers push into me. Sliding in and out, he works me like his keyboard, typing away at pretty phrases.

"You're all I want and don't deserve, and I can't let you go." He's writing words against my skin with the mastery of his fingers, and I quickly come apart, clutching at his forearm.

"You're it, Lilac," he says just below my ear, muttering into my skin. He can't mean it. He's just wrapped up in adrenaline, the drug of winning, and me breaking under him. His voice softens as his fingers remove from me and his palm flattens on my belly once again.

"This is it, angel. The monster demands a mate."

Chapter 23

Wind Knocked Out

[Pam]

After we exit the shower, Jacob slips into bed behind me. It's our final night in New York and my thoughts bounce all over the place. What we've done. What he's said. Where will we go next? He curls me into him and murmurs final words to me.

"I feel so alive with you, Lilac. I'm becoming addicted to that feeling."

I smile to myself, stroking over his arm around my waist. He tightens his hold on me, pressing soft kisses at the nape of my neck.

"Heaven," he whispers as he inhales and quickly slips into sleep. However, I lay awake for a long time, wound up from his touch and his words. I want to believe all he says. I want it so much it almost hurts. I'd no longer be the one without a partner at my side. I'd no longer be the token single woman. I'd no longer be holding all these feelings inside me, but I can't say Jacob's committing to being more.

In the morning, I wake alone but not surprised. Our flight leaves midmorning, and we need to pack. Ethan and Ella are on our flight, and we're a mixture of chatter and laughter as we exit into Jacob's hallway. He's holding my hand, not shy before his sister and her boyfriend. He even kissed me openly, in front of them, when I came down the stairs. My cheeks flamed, but it was so nice to be recognized by him before them. He was making a statement.

I'm his.

But as we near the elevator, the doors open, and a woman growing all too familiar steps out.

"Now what?" Ella mutters as we each stand still with our suitcases.

"We're just leaving," Jacob snaps, holding his eyes forward as he nods for all of us to enter the elevator. He's still holding my hand, clutching at it.

L.B. Dunbar

"I need to talk to you," Mandi says, her voice low, almost broken. She looks different this morning, younger without layers of makeup, and her dark hair pulled up into a ponytail. Ethan takes my suitcase from under my hand and enters the elevator. His hand holds the door open, and I step forward, still holding Jacob's hand. His hold tightens on my fingers.

"This can't wait, Jakey," she says, and I cringe at the nickname. Jacob looks equally put off by it and takes a step forward, but her hand settles on his forearm. Time seems to stand still as Jacob stops. "Jacob, don't make me say this in front of them."

Her eyes peer upward, devoid of emotion. While Jacob stares at Mandi, I observe him, his body tense, his eyes bright. He next glances at Ethan, something transpiring quickly between them.

"I'm not doing this anymore with you, Mandi." Jacob turns to move away from her, his arm dropping, so she releases him. We both step forward, almost crossing the elevator entrance when Mandi speaks.

"I'm pregnant."

Our hands drop as Jacob spins to face Mandi.

"Bullshit," Jacob spits, leaning toward her. The elevator alarm starts to ring as Ethan's been holding the door too long.

And my heart drops to my feet, like the plummet of the lift waiting for us.

"Even for you, this is the lowest of lows," Jacob hisses at her.

"It's true. I have the doctor's report to prove it."

"It can't be mine," he states, rubbing a hand over his head, but all I see is frustration and a twinge of something else. "You know I don't want them."

The comment hits hard, but it's almost the ultimate way to keep him. She got pregnant on their trip even though he told me he wasn't with her. They had sex then, and he lied to me.

I step into the elevator, the motion reminding Jacob, I'm standing here, witnessing this shitshow.

He turns to me as I enter the box.

"Lilac," he whispers. "You know this isn't true."

172

I fight the pull to look at him, but then I decide he needs to look me in the eye. I don't know what to believe.

"You're it," he says again to me, but he's still standing outside the elevator, and I'm inside.

"Listen to your heart," I remind him. Ethan's hands slip from the door as the annoying blare continues to drown the silence between us, and the doors slide closed.

Without Jacob.

+ + +

His silence is deafening. He doesn't make the flight, and he doesn't respond to any texts of concern other than one to his sister.

Sad eyes meet mine as she says, "He says to go on without him." Ethan wraps his arm around my shoulder, but I shrug him off. I don't want his touch. I don't want anyone to touch me. I'm suffocating under my thoughts.

"I need a minute," I warn them both, briskly walking to the restroom as my stomach roils. I'm thankful there isn't a line as I fall into a stall and heave, although there's nothing in my stomach. There's nothing inside me but disbelief.

How had this happened to me again? How had another man in my life chosen the other woman? Then again, I was the other woman. I was the second one, the runner-up. My hands plaster against the stall walls as I bend over the toilet, heaving once again.

When I finally return to a waiting Ethan and Ella, they're in line to board the plane, and Ella wrings her hands, watching me. "He doesn't love her."

"It doesn't matter, does it? She's having his baby."

Ethan shakes his head. "I don't believe her."

"I don't think it matters what we believe. He stayed with her." I take a deep breath. "As he should, right? He's going to be a father with another woman."

I glance at my phone one final time, for some sick reason, and hate that there isn't a message from Jacob. I hate that I want there to be one.

L.B. Dunbar

He's a complicated man, and I've been holding out for him for too long without reason or promises. Just waiting.

My thumb moves to the side of my phone, and I power it off.

+ + +

Jacob: I didn't want to do this by text, but you aren't answering me.
Jacob: She's lying, and I can prove it.
Jacob: Please. Don't give up on me.
Jacob: On us.
Jacob: Lilac?
Jacob: My heart.
Jacob: I can't let you go.
Jacob: I need you.

I stare at the words once I power on my phone on Monday morning. I've just pulled into the parking lot at Mae's, and as I need the phone for work, I don't have a choice but to turn it on. The texts light up the message app, and as much as I don't want to look, my eyes are pulled to his words as they've always been with his writing.

My finger hovers over a response, but my heart holds me back. Jacob has needed me for years. He's told me over and over again—in concerns of his writing, in needs for his home—but it's never been me directly. He's never wanted me. Sure, he wanted sex, and we have that pull to one another that was finally acted upon, but I'm not the girl for him.

The monster demands a mate.

He has one now, and as much as he says he can't let me go, he'll need to. She'll give him the baby he claims he doesn't want. Jacob will not deny his responsibility. He's felt guilty for his sister's condition, so he'll step up for Mandi.

Before I exit my car as I'm parked in the lot at Mae's staring at line after line of text, I have only two words for Jacob.

Me: I quit.

174

Finding strength I don't feel, I enter Mae's Flower Shop. We share an office, and our desks sit at right angles, each under a window providing us a view of the large garden center. I'm seated in my chair when I'm accosted by Mae's jovial voice.

"Spill," Mae calls out, dropping into her seat. "Tell me every sordid detail. I want positions and poses. He rocked your world, didn't he? Tell me everything. I'm living vicariously through you." Her enthusiasm would be catching if it weren't for my breaking heart.

"It wasn't like that," I state, swiveling in my chair as I turn to face her. He rocked my world but not in ways she might imagine.

"What happened?" she asks, slowly leaning forward in her desk chair.

"Mandi's pregnant."

"Who's Mandi?"

"His girlfriend."

"Are you fucking kidding me?" Mae's expression morphs to shock as her mouth hangs open, and her eyes widen. "The one he wasn't going to marry? Now he's having a child with her?"

Hearing it said aloud is like an arrow through the heart. "Yep." I reach forward to straighten a few things on my desk, which don't need straightening.

"Pam?" she questions.

"I'm okay," I state, shrugging a shoulder.

"You are not okay. You've been in love with the mystery man for years. How did this happen?" she asks. Taking a deep breath, I back up and tell her about his vacation with Mandi and Jacob's declaration not to marry her or anyone. If I do some basic math, it doesn't add up that she'd know she's pregnant within weeks, so it had to have happened before their vacation together. Perhaps New Year's when he was in New York with her, and I started another year alone.

"I'm so sorry. What's he going to do?"

"I don't know, and it's not my concern," I lie as it's all I've been thinking about for twenty-four hours. After arriving home from a day of travel, I finally allowed myself the breakdown I needed. I folded onto

L.B. Dunbar

my bed and cried. Waking up this morning, I found myself still in my clothes from the day before, and I refused to be that girl. The girl I once was when Brendan and I fell apart. I curled into myself, hating myself, and walked through the motions of each day for months. I can't go back to that person.

"You don't mean that," Mae hesitantly states.

"I quit."

Taken aback, Mae blinks several times as she sits straighter in her seat. "You what?"

"I can't keep going back for more with that man. We had sex, and we shouldn't have. My heart was already too involved." Heartbreak was inevitable, I'd told her a few weeks ago.

Mae reaches out for my hand, and as much as I don't want any human touch, I accept her comforting fingers. "You'll get through this," she says, encouraging me as she knows what I've already been through with Brendan. I nod, but my heart disagrees. Tears blur my vision.

"I don't want to cry," I whisper, and Mae releases my hand to flap hers before her face.

"Okay. Okay, there's no crying at the flower shop. Only happy thoughts," she teases, but she doesn't believe her words any more than her saying them. "Drinks tonight. That's a happy thought."

Mae isn't wrong, and we find ourselves at Town Tavern on a Monday where cheeseburgers are their specialty. I'm so hungry I could eat three of them when I hardly finish half of one on a typical night. To my surprise, my sister, Tricia, and Leon enter the bar.

"Hey," Tricia says, nearing our booth. I'd invite her to sit with us, but I can't handle happy. Glancing from Leon to Tricia, their fingers entwined and rings on each of their left hands, I just can't deal with their happily ever after tonight. Instead, I want to get drunk off my ass kind of happy. "How was New York?"

I groan, and Mae shakes her head. Tricia's face falls. "What happened?"

It's a familiar question, one I answered over and over and over again when Brendan and I broke up. People who heard we were engaged, assumed we were married, or those who knew we fell apart wondered

176

what happened. At least this time, it won't be the entire town that knows my plight. Just my family and Mae.

"He…" Suddenly, I don't feel like telling Jacob's tale. It isn't my place to spread his situation to others, and honestly, it makes me feel like even more of a fool for falling in love with an unobtainable man. "It just isn't going to happen for us."

Tricia skeptically eyes me for a second. "Leon and I were in Traverse City looking at baby things the other day." Her voice lowers on both his name and the future baby. "We saw Spencer Campbell. Remember him? He had the biggest crush on you in high school."

Mae's brow arches as she knowingly gazes at me over the table. What she knows is Spencer asked me out, and I went to New York with Jacob instead.

"He said he's been trying to connect with you. Saw you here a few weeks ago and wanted to see you again."

Both of Mae's brows lift, and I'm curious why the man is telling my sister he wants to see me.

"Maybe you should call him. You know, see where it goes."

"Maybe," I state.

While I appreciate my sister trying to play matchmaker, I also don't. She knows I've had feelings for Jacob for years, even if I didn't discuss him much. It won't be so easy to give him up. I recall how less than two weeks ago, we sat in this bar where he kissed me before my family, making a statement to them about who I was to him. They even had that freaking bet going, which Ethan won, claiming he knew Jacob had fallen for me. Ethan knows nothing about literature, so he doesn't realize it's always the angel who falls and never the villains.

My chest pinches at the thought. Jacob isn't evil, just misguided. He's been hurt and never looked at the source, initiating and encouraging the same kind of abuse in adult relationships. I feel sorry for him when I shouldn't feel anything for him.

"Okay, well, be safe tonight," Tricia breaks into my thoughts and smiles at Mae before excusing herself.

L.B. Dunbar

"Maybe she's right. You should call this Spencer guy. Get back in the saddle as they say," Mae teases once my sister and her happily ever after walk away.

"Who is 'they' and why does it have to be a 'saddle'?" I joke.

"Whatcha want? A Harley? The point is to get anything between those thighs that would rev them up again."

I laugh. "I'm not ready, Mae."

"Honey, you've been ready for years. You got sidetracked."

Sidetracked, I want to snort. More like waylaid. It's been eleven years since Brendan. There's a reason I've been single for so long. I suffered from a fear of opening my heart. Maybe my interest in Jacob was because he was unobtainable. I didn't have to worry about losing him because I never had him. But then I let him have a taste, and like a victim to the vampire, I can't seem to walk away from my monster, falling deeper and deeper under his spell. Falling until he's sucked me dry.

My phone lays on the table, and before I know it, Mae has it in her hand, tapping at the screen and holding it to her ear. Then she passes it to me, and a deep masculine voice says, "Hello."

"Spencer?" I question, narrowing my eyes at her. "I'm so sorry, could you give me a minute?"

He laughs while he says he can wait, and I cover the receiver, glaring at my friend. "What do you think you are doing?"

"Okay, maybe he doesn't have a horse or a Harley, but he runs an adventure shop. I'm sure he has something to put the wind back in your sails." Mae's idioms are not lost on me, but I don't appreciate them.

"Or maybe you could put the wind back in his." She sets her lips around the straw of her drink, imitating what she means, and I can't help but laugh a little for the first time in two days. Shaking my head, I excuse myself and walk to the back of the bar to speak with Spencer.

+ + +

Near the end of the week, I absentmindedly answer my phone from an unknown caller.

"Hello?"

"Pam Carter?" The stern feminine voice surprises me. It's not an automated system sound or even the crinkle of a telemarketer calling.

"May I ask who's calling?"

"This is Theresa McTigue, Jacob's agent." My heart races at the thought his agent is calling me.

"Is everything alright?" I hate that my first concern is something happened to Jacob directly. I've already lived through that night of concern when his Corvette kissed a tree. He could have died that night, and it caught up to me days later when I buried my father. Jacob could have died that same night.

"I understand you've quit, Jacob, but I was wondering if you could do us a huge favor." I immediately did not like the sound of things. I'd been doing Jacob's bidding for too long.

"Did something happen to him?" I question, frustration filling my voice more than concern. Obviously, something happened to him. I wonder if his agent knows about Mandi.

"Typically, I wouldn't discuss a client's personal life with someone outside our agency, but Jacob is special to me, and I know how important you are to him as well. He's been admitted to alcohol treatment for thirty days."

My breath catches. "Is he okay?"

"He will be. By now, you know of the scandal with that ridiculous woman. Our legal team is investigating, but in the meantime, Jacob fell apart. He threatened to quit writing, and I had to intervene. He's our star." She'd said the same thing when I met her at our meeting last week. *Had it only been a week?* I'd lived another life in the past few days. I wasn't feeling well again, and I attributed it all to stress.

"I'm so sorry, but I'm so glad he reached out to you for help." I wish he'd reached out to me, but perhaps I couldn't help him. Maybe I'd been part of the problem. I rarely mentioned my concerns for his drinking until recently. Maybe I've let it pass for too long.

"He didn't have a choice. After calling me drunk, threatening to quit, I went to his apartment. I've never seen him like this." I don't know how well she knows her client or how often she's seen him outside the

L.B. Dunbar

business setting, but it's apparent she cares about him and knows enough about him to call Mandi ridiculous.

"But is he okay?"

"He will be."

We both sit in silence a second.

"So what can I do for you?"

"We'd like you to keep up his social media accounts. Continue to run his reader group. Just the usual without anything unusual, and we'll try to keep the Mandi thing out of the press as long as we can. You'll continue to be compensated, of course."

I take a deep breath. "You know, Ms. McTigue, I don't really do it for the money."

"It's Theresa, and I know," she says, letting the words soak in. "That's why I'm asking you to continue doing it, even though you told Jacob you quit."

Ah, observant woman.

"Don't give up on him yet, Pam."

The words strike their mark as it's what Jacob's been asking me over and over again lately.

+ + +

"You quit working for Jacob?" Ella's startled voice surprises me through the phone.

"I had to, Ella." Behind the desperation, I want her to understand. However, apparently, I'm still working for him. My voice drops, softening when I ask, "Have you spoken with him?"

"No. Outside interaction isn't allowed." Silence fills the phone a second. "He needs you."

"He doesn't need me." He needs the treatment he's getting, and I'm so happy he's finally getting help.

"He does, Pam," Ella whines. "You're the longest relationship he's had and the truest friend."

"We had a business relationship, and we crossed a line that shouldn't have been crossed." It's best for my heart to think of it in these

180

terms. *We made a mistake.* I fault myself for giving into him. Unavailable man, his Irish trainer called him.

"He's in love with you."

I sigh. "Even if that were true, he has Mandi," I remind her.

"Something isn't adding up there. Why hadn't she said something before?" She exhales in frustration.

"Don't you want him?" Ella's voice falls. She knows how I feel. Hell, everyone's been telling me for years how I feel about him.

"Yes," I admit. "But it's not up to me."

"He's getting help for you."

I huff a laugh. "He's getting help for himself, and that's how it should be. You should understand where he's coming from." It's a reminder that Ella needed months to figure herself out before she came back to Ethan. Not that I expect Jacob to return to me, but he's getting the help he needs for *him.*

"It still sucks, but he's going to get better, Pam. You wait and see. He's going to be a better man when he comes back to you."

"Ella," I drone. I can't hear these things. He isn't coming back to me. He has Mandi and a baby. "I really need to go."

"Listen," she grinds the word in frustration. "If there's anything he'd say to you, it's don't quit. You've told him to listen to his heart. What is yours saying to you? That's the advice you gave me once, and everything in mine told me to come back to Ethan. What held my heart lived here in this town. It's the same for Jacob."

How I wish that were true, but I've had a taste of New York. Its ups and downs, and bright lights and big city fits the chaos of Jacob's life. While our small town has been a retreat for him, this isn't his home. It's a place to escape to write and think, and I imagine he'll sell it once he finishes treatment.

"I really need to go, Ella. I'll see you Thursday," I remind her, at the weekly family get-together where I'll permanently remain the token single lady at the table.

Chapter 24

Thirty-Day Grace Period

[Pam]

The next thirty days pass in a blur as I throw myself into work. The weather heats up a bit, but is temperamental like the Midwest can be. Daffodils, hyacinth, and pansies bloom, and the garden center begins to buzz. It's almost May, and the lilacs will begin to bloom soon. The thought of them opening up and fragrancing our place curls my stomach. I don't want the reminder of Jacob's nickname for me. I'm hopeful he's getting the help he needs, and I silently wish him well as each day passes. Unfortunately, I am sick. This time it's a stomach bug I couldn't shake.

"Did you throw up again?" Mae admonishes as I exit the bathroom, swiping at my lips. Once I vomit, I feel better, and sometimes I'm even hungry afterward.

"I think I drank too much last night," I lie, as I didn't drink a thing with my family during our weekly ritual at the Tavern. I haven't had the desire for anything stronger than water lately and soda. All the cherry cola in the world sounds delicious to me, along with the tuna fish sandwich on Mae's desk.

"Are you going to eat that?" I ask like a woman desperate when I see she hasn't put her lunch in the fridge yet.

Mae's nose scrunches. "You just got sick, and you want a tuna fish sandwich for breakfast? Are you . . . ."

Crazy resonates through my thoughts, and I'm starting to think I am. I'm having strange dreams that make me restless, and I wake exhausted. It's like all I want to do is sleep, and I fight the urge, telling myself I will not fall into depression over Jacob's absence. I've missed him as I imagined, and I imagine I miss him because he's been my focus for two and a half years. It's been a non-relationship relationship where I've devoted myself to being faithful to him for no reason.

"Pam," Mae says louder, snapping me out of my head. "Are you pregnant?"

"Hell no," I immediately react, blinking at her like she's a little off her rocker. Her eyes focus on me, holding me with her questioning gaze, which shifts to concern.

"No." The single word is a wisp of air between us. "I can't be."

"How *can't* you be?" she questions.

"We . . ." My voice trails. I lower for my desk chair, still staring up at her, counting the days from my last period.

"The last time I had my period was the beginning of February," I murmur, speaking to myself, but Mae hears me. Jacob had been on vacation, so it was before Valentine's Day. Then I was sick and the snowstorm, and . . .

"But we used a condom." I look up at Mae, my voice filled with my own question. *How could this have happened?* We'd used protection. He used condoms, and I was on the pill, but I'd been sick and taking medication, and oh my *God.*

My hand hits my forehead. "I'm on the pill, but I'd been sick the week before Jacob and I . . . and I was taking medicine to help with the flu." Plus, I'd been at Jacob's for those days I was ill and then again during the unexpected snowstorm. I'd been so inconsistent for almost two weeks.

Mae slowly smiles at me.

"Oh my God," I mutter, covering my mouth as I stare at my friend. "This can't be."

It was only one night.

"I think it *might be,* and there's only one way to find out." Excitement grows in my friend's face, but I'm failing to find any emotion. I'm numb. I'm stunned. I have no idea what I'll do, but the uncertainty quickly passes to possibility. I'd have a baby. I'd raise the baby. I'd be a mother.

I'd be so happy.

"But Jacob," I stammer. Jacob had already gotten another woman pregnant. We couldn't both be pregnant *at the same time.* I feel sick all over again, only this time has nothing to do with food.

L.B. Dunbar

"Let's worry about only you for now," Mae states as the voice of reason. "We need to get to the pharmacy."

"I can't walk into the pharmacy and buy a pregnancy test." The place is located underneath my apartment. How would I explain myself because small town and rumor mongers. "The gossip will start before I even leave the store."

"We'll drive to Alton. There's a CVS there. You can do it right in the bathroom."

"I'm not giving myself a pregnancy test in a public restroom," I retort. But Mae is already reaching for my hand, and she drags me out of my seat. Calling out to Franny, she tells our employee we need to run an errand, and we'll be back in forty minutes.

"How long will the test take?" I laugh, already knowing I'll only need the time it takes to pee on a stick and wait five minutes.

Forty minutes later, it doesn't matter how much time passes. I've taken a pregnancy test in a pharmacy restroom while Mae stands outside the stall. The results are positive. Confirmed by a little pink plus on a stick, I'm pregnant.

I'm going to be a mother. Single and thirty-six, I never imagined this would be my life.

+ + +

Two weeks later, I'm still numb—not in a bad way—just a stunned way. It's been six weeks since I've seen Jacob. As I'm almost eight weeks along in my pregnancy, I'm still suffering morning queasiness along with cravings for random food like tuna fish sandwiches for breakfast. In this state of brain fog, my phone rings, and I answer when I see Ella calling.

"Are you excited?" I have no idea what she means, but she has so much to be excited about. Ethan opened his restaurant on April first as he planned, and they are engaged. I'm so sorry Jacob missed their announcement and Ethan's opening, but it couldn't be prevented. Thankfully, in the party celebration atmosphere, we didn't discuss Jacob, keeping our silence on concern for his health and well-being. Ella's been checking in with me once a week since he's gone into treatment, and I've appreciated the calls even though they've been a little painful. We avoid all discussions of her brother. She's my friend, but she's also a reminder of what I've lost.

I miss him.

"What am I missing?" I ask, attempting to fill my voice with enthusiasm for whatever has her bursting at the seams.

"I . . ." The heavy pause teases me, and I chuckle softly.

"Well?"

"I thought he told you." Her voice drops, and my heart follows.

"Who told me what?" I ask, hesitating while sensing who she means.

"Jacob. He's coming home."

A ripple rushes through me, a combination of thrill clashing with dread. He's been released. He's coming here. Then I crash because he hasn't called me, and he's probably bringing her.

"That's wonderful," I state minus enthusiasm.

Ella's sudden quiet is unsettling. "I'm certain he planned to call you."

"Ella, you don't need to cover for him. It's okay. I hope he's healthy and happy. He'll need strength for the next stage of his life."

"Pam," Ella hesitates. "He—"

"He didn't call me, Ella. I've accepted that nothing is going to happen between us."

"No, you don't understand. Mandi and—"

"I've got to go," I say, choking on the lump in my throat. I can't hear this. I can't listen to her tell me he's coming home, but he's bringing his girlfriend with him. The mother of his child. Maybe she's his wife by now. Fingers cover my lips as I click off the phone, holding back the sob until I'm clear of her listening. Then I break down again, holding a hand over my lower belly.

It's just you and me, kid.

You and me.

185

Chapter 25

One Plus One Does Not Equal . . . One

[Jacob]

When Mandi sabotaged me outside the elevator, I refused to take her to my apartment. Everything in me told me to chase after Pam. Run down the flights of stairs and catch her at the bottom of the hell we'd just been propelled into. Instead, I stood still, frozen by the cold sensation of Pam's hand slipping from mine.

Hand holding.

She'd let me go. For all my begging and pleading not to give up on me, she let me go, and I couldn't blame her. Mandi stood before me spewing lies, and I had no reaction.

"This can't be true," I hissed in the face of the woman I'd confused for love. Her aggressive behavior. Her seductive attitude. Her hits, her scratches, her promises. All of it a lie. People want to proclaim love is a lie, but I disagreed. Love was the truth. Mandi had been my lie.

Pam was my love.

"We haven't been together since . . . since . . . I don't even remember when." I'd meant what I said to Pam. I was not with Mandi on our miserable vacation

Mandi flinched at my lack of memory. "New Year's Eve. We were together then." Hastily, I counted backward from mid-March to the new year. I hardly remembered the night, hardly remembered getting it up for her.

I didn't remember because I'd been drinking.

My chest squeezed, my lungs constricted. I couldn't breathe.

Drinking.

It'd be the ruin of me after all because I couldn't remember anything, and this woman might be carrying my baby.

Fight From The Heart

Did I stop drinking as my world fell apart? Did I slow down because the love of my life walked away from me? Did I give up on my drug of choice because my life was ruined?

No, I delved into a bottle that night and the next three days, until I found Theresa McTigue standing over me.

I'd tried to quit—*not drinking*—but my writing.

I'd told my agent I couldn't finish the book I'd been writing. I couldn't continue working without my muse because my inspiration had quit on me.

Two words from Lilac. *I quit.*

She'd quit me, us, and I couldn't blame her. I was a mess. I'd hit rock bottom, and those rocks were hard and edged with the truth. I had a problem.

In my weakest moment, I asked Theresa to help me, and here I spent days, staring out at the budding spring landscape of Upper New York.

I promised myself I would not miss the blooming of lilacs in Michigan. I'd see the unveiling of purple and white flowers, no matter how much it reminded me of the scent of my personal woodland nymph.

I refused to think about how she'd run away from me.

+ + +

I'm nervous as I sit at the bar. I missed Ethan's grand opening and the announcement of his engagement to my sister. I haven't always been the best big brother, although Ella tells me I am. Part of my therapy was coming to terms with my role in her scars and then accepting that it wasn't my fault. She cried as she listened to me apologize and then explain my feelings about her situation, and she forgave me as she had years ago.

I didn't deserve her, but that's another term I'd had to accept. I did deserve things in my life—good things—and the best thing for me was my angel.

My hands sweat around the glass, slipping up and down on the condensation outside of it. Ethan helped set this up for me, and I'm grateful for his friendship. I've had to learn to let go of those who hadn't

L.B. Dunbar

been friends over the years and recognize the people who were truly friends to me. It wasn't hard to walk away from the people who held a false label.

"She's here," Ethan whispers to me, and I shift on the barstool.

She's so fucking beautiful. Her curves. Her face. Her short, loose curls. There's something that looks different about her, but whatever it is, it doesn't matter.

She's here.

She doesn't see me at first, and I watch her walk in the general direction of the bar. It's located in the back corner, not more than four stools across. This isn't really the type of place to hang out and drink but a place to eat and linger at tables. Ethan did a beautiful job of setting up the place with its crisp white shiplap, soft mini-bulb lighting, and wrought-iron contrasts. Tables scatter throughout the place with white linen and an eclectic collection of chairs per table. The kitchen entrance is flanked by the bar and a stone fireplace with a black and white painting over it.

Ella intercepts Pam, who smiles at my sister. My fingers itch to touch her again. Hell, I just want to hold her and inhale her scent. I've missed my Lilac.

I turn back for the bar again and take a long sip from my glass. My hands shake, but it's not as bad as when I first went into the treatment center. I hear Ella and Pam's voice behind me, and my heart rattles in the cage of my chest.

The demons have been set free, or at least most of them.

"He asked you out again?" Ella's voice struggles, and I stiffen with my back to them.

Did Pam go on a date? Did that surfer douche get to her? Am I too late? Panic seizes my chest, and I spin on the stool.

"Lilac." It takes her a second to register my voice and then turn to look at me.

God, she's so beautiful, I think again, taking in the sapphire spark of her eyes, the brightness of her lips, and a slight flush to her cheeks.

"Jacob." My name is a breathless exhale like the times I entered her, and instantly, I'm hard. She slowly smiles at me, and without thought, I slip from the stool, stepping up to her and kissing her cheek.

"You smell beautiful."

"I'm going to check on Ethan. I'll be right back," Ella states, conveniently excusing herself and leaving Pam and me in silence, which we should have stayed in because my mouth can't hold back.

"So you went out with him?"

The smile on her face instantly morphs in exasperation, and she looks off at the diners near us.

"I don't see how that's any of your business," she says, turning back to me.

"But you did," I press. *Dating is just a precursor to sex.* Did she have sex with him? Am I too late? My blood pressure goes from zero to sixty.

"Did you sleep with him?" I can't seem to stop myself, and her arms cross.

"Are you drinking?" She nods at the large glass on the bar.

"It's water." I steady my voice, finding her question reasonable. I'll have a lot of explaining to do for myself, and I'm not off to a good start. However, I can't give it up. "Answer the question."

Turning her head to the side again, she huffs. "No, I didn't go out with him."

Thank God.

"Maybe you'd like to take it in the kitchen, or outside," Ethan appears, noting the tension rising between Pam and myself, and a few guests who are watching us.

Pam huffs in that direction, and I follow her. Ethan follows as well, continuing to guide us to the back exit. It's a crisp early spring evening, and the scent of new growth is in the air. The fieldstone restaurant sits amid a meadow with a large red barn to the left. Cherry trees in neat lines are the backdrop to the barn.

"You can fight back here," Ethan states, leaning foward to kiss Pam's cheek. "You have my permission to punch him."

Ethan steps away from us, and Pam turns back on me.

189

L.B. Dunbar

"She wasn't pregnant," I blurt out. It's not the first explanation I wanted to give her. I wanted to explain what happened, where I went, why I couldn't call. I wanted this reunion to be a surprise, and it's turning into a shamble. The fight to accept that I don't ruin everything in my life becomes real because it feels like I'm destroying this moment.

"What?" Pam stares at me, her hand falling against her belly.

"She was never pregnant," I repeat, trying to hold her gaze, but she looks away from me, her eyes on the large barn.

"What happened?" Her voice cracks when she turns back, and I shrug.

"She was trying to trick me into marrying her. She thought if she was carrying my child, I'd ask her."

"How would that have worked when she didn't produce a baby in nine months."

"She thought she'd get pregnant once we reunited." I step up to her. "But I never planned to marry her, baby or not. And I knew there couldn't be a baby, or at least not mine. I was telling you the truth when I told you I hadn't slept with her on that vacation back in February." That damn vacation I never should have gone on. I should have seen who was standing before me. I should have seen her sooner.

"You know I didn't want children, and I didn't believe in marriage. At least not before." My voice falters. At least not before Pam.

Her face blanches, all the color draining out of it.

"Are you okay?"

Her nose sniffs. "Just something in the air. It smells bad out here." Her hand actually fists near her belly, and I don't miss the motion.

"Are you sick?"

A hand covers her mouth, and she vigorously shakes her head. "No, I'm fine." She's lying. I can read it in the widening of her eyes and the lacking color in her face.

"How are you doing with this?" Her eyes roam my face, searching for signs of anything.

"I was upset at first. I mean, I was upset when she first told me, obviously, and you heard about my breakdown." I swipe a hand over my hair. I didn't want Theresa to call Pam, but I later learned that she did.

190

"But I'm better now, so much better now." I want to assure her, but she's staring at me, hesitant of me. I don't blame her. I don't deserve her in so many ways, but my treatment has helped me learn, I do deserve someone like her. I deserve love.

I want it to be her.

You're it, Lilac.

Alcohol clouded my judgment for so long, but I see clearly what's before me. Actions *will* speak louder than words, as Ethan said, but I need the time to act. I need the chance to do right by her.

"What are you doing? Tonight, why are you here?" she questions. She's here under the guise of having dinner with Ella. A neutral place seemed best, so I didn't pounce on her the second I had her alone and beg her to take me back.

"It's called dinner. I was hoping to surprise you, and you'd join me. I'm told it's part of the process of dating." The corner of my lip curls, hoping she'll remember the lessons.

She doesn't respond.

"Lilac." I step up to her as her eyes close. "Don't give up on me. Give me another chance." I sigh. "You told me you believed in them, and love."

Could she love me? Could she love the new me?

"I'm not saying it will be easy. I know I'm difficult and moody. It's us creative types," I tease, but she doesn't smile. "I want to be good for you."

"Jacob." Her eyes close again, and she lowers her head. If I didn't know better, I'd say pain crosses her beautiful cheeks. My brows pinch.

"Well, I just wanted you to know I'm back. For good. I'm selling the apartment. I'll just get a hotel when and if I need to return to New York. I can handle so much of my business electronically." It's like I'm giving her my resume instead of telling her I love her, but suddenly, it doesn't seem like the time or place.

She's really quit me.

"I'll be at the house," I finally say when she doesn't respond to me. "My deadline is pushed back, and I lost my assistant."

L.B. Dunbar

Pam stares at me while I recall our teasing boss-assistant relationship. I lean in for a final kiss to her cheek. It isn't enough. It won't ever be close enough.

"She was a hard-ass, and I miss her."

Pam's eyes widen, but when she still doesn't speak, I nod to excuse myself, leaving behind one of the best things in my life.

Chapter 26
Love Me

[Pam]

Watching him walk away was the hardest thing to happen to me. Telling him the truth was going to be the second most difficult.

She wasn't having his baby.

I was.

He didn't want children.

As the story of how she tried to trap him settles in, I feel sick once again. I'd never want him to think I trapped him. I didn't want him to feel obligated to me or beholdened to our baby. I didn't need him, but I wanted him.

I'd been to Jacob's home several times during his absence. I let in the house cleaning service and checked on things in general around the place, just as I'd done for two-plus years.

But I shook as I let myself in the next day. I needed to tell him the truth, and the shock value seemed best as that's how he approached me last night.

When Ella told me he was returning, I was in shock, and it still stung that he didn't contact me directly. I couldn't think about those things. I needed to rip off the bandage and give him my truth because he does need to know. What he did after that would be up to him.

I climb the garage stairs with heavy feet and help myself through the door with my key. Not finding him in his great room at first glance or his office, I cross the large space and enter his kitchen. He isn't there either, although his car is in the garage.

Maybe he took a walk? It wasn't likely. Jacob would rather punch the bag when he was frustrated with a writing scene or needed a moment to think. Deciding to check the workout room, I press through the kitchen swing door to find Jacob leaning against the back of a couch. His ankles cross while his hands brace on the frame. He holds a water bottle in one

L.B. Dunbar

hand and is dressed in a tee shirt and jeans. His feet are bare, and I almost smile until I see his face, lowered toward his feet. The hard edge returns, but something softer mixes in his expression.

"What are you doing here?" he questions as I can only stare at him. He's so incredibly good-looking. He doesn't seem so much broken as pieced back together but still fragile.

"My boss returned. I came to inspect the place. See if the house was clean, batteries in flashlights in case of emergency, even firewood in the garage, just in case of a snowstorm."

"A snowstorm in late April?" His head slowly lifts, and he brings the water bottle to his lips, taking a sip while watching me over the plastic container.

"Stranger things have happened."

He nods, no longer interested in playing along.

"My assistant quit," he reminds me. "So you don't really need to check on things."

I nod. "Are you really okay?"

"What do you think?" The edge returns to his voice, and he turns toward the window, squinting at the bright sunlight streaming through the glass wall.

"I'm sorry all that happened to you, and I should have said that last night." So much was racing through my head as he stood before me, confessing to me his story.

I need to tell him my story as well, but something still holds me back.

"And you aren't upset about the baby?"

"Can't be upset about something that didn't exist," he mocks, and my skin bristles. His underlying tone tells me he was upset about the non-entity child.

"Would a baby ever make you happy? Maybe with someone else."

"There's no one else." His eyes latch onto me.

His shoulders fall. His face lowering again. His feet shift as he crosses and recrosses his ankles.

"What if there is. What if you fall in love and a child . . .." The truth so close, lying on the tip of my tongue.

194

"I shouldn't have kids, anyway," he says, glancing back up at me. "I'd be a shit parent."

"I don't believe that," I say, stepping closer to him. "You just need a little assistance."

Jacob huffs. "Always finding the best in me." His voice lacks any acknowledgment of my weak hints.

"Someday, maybe," I suggest, finding it harder and harder to tell him about me.

"I don't believe in love." He lifts the water bottle again and drinks. He's falling into safe mood, protecting himself with his words. He shakes his head, dismissing me. He doesn't really *not* believe in love. He wants to believe in it, but he just doesn't recognize it. He wouldn't know it even if it's standing before him.

"What if it was right under your nose?" I step closer, straddling his crossed ankles. My voice drops, and my gaze drops to his lips a second.

"Lilac," he whispers, my nickname so familiar and so missed from his lips. The breathy air of my name brushes over my lips.

"Jacob," I softly say his name, resting my hands on his covered chest. His heart races under my palm. "Let me love you."

His head pops up. Those dull midnight orbs panic.

"Let me show you how it can be."

His frozen position allows me to lean forward, closing in on him. He doesn't move. Hands still braced on the back of the couch. The crackle of a partially full water bottle under his fingers. My lips brush his jaw, tracing over the short, artful stubble before lowering for his neck. He swallows, and I press a kiss to the bob of his Adam's apple. My hands smooth over the soft material covering his chest, the heat of him seeping through it.

My hands lower to his belly, and his stomach muscles flinch. I remember asking him if he was ticklish.

"Am I hurting you?" I question, pressing kisses to his neck.

"Only because you let go of my hand."

I pull back to look at him. I don't recall it like that. He let go of me, but none of it matters anymore.

"I'm standing before you now."

L.B. Dunbar

I tug at his shirt, and he drops the water bottle to the floor, water splashing my ankles. Once the T-shirt is over his head, I drop it and place my hands back on the warmth of his chest. His fingers come to my hips, and he tugs me forward, but I lean back, a small smile curling my lips.

"I lead," I tease him. I still need to tell him the truth. I need him to know about my condition, but selfishly, I want this moment with him. Before I lose him again, I want him.

His hands fall back to the couch edge, and I slide mine over each of his arms. Caressing him, feeling his skin, I take my time to explore him as I haven't before—wrists, forearms, biceps, and reverse. I kiss one side of his neck and then the other.

"You're a good man, Jacob," I say. "You have it in you to be loving," I whisper to his ear before nipping him there. His shoulder presses upward, and goose bumps break out on his flesh. My lips come to his, kissing him chaste and sweet, slowly adding tongue. I'm in no rush. We aren't racing to a finish line.

This is me, taking from him what I've always wanted and giving to him all of me in return.

I love this man. *God help me*, I love him.

My hands cover his shoulders and glide down to his palms, flattening mine against his.

"Hold my hands," I whisper and his fingers quickly curl, entwining with mine. My mouth returns to his, kissing him tender and sweet with all the patience I can muster when I want to devour those sultry lips and climb his body. My fingers squeeze his.

"Lilac," he mutters against my mouth.

I have a secret but he needs to know how I feel first.

Releasing his lips, I step back and tug him to follow me. He doesn't question me but blindly moves his feet. He hesitates while willing to go where I go.

"I won't hurt you. I promise." I direct him up the stairs, taking measured steps as he's behind me.

"This is already torture," he teases.

"You can tell me no," I warn, stopping on a step above him.

"I'd never say no to you, Lilac."

With a small smile, I finish leading him to his room to the edge of his bed. Placing my hands on his shoulders, I guide him to sit and allow his hands to come to my hips. I slip off my light jacket and tug off my own T-shirt.

"Your breasts are gorgeous," he says, leaning forward, mouth ready to take one still covered by my bra.

"I lead," I remind him, pulling back, and he gives me a soft grin. He licks his lips, hungry for me, and a rush of warmth pools between my thighs. We'll be getting there, but first, I return to kissing him, hands rubbing over his skin as his slip around to my backside and tug me closer to him. The kisses heat until he can't take it. He rips his mouth from me and presses eager kisses to my chest, kissing the swell of my breast above my bra.

"You're so huge," he mutters into my skin. I've always been large breasted, but I'm swelling to accommodate the changes in me. The material of my bra grows tighter as my body adjusts to pregnancy, and it's a reminder of what I need to tell him. *You should tell him before this goes any farther.* But my breasts ache for his attention, and he doesn't disappoint.

My body overrules me.

The power shifts, and Jacob takes over. He tugs down the cup of my bra, popping my breast free of the confines. Latching onto one, he sucks hard before pulling off with a sharp pop. He examines the stiff nipple and then unhooks my bra to release both breasts. The material drops before me, and his mouth returns to the other swell, sucking at it with equal eagerness. My hands cup the sides of his head and press him off me.

"My turn," I tell him, dropping down to my knees and unbuttoning his jeans.

"Lilac," he warns, his fingers combing through my short hair.

"Jeans. Off," I command.

"So bossy," he teases but assists me in tugging them to his feet. He remains seated as I lower for his length, kneeling between his legs. My mouth opens, taking him deep within the cavern and swallowing. He gasps as his hips buck and I smile around the thickness of him. Pleasing

L.B. Dunbar

him will please me. His fingers stroke through my hair, brushing it back, as I lap at his solid shaft. Within seconds, he hoists me up under my arms to stand.

"Enough," he groans, his patience nearing its limit. "I need to be inside you."

I shuck off my skirt and underwear, slipping out of my shoes without socks. I stand before him, naked and exposed, but the way he's looking at me, I feel beautiful and powerful. Placing my hands on his shoulders, he scoots himself back on his bed, drawing me over him as he moves. He falls to his back in the middle of the mattress, and I complete the climb over him, straddling his thighs.

I position him at my entrance, rubbing slick folds over his heated tip. His hand comes to my wrist.

"I wasn't with her," he says, dousing the moment a little bit. I nod, not wanting to bring her between us ever again.

"What about a condom?"

You should tell him.

"Do you trust me?" I ask, our eyes meeting.

He nods. "Always."

"We don't need one." I hold my breath for a second, thinking he'll question me. Instead, he says nothing. His eyes shift to soft black as his hips move upward, helping himself to enter me. He looks down at where he's disappearing into me, taking his time to fill me. My head falls back at the heat of him. With a hand on my hip, he guides me lower, allowing my body to take his.

"Holy shit," he hisses, still watching us connect.

My skin prickles. My body is on fire. I'm no longer certain I can keep it slow. I'm so full from him, and I want to move.

"Take what you want from me, angel." Jacob exhales as if reading my mind. His voice strains as I slide upward and quickly slip back down. He grunts, and I repeat the movement, filling myself over and over with his thickness. My hips rock. My fingertips press into his chest. My body takes control, moving me in a way I've never moved. I'm outside myself, free of constraints. Only with Jacob could I have this experience. Only with him could I feel this alive.

198

I love you. I catch the words before they can escape, but they linger on my tongue. The phrase is not part of us today. This is a sensation, not a moment for words.

I move faster, taking him deeper. No longer in control of myself, I ride him faster—friction increases and tension builds. I cry out his name as Jacob clutches at my hips.

"Take it, angel. Take all of me."

I slam down on Jacob and toss back my head as I come. He hisses, surging into me. Clutching at my hips, he keeps me pinned to him as he releases in me. He jolts and jerks, filling me when I'm already full.

Quickly, he sits up, the strength of his abs amazing. His hands cup my jaw, and he brings my mouth to his.

"You're it for me, Lilac," he mutters against my lips, before kissing me with everything he has. I return the kiss, absorbing his words. Guilt comes quickly on the tail of this moment because I've just complicated everything triplefold.

+ + +

Jacob fell asleep shortly after we cleaned up. I lay tucked into his chest, his front to my back. However, I'm not able to sleep despite the exhaustion. Carefully, I slip out from under his arm and enter his bathroom. My mind races through what we've done and what I still need to say to him.

His rainfall showerhead douses me, and I stand under the spray, loving the heated sensation. Jacob has these bits and pieces that show his wealth while he often dresses like a college kid in ripped jeans and flannel shirts. *The Professor.* I smile to myself as my hand covers my belly.

What will our baby be like? Will he be book smart or street wise? Will he have a bit of both in him like Jacob does? I'll be the one to teach our child how to start a fire and cook. Will Jacob be by my side when that happens? A tear comes to my eye, and I swipe at it as I hear the soft click of the shower door.

L.B. Dunbar

While I anticipate him behind me, I still flinch when Jacob's hand curves over my hip and the other lands on my belly over my hand. Can he feel me changing? Does he know what I carry inside me? Would he be happy?

"Did I scare you?" He laughs a little as his mouth sucks at my neck.

"A little," I tease.

"Do I frighten you?" he asks, and I scoff.

"You have no idea." My breathless whisper surrounds us. The sound of the shower drowns out my fear or so I think. Jacob stills behind me.

"What are you frightened of?"

"You'll break my heart." I can't look at him, but I need to be honest about this one thing.

"I know I've hurt you, and I'm sorry for that. You're it for me, Lilac. Let me make it up to you."

Jacob kisses my shoulder. Then moves back to my neck.

"There's never going to be anyone else as real, as true to me, as good for me as you." His hand comes to the opposite side of my neck, massaging the juncture between it and my shoulder while his mouth continues to suck at my skin. He's so good at what he does, and within seconds, I'm melting under the steam of the shower and the heat of his touch.

"Why are you in here?" he questions.

"I just couldn't sleep," I admit.

Because I have something to tell you.

"You're tense. You okay, angel?" He works at my neck a little longer and then reaches for the shampoo bottle. Without asking, he washes my hair, shampooing it with gentle fingertips. My eyes close as my head bobs under his scalp massage.

"You like that?"

I purr in response, and he chuckles.

"Turn," he commands, and I spin to rinse my hair. His scent surrounds me. Cloves. Inhaling, I open my eyes to find Jacob looking at my lips. His curl into a crooked smile, and mine follow. Glancing down, I reach for his arm, running a finger over the intricate ink.

"What do these mean?"

"Most are symbols representing warriors, fighters, or survival."

My eyes drop to the word on his wrist, recalling the tattoo I'm most familiar with. *Nevermore.*

"My father would grab my arms hard. Hard enough to leave marks. Bruising fingertips. This art covers any impression he ever made." While the bruises would have healed, the emotional wounds run deep within Jacob.

"And what about this?" My fingertips trace over the words on his pec. *Change your destiny.*

It might be simple and obvious. He didn't want to be like his father, but I sense something deeper to the words.

"Cliché for an author, right? But the words just stuck with me. I made it my motto when I got my first contract. I was changing my destiny."

"Meaning your stories would be your life?"

"Something like that. It's more a reminder that I'll be who I want to be. I won't be him." Hope blooms in my chest as it's the first time I've heard Jacob accept that he doesn't have to be like his father. In fact, he's nothing like him. He won't lay a finger on a child. He won't disown his child for making his own choices.

I spin Jacob and run a finger over his lower back, along another set of inked words.

I am not what happened to me. I choose to be something more.

"And here?" I question, keeping my voice low and soft, hoping the tenderness of my touch tells him he can trust me with these things.

"It's the first place my father kicked me. It's the shape of a boot heel, and the words are to remind me that I will not be what happened. I will not become them. I choose to be something greater." His voice is pained as he explains the meaning. I bend to kiss the permanent scar. Jacob flinches, and I place a hand on his hip to steady him.

His upper left shoulder has another small mark. It looks like a sunburst, but on closer inspection, I see it's a puckered scar. I run a finger over it, and Jacob shudders. He volunteers an answer before I ask.

L.B. Dunbar

"Dad burned me with a cigar. It was an accident," he mocks. "It wasn't deep, but it marked my skin."

I tip up on my toes and press a lingering kiss on the spot. My eyes close, trying not to imagine the horror of a father harming his child.

Finally, I'm drawn to a larger set of words on his right side, under his arm, but closer to his hip bone.

Never give them power over you. You are not the beast. Do not let it become you.

The lines run up and down, and I have to turn my head to clearly read them. I trace each line, feeling Jacob's eyes on my action.

"My father punched me there. It gave new meaning to sucker punch to the gut. That night, I lost my appendix."

"Jesus," I whisper, lowering to kiss along the lines.

The shower has turned rather serious, and my heart hurts for all his hurts. I reach for his body wash, pour a generous helping into my hand, and lather up before massaging the liquid soap over his skin. I swipe up his chest and over his shoulders, cascading down his arms to his wrists. I press a kiss to one shoulder over the soapiness and step around to his back. Rubbing in small circles, I coat the firm muscles over his shoulder blades, pressing gently over his inked scar. My hands stretch around his waist and lower for something long and hard.

"What are you doing, my little wood nymph?" He chuckles, and I do too as it's been a while since he's called me that.

"Remind me what that story is again," I tease as I stroke over his thickness.

"Once upon a time, there was a tempting wood nymph named Syringa. The god Pan noticed her and chased her into the woods, lusting after her." One of Jacob's hands goes to the tile before him. The other lowers for my wrist while I squeeze him. "He wanted the beautiful creature more than he'd ever wanted anything." His voice drops as I tug at him. "One myth is, she hid in the form of a lilac bush. Pan discovered where she was, or rather what she'd done, and he carved her into a flute that he would carry with him at all times."

Continuing to stroke Jacob, I press my lips to his shoulder blade. His hand squeezes my wrist.

"If you ask me, by carving her into an instrument, he just wanted to put his lips on her and make her sing all day long." I don't miss the euphemism as he chuckles. I tug harder at him, slipping faster down his length with the aid of the soapy wash.

"Lilac, may I be so bold as to ask if I can make love to you again?" His words startle me, and I still my movements.

"I'll never have enough of you. You've carved yourself into my skin." Turning to face me, he presses me back to the tile. His mouth nips and sucks at my wet skin as a hand slides down my body, taking its time to coast over my breasts and stopping to circle a nipple. I hum at the attention he pays the achy swells, arching my back as he cups one and lowers to suck at the other.

"Are you my instrument? Can I play you? I want to make you sing."

While his tongue laves at the peaked nub, his fingers lower between my thighs. My head tips back as he strokes over me, ready and eager to go again with him.

"I'd like to keep you with me, Lilac."

My breath catches. I want to believe him. I want to believe that as good as we are, we can stay that way.

"Careful, Jacob. That sounds like commitment. Pan was only in lust with his lilac."

Jacob lifts his head from watching his fingers play me. His molten eyes stare into mine.

"What if it's love?"

I swallow around the lump forming in my throat. My eyes hold his, but my body vibrates.

Can I believe this? Can it be?

"You don't believe in love," I remind him, my voice croaking as fingers enter me.

"Maybe you've made me a believer." His mouth crashes to mine as his fingers work faster. My body responds, rocking into his palm.

Bending at the knees, he lines himself up and thrusts upward. Hands slip beneath my thighs, lifting me with the wall at my back.

"I'm too heavy," I mumble against his mouth.

"You're luscious."

L.B. Dunbar

I'm pregnant.

"You're beautiful," he says around another kiss.

And pregnant.

"You're everything."

I'm having your baby.

The words rest on my tongue, which tangles with his, and I'm lost to the sudden sensation of him filling me once again, wiping away the reality of our position. Syringa gave into the Greek god, letting him play her over and over again. I seem to be no different from the namesake he's given me.

Despite my position—back to the tile, legs around Jacob's hips—he takes his time to go slow until I can't take it any longer. I break free of his mouth and demand he move faster.

"The wood nymph requests, and the god follows." He hammers into me, jiggling me against the sweating tile at my back. My arms wrap around his neck, allowing him to move me as he wishes as the telltale signs flutter in my belly. Our skin slaps together. Our breaths gasp at the exertion. Jacob hoists me higher, and I slam down on him, forcing him deeper.

I scream his name, and he stills, pressing me into the tile. Denotating within me, we come in tandem. It's the most incredible sensation.

"I feel so alive with you," Jacob says, pulling back to kiss me, fierce and hungry before breaking from my lips for my neck.

"What are you doing to me?" he whimpers. Our heavy breathing mixes with the pattering of the shower. Still within me, he holds me in this position for another minute, and I wonder the same thing about him.

How am I going to tell him?

+ + +

"I'm famished," I blurt out once we exit the shower, and I wrap in a robe he offers me while he drapes a towel around his hips.

"My assistant quit, so I don't know if I have anything edible," he teases.

"God, what a bitch. Who could quit you?"

204

He mischievously smiles while tugging me close for a quick kiss. "Don't talk about yourself like that." His mouth lands on mine again, and I could spend the rest of my life kissing him. It's a dangerous thought.

"Get back in bed. I'll be up in a few minutes."

Returning to the bed, I fix the messed up spread of blankets and remove the robe, crawling under the covers. After tugging the blanket to my neck, I draw my knees to my chest, staring out the window while I wait for Jacob. It's late afternoon or early evening. I've lost track of time.

I need to tell him.

With each passing hour, I feel more hopeful he'll accept my circumstance. He'll accept the baby, but I'm still not certain. Everything is so raw and fresh. It has hardly been twenty-four hours since his return. He tells me he's staying permanently, and I want to believe him.

When he returns to the room, he carries a tray piled with an assortment of items. Crackers and cheese. Peanut butter, a cut apple, and a small bowl of raisins. A bottle of wine under his arm. He sets the tray over my legs like he did when I was sick and in this very bed. Then he holds up the wine.

"For you, not me."

I shake my head. "I don't need it."

He licks his lips. "I don't want you to stop because of me. I'm doing good. Every day, it gets better."

Reaching for his wrist, I cover it with my hand.

"I'm doing it for me. I don't need it. Water's fine."

Jacob's brows crease, but he sets the bottle of wine on the bookcase behind the bed and heads to the bathroom. He returns with a glass of water. Jacob climbs into bed next to me and holds out a slice of apple, smothered in peanut butter with a few raisins on top.

"What are you doing?" I giggle as the piece nears my lips.

"Feeding my angel. Now open." I take the bite he offers me, humming at the combination in my mouth. He's sweet, and I want to believe it can last. My thoughts settle around the truth I'm holding in. He's going to think I tricked him, like her. He's going to think I've done this on purpose, like her. My advantage is, there really will be a baby. His baby.

205

L.B. Dunbar

"You're very quiet over there." His somber voice breaks into my thoughts.

"How does it work for you? The treatment?" I pause. "You don't have to tell me, but I'm curious. I don't want to trigger anything."

Jacob chuckles, reaching for a cracker and cheese combination. "You won't trigger me, but I think to be safe, I should remove all the alcohol from the house."

"Your assistant can handle that," I say, tipping a brow at him.

"I'll get her right on that after she's on me again." He leans forward and kisses my shoulder. "But seriously. I fell hard after you left, but I don't fault you. Mandi was all on me. I wanted to chase you, but I was stuck. Like I couldn't believe her, but something held me in place. I had to face her and the situation before I could ask you to stay with me."

Jacob pauses. "And I want you to stay." His eyes soften, the words hesitant, sheepish even. "The biggest mindset change was accepting that I do deserve good in my life. You're the best part of everything, and I never want to lose you."

I smile, but I don't comment, allowing him to tell me more.

"Anyway, I wasn't allowed to make phone calls once I entered. There was a family weekend toward the end, but I passed. I didn't want anyone to see me there, see me like that."

"But you called Theresa." It lingers in the unsaid that he didn't call me.

"I tried to quit Theresa, that's what worried her. That and the fact I could hardly form the words. She crashed my place and demanded I get my shit together."

"I'm glad she did that for you." My voice lowers, and his hand comes to my chin.

"I did it for you," he whispers.

Shaking my head, I retort, "You did it for you because you needed it. But I'm happy you did. You seem better already."

"Every day, a little more." He smiles. He's been perched on his elbow, but he sits up, slipping his finger down the side of my face like he does. "You make me better."

I try to stifle a yawn, and Jacob chuckles.

"Am I boring you?"

"I'm so sorry, I'm just tired. Someone wore me out." Between the sex, the snack, and my rambling thoughts, I'm exhausted.

"You work too hard."

I laugh. "I'm about to work harder as my boss is back."

"Hmm. Your boss likes it hard."

I laugh again. "You're insatiable."

"Only for you, Lilac. Only for you." He leans in to kiss me, taking his time to savor my lips before his tongue sweeps along the bottom, and he pulls back.

"Okay, time for bed then, angel." Jacob hops off the bed, moves the tray to the floor, and crawls back in next to me. We curl to our sides, my back to his front, and he nuzzles his nose into the back of my neck.

"You smell like me. I need to change that," he teases. "But I like you in my bed. I never want to sleep without you in it again."

My vision blurs, and I close my eyes in the dark room. A tear slips from each of them.

"I like being here," I admit, my voice thick. Jacob presses a kiss to my nape, and I swallow again. He's so tender, and it's ripping me apart. With everything he does, he's saying he loves me without the words, but it's not safe to make assumptions. He's not going to want to marry me, and he's definitely going to be upset when he learns about the baby.

And because I'm a fool for him, I'm selfishly soaking up this minute before we fall apart again.

L.B. Dunbar

Chapter 27

Things Fall Apart

[Jacob]

From my position inside the walk-in closet, I see Pam bolt upright in my bed and twist side to side as if looking for me. I chuckle softly to myself. "I'm back here," I call out. Would she feel lost without me like I've felt the last six weeks without her? It's been hell. A living hell.

The closet light illuminates a small portion of my room, so for the most part, Pam is only a shadow in the dark. I watch as she turns in my bed, glancing over her shoulder at me. She's so fucking beautiful, and she's in my bed. Not because she's sick. Not because of a storm. She came to me willingly and seduced me.

Let me love you, Jacob.

Jesus, the thought alone stitched up my heart. Hearing those words from her lips, and then her kissing me like she did, it just meant everything. It was enough to make a strong man weep, and I almost did last night as I finally entered her again. And when she kissed all my tattoos and scars in the shower, if that doesn't break a man and put him back together, nothing would. Where did this woman come from? What did I do to deserve her? In therapy, we learn to allow deserve as a word. We deserve better, we can be better, and I meant what I said to her. Every day is better, and with her, I expect life to stay that way.

Looking at her sitting in my bed, I feel my heart hammer in my chest. God, do I want her again. Unfortunately, I don't have time this morning. I slip on the shirt in my hands and cross my room to a sleepy Pam.

"Go back to sleep, angel." We didn't get much sleep last night, but even before we did what we did, I noticed she looked tired. But there was also something else about her. She glowed in a way I can't put my finger on. My eyes dip to her breasts, loosely covered by the sheet. They

208

look bigger to me, fuller even. My mouth waters, but I can't get distracted yet. I reach out for her hair and brush back the locks.

My phone buzzes on the bookshelf, and Pam and I both look at the screen.

Theresa.

I avoid Pam's eyes, but hers press into my face, begging for an answer.

"What's going on?"

I sigh, hating this already. "Theresa booked me a lecture at U of M as long as I was coming back here. She wants me to get back to work immediately. There's a dinner with the writing department and then a presentation at seven. She booked me a room as it might be late when I finish."

It's almost four hours or so from here to the east side of the state, and I hate that I'm already giving up a night with Pam.

"You've been out of the center for two weeks. What were you doing then?" We talked only a little bit last night about the time we've been apart, and we have so much more that needs to be said.

"I had outpatient visits, plus I put my apartment on the market to sell." I meant what I said the other night. I'm here to stay. I packed up my things, ordered movers for what I wanted shipped, and left the rest. I leave out how I had to get a restraining order against Mandi. I didn't need some off the rails behavior like she already pulled. I don't want to get into Mandi shit. It's over.

What I want is to keep soaking up moments with my Lilac. What we did last night. What she said to me.

"I could come with you," she quietly suggests.

"How about if I find you in my bed tonight instead? I can skip the hotel and come back after the lecture."

"I don't want you to drive back late. It might be midnight or later. Plus . . ." Her voice drifts.

"I'm not going to drink," I assure her. "If anything, coming home to you is a good excuse to skip the bars and drinks afterward with the department."

L.B. Dunbar

Pam nods, uncertain of me, and while I'd love to prove myself to her right now, I can't.

"I hate to do this, but I've got to go."

She shifts to kneel on the bed and takes the sheet with her, covering herself. I hate how she's hiding from me. Despite our closeness throughout the night, a wall remains between us. It's thin but present. Her concern isn't unwarranted, though. I promised myself I'd be good enough for her. I'll do right by her, but I have a ways to go to prove myself.

"I want to wake up with you every day," I blurt out, sounding like a sap as I lean forward to brush at the hair along the side of her face. Her blue eyes widen in the dim light. She softly smiles at me, but it's not reaching her eyes. Am I misreading something here? Did last night not mean what I thought it meant? I want Pam in this bed every night and waking here every morning—with me.

She slowly moves, pushing down the sheet and crawling on her knees to get closer to me. Naked, she reaches out for me, wrapping her arms around my neck and latching her mouth to mine. The kiss is instantly intense and telling me something like her kisses last night.

Let me love you, Jacob.

I want her to, and I want to give her what I can in return. Maybe she can teach me how to love because I want to love her. I want a future with her.

I return the kiss with equal intensity, soaking up her taste, inhaling her scent, and memorizing her touch. She's sensory overload, and every part of me feels pulled to her. Why have I waited so long for this moment? I've wasted so much time holding back from her.

Pam slows the kiss and pulls back from me.

"What was that?" I tease, feeling the heat of that kiss through every inch of my body.

"Just saying goodbye."

My forehead furrows. A current under her voice scratches at me, like sandpaper going in the wrong direction, but I dismiss it.

"I'll call you later," I say, not liking the sound of my own voice any more than hers.

"Later," she whispers.

"Oh, and if my assistant happens to show up today, can you tell her I'll be back later to thank you for her services?"

Pam's eyes narrow. "What services?"

"When I was gone, I heard she kept things together for me. Holding up my social media presence like she does and even editing some chapters in case I wanted to work." Theresa told me what Pam did for me. "I heard she didn't take the money offered to compensate her for her time."

Pam's head lowers while she licks her bottom lip.

"I want to pay her for her time."

Her head pops up. "Throwing more money at her?" Her lips twist, fighting a smile instead of chewing me out.

"I'll be making payment in kisses."

"Funny, I know a guy in New York who took those, too, for tour guide services." Her smile grows.

"Interesting," I tease. "I heard he went out of business because he wasn't paid by some wayward tourist."

"Goodness, I'll have to have your assistant look into that. She'll see what she can do to find the guy and pay up."

Curling my hand about the back of her neck and bringing her back to me, I say, "I don't want my assistant looking for any other man. Only me."

"Only you," she whispers before I take her mouth again, heating us up once more. My phone vibrates again. Dammit, Theresa might be the death of me. Then I reconsider as Pam's the one jolting my heart back to life.

"Maybe we can consider some kind of trade. Tour guide. Assistant services. We could work something out." I hold the nape of her neck as my sight skims over her face, taking in all of her like a photograph before I hit the road.

"You're so beautiful in the morning."

Her eyes hold mine for a long minute before I can't take the heat. I'm so tempted to strip my clothes and get back under those sheets with her. Hold her tight and prove to her I'm hers.

L.B. Dunbar

My phone hums in my back pocket again—fucking Theresa—and the moment between us breaks.

"Bye, angel."

She smiles at me, causing my heart to feel freer than it's ever felt, and I step away from her with a final glance back at her in my bed, feeling the rightness of it.

+ + +

I drive a Cadillac Escalade SUV now instead of my fancy red Corvette, which doesn't have the same flair as my sports car and guzzles gas, but I love the comfort of this beast. After a day of driving hours, dinner, and a two-hour presentation with questions and answers, I'm spent, but I meant what I said to Pam. I want to find her in my bed, so I start the trek back to Elk Lake City, especially after an ominous text.

We need to talk. Call me when you can.

The text haunts me as I drive. Is there any combination of words that sound worse? It's like a death sentence to a relationship, and I feel sick. I don't want us to be over before we truly start. The niggling sensation from the morning triples in potency. My gut keeps telling me I've missed something, and a sense of impending sorrow hovers over me like a dark cloud.

I'm living in one of my novels.

I tried calling earlier and excused her lack of response to her work. As it's the beginning of May, the busyness of the flower shop increases every day. However, it's late enough she should be at my place. Maybe she isn't there. Maybe she won't be in my bed when I get home. Home. Pam is my home, but I want us both in that house. I've already slept without her for six weeks. I don't want to do it ever again. It might feel like I'm rushing things, but I want her in my bed each night and morning, which means I want her to move in with me.

When I don't reach Pam after another attempt, I decide to call my sister despite the later hour.

"Hey," Ella greets me, her voice quiet.

"Hey. I hate to call so late, but I was wondering if you've seen or heard from Pam today." I jump right in, sounding obsessive, possessive, and out of control because I'm coming out of my skin. Despite our lovemaking session, I'm still a little shaky where we stand. I know where I want us to be, but Pam's right. We need to talk.

"Haven't you heard?"

My tongue thickens. My mouth goes dry. "Heard what?" I bark, choking on the heaviness in my throat.

"Pam was in a car accident earlier this evening."

"What?" I choke, my vision immediately blurring. "What happened?"

"She hit a deer just off Winters Trail, your road. It was evening, and the EMT guesses the deer was crossing the road. How she didn't see it, we don't know. It was huge." Ella pauses, and I hear the swallow. "He had spring antlers and landed on her Jeep, breaking the windshield. His antlers punched the airbag, Jacob."

My eyes close a second while I'm driving. *Please, no.* If there is a God, don't take the good in this world.

"Ella," I croak, needing her to continue.

"She hit that steering wheel hard, but thankfully, the deer didn't hit her."

"What does that mean?" The question is a choked whisper.

"It means, another inch closer and . . . I don't want to think about what it would mean. We're all at the hospital in Traverse City."

"How bad is it?"

"I haven't seen her, but she's still unconscious and has been for hours. Bruises and broken ribs from what I'm told. They're keeping her for observation."

Fuck. Fuck. *Fuck.* My palms sweat as they grip the steering wheel, and my foot grows heavier on the gas. The darkness outside my window turns into a vortex, rushing past me as I fly down an empty highway. My world feels like it's spiraling out of control.

"I'll be there as fast as I can." I quickly tell her where I'm at and click off the phone. Sending up a silent prayer for Pam to hang on, I try

L.B. Dunbar
not to think about how just when I thought everything good could fall
into place, I could also lose all that's important to me.

Chapter 28

Moment of Truth

[Jacob]

When I enter Pam's room in the early hours of the morning, I take several short breaths. I'm certain I broke every speed limit on what should have been a four-hour drive to get here in two, and I'm a wreck, especially when I see her in a hospital bed looking broken and small.

A woman in her sixties sits at Pam's side, and I assume she's her mother as their eyes match.

"How is she?" I ask before even introducing myself. This isn't exactly the way I hoped to meet her mother.

"She'll be alright. She's a survivor. It's in her nature." Her mother kindly smiles at me, the curl of her lips matching her daughter's.

"I'm Jacob," I offer. "Jacob Vincentia, the writer and the man she works for. I called you when—"

She holds up a hand to stop me as the words are falling out in a rush.

"I know who you are. You're the boss." She smiles again, but this time it does reach her eyes.

"I'm also in love with your daughter." The curl of her mouth grows larger, and her eyes finally show a spark.

"It's nice to finally meet you in person. I'm Mary." Instead of just shaking my hand, she cups mine with both of hers and then steps aside. "Why don't you sit here?"

Taking her seat, I sit and stare down at the woman who breathes life into me. I hate how helpless she looks.

"Angel," I whisper, holding her hand while brushing back her hair. She looks beautiful and awful, and I'm just so glad she's alive. Being in this hospital is a déjà vu to our first official meeting—well, actually the second—and I'd reverse our roles if it would prevent her from being hurt. I'd gladly put myself back in that bed instead of her lying there, looking so broken, but I also promised her, and myself, I'll never be in that position again.

Her eyes are swollen, both black and blue. Her nose bruised as well. I scan her midsection as if I can see through the blanket to the broken ribs and any other bruises. "She's so beautiful," I say to her sleeping form and the presence of her mother. A sob chokes me, and I lower my head for her hand. A hand comes to my shoulder, and a soft voice follows.

"We're just glad you're here," her mother tells me, and she has no idea how grateful I am to be here as well.

+ + +

Brightness fills the hospital as I wake with a kink in my neck. I slowly lift my head and rub at the sore muscles while still holding Pam with my other hand.

Blue eyes meet mine.

"Hey, angel," I softly greet her, more overwhelmed than even last night. The relief of her open eyes, staring back at mine, is almost too much, but I'm not looking away from her.

"What are you doing here?" she questions, wincing as she asks.

"There's nowhere else I'd be, Lilac." I squeeze her hand harder, fighting the emotion in my throat. Tears fill her eyes and spill from the corners, rolling to her hair. "Hey. Hey," I whisper. "None of this."

My fingers brush at her cheeks, and someone clears their throat. I turn to find her younger sister sitting in a chair at the end of the bed.

"I think I'll give you guys a few minutes." Her sister stands, and although she isn't showing much, I recall Pam telling me she's pregnant. The way she lifts herself from the chair is more telltale than the bump that shows once she's upright. She repeats her mother's words during the dark hours of the morning. "We're all glad you're here, Jacob."

I've only met her once before, but her words do something to my insides. She gives her sister a long look before leaving the room, and I turn back to Pam, my eyes catching on the monitors. When I first arrived, I hadn't noticed the machines and wires as I did while drifting off to sleep. Between the soft bleeps and jagged digital bumps, I'd drifted off, but I remember wondering why Pam had two machines hooked to her, like two heart monitors. Dismissing the thought, I glance down at her.

"How are you?" I want to wrap my arms around her and take care of her, but I don't want to mess with these machines.

"We need to talk." Her serious tone frightens me, and I try to tease when I say, "Don't you dare leave me." It's what she said to me when she pulled me from the wreckage of my crash all those years ago, but I also mean it on a deeper level. I don't want her to leave me.

"Jacob." She chokes, and I reach for a Styrofoam cup with a straw, holding it up for her. She licks her lips but shakes her head. "This is important."

"Lilac, whatever it is, can wait." My voice grows stern.

Thankfully, a nurse immediately enters, and I consider her a reprieve from the inevitable. Pam is about to break up with me before we even have a start. The nurse's expression is cheerful as if she isn't interrupting anything, isn't preventing me from getting my heart ripped out because that's all I can think about with Pam's words.

We need to talk.

The nurse speaks instead. "Time to check your vitals and the baby's."

My neck cranes, attention turning toward the nurse, when my sight catches on the monitors. Everything else moves in slow motion. The nurse checking the machines. A thermometer over Pam's forehead. The fear in Pam's eyes.

"Excuse me. What did you say?" I question the nurse as sound rushes back into my ears, filling them with the monitor's beeping. The click of the thermometer. The tap of her plastic clogs on the tile.

"The baby? Are you the daddy?" Her eyes lower for my hand holding Pam's. Her smile is hopeful as she tucks Pam's blankets around her.

I turn back to Pam.

"What is she saying?" I glare down at her bruised eyes, struggling.

"I'm pregnant." The announcement is hardly a whisper.

L.B. Dunbar

After dropping her fingers, I raise both hands to the back of my head and pace a small circle next to the bed before facing Pam again.

"You're what?" I snap, unable to contain the emotion rippling through my body. *How could this be?* My heart actually caves within my chest. I know we were apart for six weeks but still, this hurts. This hurts so much. "Who?"

The demand startles her, and tears start to fall in earnest.

"Maybe now's not the time for this," the nurse says, a witness to my heartbreak.

"It's yours," Pam whispers, and I stare at her. My heart slowly restoring.

"How?" I ask louder, still in a state of shock. Her liquid-filled, swollen eyes stare back at me as more tears fall. Typical to my Lilac, she gives me an incredulous look like she can't believe she'd have to explain the process of reproduction to me. I don't need her explanation.

"I'm always covered," I remind her. "I keep it wrapped up tight, and you're on the pill."

"Are you okay?" the nurse asks Pam, eyes wandering to one of the monitors. "Do you want him to leave?"

I'm not going fucking anywhere.

"Could you give us a minute," I command, my voice brooks no argument. I want her out of here. In the background, the monitors are rising in tempo. Ignoring me, the nurse continues to watch Pam. Clearly, she's not leaving the room either.

"Explain this to me, Pam," I demand, pretending we don't have an audience. Her face crumples, and Ethan picks this moment to enter the room.

"What's going on?" His tone expresses his immediate concern at the distress he sees on Pam's face. I ignore him as well.

"It just happened." Pam finally answers me. "The night of the snowstorm." The timing makes sense. It's the only night we were together before the other night, but I still can't seem to comprehend how this could be.

"Sometimes these things just happen," the nurse interjects, her voice cheerful and positive as she adds, "The Lord works in mysterious ways."

"Whoa, whoa, whoa. What are we talking about here?" Ethan hesitantly laughs, but I'm not finding any humor at this moment.

"Why are you still here?" I snap at the nurse as I glare at her and then turn on Pam again. "How long?"

"I'm eight weeks along."

"No, I mean how long have you known?" I can hardly contain my growing frustration. *Why didn't she tell me?*

"A few weeks after our trip to New York."

"A few weeks!" I shout aghast.

"Hey man, settle down," Ethan states, stepping closer to me, and I spin on him.

"Did you know about this?" I can't read his blank face, so I give him the information. "She's pregnant."

Ethan's eyes leap from me to Pam. "Really?" His voice softens. "That's wonderful, Pam."

"Why didn't you tell me?" My voice lowers, but my heart still races with this news. What does this mean? Why hasn't she said anything? Is she not happy? Is she upset I'm the father?

A hand scrubs down my face. Shit. *Just shit.* My brain screams. I ruin everything. Looking up, I watch Ethan lean forward and press a kiss to Pam's head, pushing back her hair. She remains there, crying through his congratulations.

"Get him out of here," the nurse demands, addressing Ethan.

"Outside," he barks. "Now."

"Fuck you," I hiss. "I'm not leaving her." Ethan pushes me, and everything in me tells me to fight back. To shove him aside, but my eyes fall to Pam, who has closed hers and rolled to her side. She must hate me. Oh my God, the one thing I never wanted is for her to hate me, and I've gotten her pregnant. In my weakened state, Ethan grabs the shoulder of my shirt and drags me into the hallway. I shrug him off me and slam my back into the wall.

L.B. Dunbar

"You're a dick," Ethan states, venom in his voice, which matches the blood roiling through my veins. "Did you not see her condition? She just had an accident. She could have died," he reminds me. "She could have lost the baby, and she doesn't need this." He waves his hand up and down before me.

"What's going on?" Ella says, rushing to Ethan's side. She reaches out for me, but I slide along the wall, away from her. "Jacob, what happened?"

"Pam's pregnant."

My sister's face quickly breaks into a blinding smile, beaming with excitement. "That's wonderful."

"Why didn't she tell me?" My voice cracks as the shock settles in, and I vibrate with the anxiety of her rejection.

We should talk. She was going to tell me. She was going to break things off.

"Let's evaluate this situation," my sister says, learning all this new shit from her therapist. "You thought you'd gotten another woman pregnant. The woman of your dreams needed to accept this. She walks away from you to give you the space you need. You go into treatment and get yourself clean because that's what you needed to do for you. And she's been here waiting for you."

"Pam's been waiting for me," I slowly repeat Ella's words.

Let me love you, Jacob.

My head lowers a bit, but I'm still breathing heavy.

She made love to me and kissed my scars. She healed my heart. She's been standing right in front of me.

"Then you find out the truth. Mandi faked her pregnancy to keep you. She tricked you." Ella continues to eye me, emphasizing her words, and letting the sad truth of my life sink in. "Do you think, just maybe, Pam might have worried you'd think she did the same?"

"I would never—"

Ella holds up a hand to stop me. "Uh. But you're reacting right now."

"I'm in shock." I state the obvious. My sister and I stare at each other until I have to look away.

220

"Jacob, she has loved you unconditionally," Ella reminds as if I should know this, but I do. When I think back on the years, the dedication to me and my work, to my house and our friendship, she's always been there for me. And what have I offered her?

"She's taken all your crap for years, man," Ethan interjects. "We didn't even know who you were, but every time she mentioned '*the man she worked for,*' we saw it in her face. It was written all over her. She was in love with you."

Ethan pauses to exhale in frustration and pulls his hair from his forehead to the top of his head.

"And if you don't get your ass back in that room and apologize, you don't deserve her," he adds. Ella glances up at Ethan and scowls. His face instantly falls, and he drops his hair.

"Sorry, princess," he mutters before leaning in to kiss her temple.

Ella twists back to me. "You need to fight for her, Jacob. Instead of always fighting against life, it's time to step up and fight *for* it. This is what you've been waiting for, a chance to be loved. A chance to give love."

"You don't think I want this?" I'm confused. Of course, I want Pam. Of course, I want the baby, I just . . .

My head turns back in the direction of Pam's hospital room.

She's having my baby.

I love her.

What am I doing in the hall?

221

Chapter 29
Reactive Reactions

[Pam]

With Jacob still in the hall, I curl to my side, which hurts like hell, but I just want to tuck into myself. This didn't go as I had planned. Nothing has gone as I hoped. I wanted to tell Jacob on my own terms. Maybe after I heard the heartbeat next week. Then again, they ran an ultrasound as a urine sample showed I was pregnant. My family didn't know to offer that information to the doctors as I hadn't told anyone yet but Mae. Thankfully, the baby is protected, and my little peanut's heart is pumping away. I, on the other hand, feel heartsick.

"He's just a little in shock," the nurse says, still by my side. "Apparently, he didn't know." The question lingers in her voice, and I shake my head. With her still rubbing my hand, I wipe away the last of my tears, telling myself I will not cry over Jacob anymore. When he left me yesterday morning, I had this weird sensation something was going to happen, almost like a premonition of something bad occurring. Unfortunately, it had been my own stupidity. After going to work, I broke down from the emotional high of being with Jacob again. I told Mae everything from the seduction to my lack of telling him about the pregnancy.

"What are you afraid of with him?" she questioned, truly concerned. In her eyes, Jacob had returned. He'd come back to me. She didn't understand.

"He doesn't want children, or marriage, or even believe in love. I don't want him to think I tricked him like Mandi tried to do." It'd certainly been a shock to learn the truth. She tried to manipulate him into marrying her, and I didn't want Jacob to think I'd done the same thing.

"That's ridiculous," Mae stated, still full of sympathy for my stress. *"He loves you. I haven't even met the man, and I'm certain he does."*

Storming out of my hospital room seems to prove quite the opposite.

"Lilac." His quiet voice startles me, and I squeeze my already closed eyes even tighter. "Lilac, look at me."

I cannot look at him. *Go away.*

"Lilac, please. I don't want to say what I have to say to your back." His voice is calmer, and the nurse continues to rub my arm, soothing me. She's not telling him to get out, so I assume she sees something in him.

I flip with a cry of pain, and Jacob's eyes widen, but I dismiss his concern. "You have nothing left to say to me, Jacob. For over two years, I have given you my dedication and devotion. I've given you my heart," I emphasize, poking at the hospital gown over my chest. "I've been loyal and faithful for God knows what reason, and I don't need this from you. I knew how you felt. No love. No marriage. No children. I don't expect anything from you. I just wanted to love you."

Dammit, the tears begin to fall again.

"I wanted you to let me love you. I *want* you, but I don't need you, Jacob, and there's a difference. I can raise this child on my own. I just thought you should know the truth."

I try to roll back to my side but cry out again in pain. Jacob's hand comes to my arm, keeping me on my back.

"Are you finished?" he softly questions, and I huff while quiet tears stream to the sides of my face.

"Lilac," he begins, swiping a hand over his head and then reaching for my hand to entwine his fingers with mine. "I fucked up. I always do. I told you once if I ever had anything good in my life, I'd mess it up, and I did. Look at you." He swipes a tear from my cheek while squeezing the hand he holds. "I'm wrecking you, and it's killing me. I love you, angel."

The tears fall harder just when I thought they'd subside.

"I love you, and I want you to love me. I want you to *need* me because I certainly need you. I don't want to live without you."

Through blurry eyes, I try to focus on him. "What about the baby?"

"Angel," he addresses me, swiping his finger along the edge of my face. "You've given me life in more ways than one. I'm not upset about the baby. I'm in shock. And I thought you weren't telling me because

223

you were upset. You didn't want me to know I'd put my demon in you." His voice falters as he tries to joke.

"It's not a demon," I admonish through the subsiding tears. He lifts my hand cradled in his and presses kisses to my knuckles.

"Of course not. Any child of yours must be an angel." More kisses cover our joined hands. "I'm sorry I lost it there for a moment."

The nurse reminds us of her presence. "If you two are good now, I think I'll step out." Jacob's head turns to her, and she warns him directly. "No more funny business from you, or I'll toss you out myself."

"I apologize for that." He pauses, taking a deep breath and then adds, "I'm going to be a dad."

The nurse grins, and I watch Jacob's face morph from cautiously concerned to contagiously happy.

"So I've heard," she tells him. "Congratulations, Dad. When are you due?"

Jacob turns to me, raising his brows in question.

"January first."

"Just in time for the new year," the nurse states, and Jacob's dark eyes soften.

"It's already a new year," he says, shifting to glance at my belly. "It's a new life."

The nurse pats my arm before excusing herself, giving us the privacy we need.

"I was surprised myself," I finally admit once she leaves. "Are you sure you're okay with this?"

"I didn't think I'd want children because I thought I'd be like *him*. But you won't let me be like that, and I don't have it in me anyway. *I am not my beginning. I will not repeat my past.* I'm going to get both of those lines as new tattoos, along with a lilac right here." He sits back and points at his right pec. "You're my future, Lilac. You've changed my destiny. You've pointed me in the right direction after I've been on the wrong path for too long." He lifts my hand and kisses my knuckles. "I do want this baby *with you*."

224

His other hand comes to my belly. "We're going to have a baby." His voice drops. "Through a condom. Despite the pill. I must have super sperm, and we're having a baby. Us. Together."

"Are you really joking about your sexual prowess?"

He lowers himself for the chair next to the bed, still holding my hand.

"Do you know what this means?" he states, still focused on his other hand over my belly. I shake my head.

"It means dinner, hand holding, *and sex*, all the time."

"Jacob," I groan. He pushes down the blanket over me and pulls up my hospital gown.

"What are you doing?" I choke out, stumped by his actions.

"You're having my baby," he says to my belly, placing his palm flat over my stomach once more, spreading his fingers over my skin. I shiver at his touch. He lowers his face to my abdomen and kisses me. Tender. Soft. Telling. He continues to press his lips to my stomach over and over again.

"My baby's in there," he coos to my skin.

"Does this hurt?" His head pops up, eyes filled with concern. I shake my head, too flabbergast for words.

"Let me love *you*, Lilac. Let me learn to love you and the baby." He lowers once more for my belly, setting a kiss over the nonexistent bump, and then turns his head to rest on me. His arm over me tightens, and he closes his eyes.

"I love you, angel, and I'll fight for you, fight until the end to deserve your love in return."

I swipe at my eyes with my free hand, still holding Jacob's hand. My heart has just ridden a roller coaster of emotion, and I'm drained. I need rest. I need not to think, but I'm also so full of love.

"I love you, Jacob." My free hand covers his head, swiping over his hair as his head lies on my belly.

"I meant what I said the other day. I want to find you in my bed every night and wake with you every morning. I want to take care of you, Lilac, like you always take care of me. Let me try. Or teach me." He sits up straighter. "Just don't quit on me."

L.B. Dunbar

"I'm right here, Jacob."

"Move in with me."

"Jacob," I drone. "We don't need to jump ahead."

"We can step back. We can go on dates that don't lead to sex. We can go back to hand holding. Just be in my house. Tell me you'll move in with me. Promise me you won't leave."

"It's too much," I tell him while laughter fills my voice. *Can this really be happening?*

+ + +

Within a day, I'm sent home—Jacob's home—because he refuses to let me go anywhere else. True to his word, as my body heals, Jacob tends to me.

He gives me baths but doesn't turn them sexual.

He massages my body, avoiding the bruised areas, but doesn't attempt to make them sensual.

He holds me at night, kisses my shoulder or neck, but it's nothing heated.

It's pure torture.

He also does lots of hand holding.

A week passes like this, and he's romantic. As it's mid-May, lilacs are in bloom, and he brings me handfuls that I'm certain he stole from other people's yards as he doesn't have any bushes of his own.

"White, for innocence." He'd hand me the flower and kiss my belly.

"Dark purple, for passion." He wiggled his brows, and I'd groan as I'm desperate for him.

"And true lilac, for first love." He swiped the flower at my nose before giving it to me.

I also find poems on his pillow if I wake alone. My favorite of them is "Romance" by Edgar Allen Poe, about a man who didn't believe he'd care for love, didn't think it could happen for him, but when it does, he can't stop himself from falling into it. It's rather appropriate for my dark writer.

Then one day, I wake from a nap with a poem titled "Evermore."

Not a poet myself, by trade,
I'm taking a chance to persuade.
A man of words in many ways,
Yet I have not the ones to say,
All that I feel and need and want,
And so I cheat with words of yours.
Dedicated to my heart, I
Must now be true. The fact being
I'm in love with you, my angel.
To explain the depth of my love
For you, unconditionally,
I must admit my loyalty.
And to fulfill my destiny,
To keep you and mine safe with me,
I promise to love evermore
And ask you to forever be
Mine.

I sit up to discover Jacob in his writing chair beyond the bookshelf in his bedroom.

"Who wrote this one?" I ask, finding its meaning abundantly appropriate. Jacob doesn't answer but stands, setting his laptop on the floor. He circles around the bed and kneels next to it.

"I wrote it," he states sheepishly.

"It's beautiful," I tell him, reaching out to cup his face.

"You know, I want you to be with me for the rest of my life."

"Yes," I reply uncertain where this is leading.

Jacob leans back on his knees and pretends to pull something out of his pocket. He cups his hand as he presents me with the invisible something. Literally, there's nothing in his palm, which he flattens but holds out toward me.

"Play along?" he questions, and I glance up at him.

I reach forward and take the air between pinched fingers like I'm picking up a delicate package.

L.B. Dunbar

"It's a box," Jacob explains, and I nod as if I understand, as if I see it, which I do, but it's not the kind of box I expect from him. I wipe away my imagination. I'm in his home for now. He's accepting the baby. It's more than I could have asked for.

"Open it," he suggests, but when I sit there dumbfounded, uncertain if the lid is loose and pulls straight upward or on a hinge and tips back, Jacob continues his pantomime. He pretends to flip the lid and present me with something. I'm confused, and the crease to my brow expresses it as I glance up at him again.

"I want to clarify something before I do the actual asking because I want there to be no misunderstanding."

The crease of my forehead furrows farther. "Okay."

"When we were in New York, I went on an errand the day you went to the spa with Ella." He shifts to dig in another pocket and pulls out something I can't see with his hand fisted. "And I bought something, thinking it would represent a promise. A promise to try. A promise of hope. A promise from me to you."

I'm still sitting as if I hold an open box inside my hand—the invisible box—and its weight is suddenly real. Its shape I can feel pressing against my palm, which begins to sweat. I can almost see the box within my hand. It's white, with a white cushion, but I can't picture what it holds. I'd never imagine what came next.

"But I'd like this to be more than a promise." Jacob holds out the real item in his other hand. A square-cut diamond with small purple stones around it. Lilac-colored stones. "This is my proposal, Lilac. Let me love you. Teach me to be a better man, and I promise to love you in return. I'll be loyal and faithful, trustworthy and true. I'll fight for you every day, fight to deserve you if you'll be my wife. Be my *ever*more and marry me, angel."

I stare down at the ring, placed where the invisible box rests in my palm. Silent tears stream down my face, and I glance up at him, finding his expression hopeful but hesitant.

"I love you," I whisper, and his face lights up. He rises higher on his knees at the side of the bed, hands curling into the blanket over me.

"Is that a yes?" he questions.

"Evermore. That's a yes, Jacob."

He picks up the ring with shaky fingers, and I flip my hand so he can place it on my ring finger. We both stare at the sparkling gem surrounded by light lilac-colored jewels.

"It's so beautiful," I whisper.

"You're beautiful, Lilac," he says, and finally kisses me, really kisses me. Our mouths meld together, sipping and savoring one another. My hand cups his cheek while his arms wrap around my waist. Jacob stands and climbs over me with our lips still connected, and I tip back to take his body over mine.

"Does this mean the hand-holding phase is over?" I tease. It's been a week.

"We are moving on," he says, propping up on his elbows and brushing back my hair with one hand. "But the hand-holding phase is indefinite. I'll always hold your hand, angel. You don't even have to ask, or sometimes you might have to ask. Say Jacob, I need you." His eyes pierce mine. I told him in the hospital I didn't need him. I wanted him but didn't need him. I lied.

I nod to accept his suggestion. His eyes shift, watching his fingers comb at my short blond locks.

"You've been my destiny all along, Lilac. You found me when I had that accident years ago. You *saved* me. You've put up with my bullshit and patiently waited for me to get that bullshit in order. I only wish I'd done it sooner," he says. "It's the only thing I've ever regretted."

"We have all the time ahead of us," I tell him. We're both a little scared. Between a budding relationship and our baby's birth, a lot is going to happen in the next few months.

"I didn't need to change my destiny. I needed to recognize it. I needed to *find* you, angel. I'll never need to change mine again." His mouth comes to mine, soft and delicate like the petal of a flower, and too quickly, he pulls back. "Thank you."

"For what?" I giggle, reaching up with my thumb to trace over his lower lip.

"For not giving up on me. For fighting with me, against me, and eventually *for* me. I love you, Lilac." His mouth returns to mine, and

L.B. Dunbar

finally, we move on from hand holding to eager kisses. Next comes the sex part, but we both know this is about love.

Epilogue
Back in Bed

[Jacob]

I needed to take a quick trip to New York once my apartment sold and to meet with Theresa about a book tour. I wouldn't be taking one until after the baby was born. I enter the house to find a pair of shoes haphazardly in the middle of the front hall. My forehead furrows as it's not like Pam to be messy. Stepping into the living room, I notice a shirt on the floor near my office door. The stairs start just outside the entrance, and I turn to find a skirt on the steps leading upward. My heart races as do I, suddenly taking the stairs two at a time to my room.

Our room.

I find a purple bra at the top of the stairs, and just inside the entrance to our bedroom is the matching purple thong on the floor. Ignoring the clothing, I glance at the bed to find my Lilac sitting in the middle of it. Her back is to me, exposing her skin. A sheet is tucked up against her front, but I'll be removing that quickly, once I figure out what she's up to.

"Lilac?" I question, walking to the side of the bed. Her head tilts, glancing up at me over her shoulder.

"Welcome home, Professor."

I chuckle at the ridiculous nickname from the gym. "What are you doing, my little wood nymph?"

"You said you wanted to sleep each night and wake each morning with me in your bed, but we missed the past two days." Her lips pout in the cutest of manners. "So I thought I'd surprise you by being in your bed when you returned home."

"Does my assistant know you are here?' I tease, tugging off my own shirt as I kick off my shoes. Pam never really quit me, not in my writing career or my personal life.

"I told her she had the day off."

231

L.B. Dunbar

"You know I'm going to have to pay her for that time off."

"Kisses?" she asks, arching a brow at me.

Pam stares at my left pec. True to what I promise, I had two additional lines added to my chest. *I am not my beginning. I will not repeat the past.* The font matches the previous work—*change your destiny*—so it reads seamlessly. In addition, I added a bright purple lilac. Working at my pants, removing my boxer briefs at the same time, I speak to her. "This tops the surprise of finding you sick on my couch."

"What about the surprise of the baby?"

"Yeah, that was a surprise, too." I chuckle, standing before her in all my glory. I reach out and swipe a finger along her hairline.

"But you're happy, right?" Her voice turns serious as those blue eyes that match heaven stare back at me.

"Lilac, I've never been able to define happiness until now." My hand pulls down the sheet covering her, revealing her luscious, swelling breasts. I'll get to savoring those in a minute. First, I place my hand on her belly. "This is happiness to me." I lower to kiss her there, and her stomach flinches with the tickling touch.

"And this is happiness to me," I state, sitting up and placing a kiss on her mouth. Without words, I'm telling her that her in my bed, at any time of day, brings me the best of feelings.

"I love you," she says to me as she says every day, and I feel it around me like a constant embrace. I see it in all the things she does for me, and I still kick myself that I hadn't seen it before. Here's the thing about love. When you haven't had it, you don't know what to look for. You just know it's different from anything else. Pam is my different. She's everything I never thought I could have, but I'm so thankful she's mine.

"I love you, too," I tell her. "Now, let's get to the part of you in this bed."

"Are you going to be a big grumbling bear?" she teases as I lean toward her, pressing her back to the mattress.

"More like a beast," I reply, groaning into her neck.

"Hmm, I might like grumbling Jacob." She falls to her back, wrapping her arms around me, and I shift to lay over her.

"I promise to be a giant teddy bear afterward," I tease, and Pam laughs under me, rumbling against my skin. Her laughter is the best, and I cover her mouth with mine to capture the sound. My hands roam before I remove my mouth from hers and lower for a breast, savoring the fullness. Her body is changing, but it's proof of our connection. We did this together, and I've never been happier.

My fingers lower, slipping between her thighs while her hand wraps around my dick. As she squeezes, I moan. "Two days was two too many." I don't want to sleep in a bed without her again.

Her mouth seeks mine as we touch each other, reacquainting despite it only being days. Touching her is never going to get old.

"Soon, I'll be too big for you to climb over me," she says, wiping a hand over the slight bump at her lower abdomen.

"We'll be creative like we've always been." Two fingers easily enter her, and her head falls back.

"You're so beautiful," I hum at her throat.

"I love your sense of creativity," she murmurs as I bring her to the edge. She's so close, and I love to watch her break, but I need to be inside her. I need to feel her release around me. I pull out my fingers, and she whimpers, but I'm quick to replace my fingers with something more. Sliding into her heat, I groan with an overwhelming sense of home. And rightness. And happiness. She's my light in the dark, and she's brightening that darkness more and more every day.

"You're going to be my wife," I grunt as I thrust into her. Her arms lift, hands flattening on the bookcase behind her head. My hands cover her wrists as I rock my hips, filling her repeatedly.

"Your wife," she strains, her orgasm building.

"And the mother of my child," I stammer, hammering into her faster.

"A mother," she whispers, a faint smile gracing her face. That smile does something to me. I'm unleashed, rocking into her harder, reaching deeper within her. For the first time, I feel as if I've given something to her. I don't always take. My seed inside her will make her a mother, and I'll do it again and again if she'll give me the present look on her face—the one of pure bliss.

L.B. Dunbar

"Jacob," she warns me, my name like a prayer on her lips. Her legs wrap over my hips, and she arches her back, forcing me deeper as she comes around me in wave after wave. I still my own motions, jolting inside her, giving her all of me in return.

Nothing will ever be the same for me, and I'll fight to the end of my days to keep it this way.

+ + +

I have another book to write, a baby on the way, and my angel in my bed with me. We decided Ella's old room would be a good nursery, although at first, the baby will sleep in a bassinet in our room. I don't know any of this baby lingo, but I am learning as I promised Pam I would. She's an excellent teacher. I especially love it when she rewards me with things, like sex on the future nursery floor.

"What if we have more than one child?" I asked her once we finished, staring up at the large empty space too big for a single child's bedroom.

"You'd have more than one child?" she questioned, turning her head to face me.

"I'd have more than one child with you, Lilac," I told her, returning my spent body to blanket hers. *"How many do you want?"*

I'll admit, I held my breath.

"Three seems like a good number," she said, so three will be what she gets. I have faith in my super sperm to get the job done. We wouldn't be using protection in the future, which heightens my odds.

My love for her blooms daily and now it will blossom with the birth of a baby. I never knew how much I longed for love, and my heart is near exploding with how much it wants to give.

Three babies and my Lilac. Some days, it seems like too much. I don't know how I got so fortunate. It couldn't have only been an accident, but destiny with an angel dropped from heaven.

My evermore.

Thank you for reading.

Up next in the Heart Collection: View With Your Heart

If you like small town romances, you might also like The Silver Foxes of Blue Ridge. Start here: Silver Brewer

Want to stay up to date on all things L.B. Dunbar: Love Notes

+ + +

Thank you for taking the time to read this book. Please consider writing a review on major sales channels where ebooks and paperbooks are sold.

More by L.B. Dunbar

Sexy Silver Foxes
When sexy silver foxes meet the women of their dreams.
After Care
Midlife Crisis
Restored Dreams
Second Chance
Wine&Dine

The Silver Foxes of Blue Ridge
More sexy silver foxes in the mountain community of Blue Ridge
Silver Brewer
Silver Player
Silver Mayor
Silver Biker

Collision novellas
A spin-off from After Care – the younger set/rock stars
Collide
Caught – a short story

Smartypants Romance (an imprint of Penny Reid)
Tales of the Winters sisters set in Penny Reid's Green Valley.
Love in Due Time

L.B. Dunbar

Love in Deed
Love in a Pickle (2021)

Rom-com for the over 40
The Sex Education of M.E.

The Heart Collection
Small town, big heart - stories of family and love.
Speak from the Heart
Read with your Heart
Look with your Heart
Fight from the Heart
View with your Heart

A Heart Collection Spin-off
The Heart Remembers

The Legendary Rock Star Series
Rock star mayhem in the tradition of King Arthur.
A classic tale with a modern twist of romance and suspense
The Legend of Arturo King
The Story of Lansing Lotte
The Quest of Perkins Vale
The Truth of Tristan Lyons
The Trials of Guinevere DeGrance

Paradise Stories
MMA romance. Two brothers. One fight.
Abel
Cain

The Island Duet
Intrigue and suspense. The island knows what you've done.
Redemption Island
Return to the Island

Modern Descendants – writing as elda lore
Magical realism. Modern myths of Greek gods.
Hades
Solis

Turn the page for an excerpt of <u>View With Your Heart</u>.

L.B. Dunbar

Excerpt –

View With Your Heart – Book 5 in the Heart Collection

Take 1

[Gavin]

The view around me brings a wave of memory.

Blonde hair bright as the sunshine streaming across the water. Blue eyes the color of the deepest portion of the lake.

The soft lull of the lake water lapping at the shore suggests summer, a time reminiscent of light breezes, hurried kisses, and Britton McKay.

Neither she nor I have been in this area in thirteen years and it feels surreal to be here at all.

Home.

I didn't exactly grow up on the shores of Elk Lake but in the countryside around it. The land filled with cherry orchards, chirping crickets and chattering cicadas. My parents still live on the century old farm, and I haven't seen them in over a decade.

As I sit on the third-floor balcony of a condominium rental that wasn't built when I left twenty years ago, I stare out at the glimmer of sunlight rippling across the lake before me. I'm a long way from the place I now call home—California. I've rented this condo for the next two weeks, encompassing my business at the Traverse City Film Festival, an event thirty minutes from my current location, and the upcoming nuptials of my childhood best friend, Jess Carter.

I'm honored to stand up for him. Jess was practically another brother. I've been thinking a lot about friendships and family this summer. How I've been a shitty brother to my real one and even shittier as a son. I pulled away for my own sanity, but now, I feel like I'm missing out on something. Something I can't quite put my finger on. The last time I was in the area I holed up for the weekend with a beautiful girl. The weekend turned into something wild and unpredicted, and I smile once more with memories of Britton.

My eyes remain on the dancing waves. They don't crash here like the angry Pacific against the sandy beaches of the west coast. They softly glide and skitter back. The movement is graceful and reminds me again of Britton. I was eighteen when we met and on my way to the Baseball Hall of Fame, if my father had anything to say about it. In the end, he had no say in the course of my life. I'd been eager to bust from here. Baseball was my future. However, when your world centers around sports, the axis feels unbalanced when you quit.

And I quit, according to my father.

I lean forward in the balcony chair, continuing to gaze out at the slice of lake before me. The liquid expanse runs for miles to my left. The homes circling this lake have certainty changed in the course of my thirty-eight years. Most are huge and valued at close to a million dollars. Who'd a thought?

I wonder if Leo still has a place here.

It'd be a long shot that Britton's uncle still owned a home on these shores. Swiping a hand through my thick hair, I realize he'd be almost a hundred by now. Slowly, my smile fads when I consider the alternative for an old man.

I'd been thinking of death too much lately as well. Or perhaps it was life I was contemplating. What have I accomplished in nearly forty years? What will I do next?

I sigh, knowing part of the answer. I'm here for the festival to showcase an independently produced film. It's a passion project and I'm proud of it.

Swiping fingers through my thick hair once more, I lean back in the rickety outdoor seat. My long legs slide forward, and I stretch. My eyes catch on a woman walking on the beach. Her blonde hair blows in the early evening breeze. Her summer dress billows around her thighs. It's one of those scenes that looks unreal, almost staged, and I'd love to capture her with my camera.

Instead, I freeze frame her in my mind.

The waves lick at her bare feet as she carries a pair of sandals in her hand. On occasion, she whips her head to clear her face of the loose hairs floating about her. She looks effervescent as if she doesn't actually exist on this beach. She's elegant despite the awkwardness of walking on the uneven sand. She has the grace of a dancer.

The thought makes me sit taller and narrow my eyes at her.

Once upon a time, Britton wanted to be a dancer, and I curse myself for thinking of her again. She was a summer girl when we met, which meant she didn't live in the area. She was only visiting for three months. The timing was after my high school graduation and before I left for college. That was the best June, July and August of my life. I was reckless, thoughtless even, but not with her. She was all I thought about that summer. We had temporary written all over us, but perhaps that was the appeal. Summer loves are like that—unparalleled because of the limitation on them.

As I have a good view of the woman, I continue to watch her from my seat on the third floor. She stills a second, spinning in a half-circle to again settle that hair dancing around her face. The breeze blows it back as she faces west. With her back to me, I imagine her eyes closing as she feels the sun heat her cheeks. I'm enthralled by her movements which are nothing out of the ordinary. Any woman might move in this manner to clear her face on a breezy, late afternoon.

It's when she turns back around, dips her head and brushes only one side of her hair behind her ear that I stiffen. I do a double take and squint harder at her.

It can't be.

Britton was just as hell bent on being somebody as me. New York called her name, she said. We were headed to opposite coasts.

Yet, the movement of her hand, the way she holds it on the side of her neck a second after brushing back her hair feels too coincidental. She begins walking again, coming almost parallel to my view, and stops before the condo building. Putting her back to me again, she looks at the water once more and more memories rush over me.

A tiny boat, a dark night and fireworks bursting over the water.

Shaking my head, I realize I'm imprinting, merging my history with reality. I blame it on my emotions which are a roller coaster ride of peaks and valleys at being so close to home and soon to see my family.

Still, I can't take my eyes off the woman who spins and faces the building a second time. A hand at her brow, shields her eyes, and it's as if she looks up at me. For some reason, I wave. Her hand drops and I chuckle to myself. I'm an idiot, and I'm relieved she didn't see me.

Then, her hand lifts, and a hesitant, short wave returns mine. My breath catches.

Again, it can't be, can it?

Because if I could do any imprinting, it would be Britton McKay standing on that beach.

What would be the odds?

Considering this thought, a young boy runs across the sand to her, and she extends an arm to him. He looks like he's more than a youth but not quite a teen. However, I'm not a good judge of ages. I'll probably never have children. Zoey hadn't wanted them, and I guess, I hadn't either.

Still, I've been thinking so much about family.

My sight follows the woman, wrapping her arm around the kid's neck. He's carrying a wakeboard in his hands, a favorite pastime of kids in the area. Surfing isn't really a thing in these parts. He's nearly as tall as the woman, and she presses a kiss to the side of his head. Quickly, he slips out from under her arm. Her head tips back like she's laughing as he runs off before her, drops the board and skims a few feet in the inches deep wave. He stumbles and she bends forward laughing harder.

I can't remember the last time I laughed like that. Belly shaking. Eyes tearing. Full body immersed in the depths of something funny.

Again, I remember someone laughing just like that, and as much as I don't think it's a possible, it seems undeniable.

Britton McKay is here.

Continue reading: <u>View With Your Heart</u>

Original Playlist from *Fragrance Free.*

I love when books have a playlist, like a soundtrack to a movie, and every time you hear that song you can picture the scene in your head.
Here's Pam and Jacob's playlist. Enjoy.

"Wake Me Up" - Avicii
"Safe & Sound" (From "The Hunger Games Soundtrack") – Taylor Swift
"Make You Feel My Love" – Adele
"Bad Things" – Meiko
"Winter Song" – Sara Bareilles & Ingrid Michaelson
"Winter" – Tori Amos
"Glitter in the Air" – P!nk
"Closer to Love" – Matt Kearney
"Rumor Has It/Someone Like You" – Glee Cast
"Flightless Bird, American Girl" – Iron & Wine
"Wicked Games" – Chris Isaak (added 2020)
"Best Day of My Life" – American Authors
"Empire State of Mind" – Jay Z
"I'm Not Sorry" – Meiko
"My Heart Can't Tell You No" – Sara Evans
"Think of Me" – Andrew Lloyd Webber
"Dreaming With a Broken Heart" – John Meyer
"Thinking of You" – Katy Perry
"Kiss Me" – Ed Sheeran
"Gravity" – Sara Bareilles
"Smother Me" – The Used
"Stuck On You" – Meiko
"Marry Me" – Martina McBride & Pat Monahan of Train
"Never Gonna Leave This Bed" – Maroon 5

(L)ittle (B)its of Gratitude

It takes a village, and in 2020, in the heart of a world pandemic and the decision to rewrite a five-book series, it takes miracle workers. Those miracle workers are my editors Jenn and Mel who did edits under fire when I fell behind. The theme of 2020 has been write, write again, write one more time, and then edit, edit, edit…and these ladies deserve all the wine for being there for me.

Once again, thank you to Shannon for another beautiful cover and Karen for final eyes on this project. Also thank you Rox for catching a few other oops! To all the readers on my Always ARC team, thank you, to you as well for your patience and support. Launching L.B. is a collection of amazing people!

Another group of amazing people is my reader group, Loving L.B. Thank you again and again and again for loads of laughter and sexy silver fox images. To Sylvia and Tammi, for continually taking over days and adding to the fun, thank you for showing up and sticking around.

The changed man (person) who gives up an addiction is a worthy hero in my book, and in my life, so I applaud anyone with an addiction who fights their way through the darkness and finds light, first in him or her-self, and then finds love with someone who sees your greatness. Never give up. Love is always worth the fight.

And on that note, to the people I'd always go to the mat for: Mr. Dunbar, a worthy hero, and our four fighters: MD, MK, JR and A. May the world be a better place for your futures.

L.B. Dunbar

About the Author
www.lbdunbar.com

L.B. Dunbar has an over-active imagination. To her benefit, such creativity has led to over thirty romance novels, including those offering a second chance at love over 40. Her signature works include the #sexysilverfoxes collection of mature males and feisty vixens ready for romance in their prime years. She's also written stories of small-town romance (Heart Collection), rock star mayhem (The Legendary Rock Stars Series), and a twist on intrigue and redemption (Redemption Island Duet). She's had several alter egos including elda lore, a writer of romantic magical realism through mythological retellings (Modern Descendants). In another life, she wanted to be an anthropologist and journalist. Instead, she was a middle school language arts teacher. The greatest story in her life is with the one and only, and their four grown children. Learn more about L.B. Dunbar by joining her reader group on Facebook (Loving L.B.) or subscribing to her newsletter (Love Notes).

+ + +

Keep in touch with L.B. Dunbar
www.lbdunbar.com
Stalk Me: https://www.facebook.com/lbdunbarauthor
Instagram Me: @lbdunbarwrites
Read Me:
https://www.goodreads.com/author/show/8195738.L_B_Dunbar
Follow Me: https://www.bookbub.com/profile/l-b-dunbar
Tweet Me: https://twitter.com/lbdunbarwrites
Pin Me: http://www.pinterest.com/lbdunbar/
Get News Here: https://app.mailerlite.com/webforms/landing/j7j2s0
AND more things here
Hang with us: Loving L.B. (reader group):
https://www.facebook.com/groups/LovingLB/

Made in the USA
Middletown, DE
25 May 2022